Autographed Edition
Nina Foxx

just short of crazy

Nina Foxx

BY NINA FOXX

Just Short of Crazy

Marrying Up

Going Buck Wild

Get Some Love

Don't miss the next book by your favorite author.
Sign up now for AuthorTracker by visiting
<u>www.AuthorTracker.com.</u>

just short of crazy

NINA FOXX

AVON
TRADE

An Imprint of HarperCollins*Publishers*

HarperCollins books may be purchased for educational, business, or sales promotional use. For information please write: Special Markets Department, HarperCollins Publishers Inc.,10 East 53rd Street, New York, NY 10022.

FIRST EDITION

Designed by Stephanie Huntwork

Library of Congress Cataloging-in-Publication Data

Foxx, Nina.
   Just short of crazy / Nina Foxx.—1st ed.
       p.   cm.
ISBN-13: 978-0-06-084799-9 (alk. paper)
ISBN-10: 0-06-084799-9 (alk. paper)
1. African American women—Fiction.   2. Women lawyers—Fiction.
3. Triangles (Interpersonal relations)—Fiction.   I. Title.

PS3556.O98J87 2006
813'.6—dc22   2005057195

06   07   08   09   10   DIX/RRD   10   9   8   7   6   5   4   3   2   1

new attitude

"Cut it off." Alexis spoke before Angel even opened his mouth. Walter had loved her with long hair so it had to go. Part of making a clean break.

Angel acted like he didn't hear her. He stood looking at her in the mirror with his cutting scissors frozen in midair.

She repeated herself. "All of it. Almost a buzz cut."

"Girl, you crazy," he said. "I can't attach no weave to that." He laughed, along with everyone around her. Alexis waited for the laughter to die down and then simply smiled. "I know. I don't want one. I think I just want to go natural. Uncover the new me."

Angel was reluctant, but he poked out his lips and turned on the clippers. The shop was quiet the whole time. They all watched as Alexis lost what must have added up to five pounds of hair. To not want mounds of Texas big hair was akin to blasphemy.

She left the shop and ran her hair through her new hairdo. It felt great. It had been years since she'd felt her natural hair and it was softer than she remembered it being. *Why in the world had I been hiding under all that rug for so long?* Alexis almost couldn't keep her hands out of it. She chuckled to herself and hopped in her car. Had she become a cliché, the scorned woman who made all sorts of changes after shedding one hundred and eighty pounds or so of dead weight? This new hair was part of the post-Walter Alexis. What a way to spend a lunch hour. This was the first time in years she'd had anything done other than her weave tightened or relaxer touched up. It had only been a few minutes and already the butt-length, ultrastraight tresses that used to define her felt passé.

The cut had certainly taken less time; there was still time left before her next appointment at the office.

Alexis grabbed a cup of coffee and headed back to prepare. Her phone buzzed almost as soon as she walked through the door. She stumbled across the floor, then snatched the phone off its hook.

"Alexis Montague Pearson."

"So serious." It was Shana, the legal assistant to her boss, the head lawyer. The one whose name was on the building. Alexis could hear the smile in the woman's voice.

"How can I help you?" She failed to understand how some people could always wake up happy. Shana was happy all damn day long.

"Monty would like to see you. This morning."

A few butterflies flitted in her stomach. She cleared her throat. "Okay. Am I in trouble?" She tried to make a joke out of it.

"Not that I know of. In half an hour?"

As if I have a choice. "Of course." She hung up the phone. What now? They couldn't possibly have anything to complain about. She was doing more casework than she had in months.

Alexis finished up what she had been doing before lunch, then straightened up the papers on her desk. The elevators in the building were ancient and slow, so it would take her a minute or two to get to Monty's office. No need to keep the boss waiting.

She put everything in its place and stood up just as her phone rang again.

"Yes, Auntie." Alexis glanced at the clock. A gnawing feeling in the pit of her stomach told her she should have let this one go to voice mail. It was her Aunt Athena.

"Don't sound so happy to hear from me."

"I'm sorry. I was on my way to a meeting."

"That's fine. I understand, you have been busy lately. Too busy even for the auntie that took you in and gave you a good life."

Alexis rolled her eyes. How many times had she heard that? Yes, she had been raised by her Aunt Athena, alongside her cousin and best friend Paris. Back then, her mother had been unmarried, pregnant and fourteen years old. It had seemed like a good idea; growing up in smaller and more rural Austin with two home-owning parents would surely be better for her future than the meager existence her single mother could provide. Alexis bet all her money that her own mother, God rest her soul, had no idea that her daughter would be paying for that decision in perpetuity.

"I won't keep you long. I just called to remind you to go

and get fitted for your bridesmaid dress. You do have the details, right?"

How could she not have them? After the wedding information had been e-mailed to her, her aunt had set up some wedding site that sent almost daily countdowns with never ending wedding updates. And there were a lot of them. Paris could not seem to make up her mind about anything. "Yes, I do. I wouldn't miss it for the world. I made sure that I would be done in time to get there by eight tonight." Not exactly true, but it seemed to satisfy her aunt. *Surely everyone was rushing to wear an unflattering sherbet-colored dress.* Alexis gritted her teeth, then hung up and locked her small office.

It was unusual for Alexis to be summoned to the executive suite, and she had no idea what the reason was this time. Her performance had been exemplary, more so than usual. She'd logged more than the necessary hours, and done all of the research and depositions they'd asked her to do, even interviewed other people's clients when necessary. Alexis frowned. She knew she had taken a hard-line approach to many of the clients lately, especially the female ones. Maybe the people upstairs didn't like that or had received a complaint.

Before she and Walter broke up, she'd coddled most of her clients. Usually she pitied them, feeling sorry for the way most of them let men walk all over them. When the women finally woke up or couldn't take it anymore, then they would end up in her office. She wasn't a partner or anything, so new that she was barely above a paralegal, but the firm she worked for handled many of the high-profile divorces in Austin.

The women she pitied before had now become sisters in the cause. It was easy to take their sides. Most of them were better off without men in their lives. She tried to show them, in her own way, that a modern woman would just be slowed down by traditional marriage. They didn't need it.

Alexis certainly didn't. She came up with so many new ways to word divorce demands that her ruthlessness surprised even her. She nodded to no one in particular. If this was the problem, she would apologize and get on with it.

Shana was on the phone when Alexis arrived. She barely looked up, instead waving Alexis through to where Monty was waiting for her.

He stood with his back to the door, staring out over the downtown skyline. His jacket was off and his hands were in his pockets.

Butterflies fluttered in Alexis's stomach as she appreciated the way his expertly tailored jacket hugged his body. Her thoughts made her blush as she cleared her throat so he would know she was there.

Monty spun around, immediately flashing his ultrabright smile. He quickly gave Alexis the once-over. He had not remembered that she had such an attractive face.

Alexis smiled in return. *How in the hell did he get his teeth so white?* "You wanted to see me?"

He nodded. "I did. Thanks for coming up. I hope I didn't alarm you."

"Not really," she said coolly.

"Have a seat." He waved toward the chairs by the side of his desk and then came around to join her. "No big deal, really. I have been meaning to check on you for a couple of days now."

Alexis swallowed hard. It was a little hard to read him and

if she didn't know better she would think that he was check-ing her out. The office mill had all kinds of rumors circulat-ing about her and her breakup. One of them even had her experiencing a nervous breakdown. Her face reddened at the thought of him wondering about that one.

She was aware how much she stuck out in her firm. She was the only in a lot of categories. The only African-American female. The only lawyer who didn't go to UT Law School. The only single lawyer.

"We noticed that your billable hours have gone up signifi-cantly here recently."

"That's good, right?"

"Oh, it is good, but it worried me. You might not believe this, but we like our lawyers to have a little balance in their lives." He smiled. "A little fun every now and then. Every-thing okay?"

Alexis relaxed a little. "Yes," she said. "Everything is just fine. I have just set some new and different goals for myself over the next few months." *That should be the answer he was looking for.* She held back from what she really wanted to tell him. *None of your damn business.* He probably would not ap-preciate that at all.

He cocked his head to the side. "Is that so? That is very commendable. I don't mean to meddle, but are you aware that the office buzz is that you have broken up with your fiancé? Didn't you two live together for a bit?"

A bit was about all it was. Was nothing private anymore? "I'm fine. Never better, in fact." She paused. "I pride myself on not letting my personal life interfere with my work."

"Good. I just wanted to check for myself. But everyone needs some kind of outlet. When people don't have them, they need to see shrinks, and well, that makes our health insurance premiums go up. Not to mention it is bad for business." He grinned.

Was he trying to make a joke? That was all she needed, the office gossips making light of her love life. "Look, Monty, I assure you. All is well. I got rid of some dead weight over two months ago and have even taken up a new hobby or two."

He stood up, nodding. "That's good. Whatever you are doing, I'm glad to see that it agrees with you. And you have even gotten a new hairstyle." He paused. "It is very becoming. I knew you had things under control. You have always appeared to be that type of person. In control of things, that is. We wouldn't want to have you burn out. At least not yet." He flashed a thin smile.

Alexis tried to suppress her annoyance. She silently counted to ten to make sure her feelings would not come through in her voice. "So, are there any other problems or concerns? I have a six P.M. that I don't want to be late for."

Monty shook his head.

"So, I should be expecting a larger-than-life bonus then?" Alexis returned the same cheesy-looking grin he had given her. She glanced at her watch.

He cocked his head to the side, then shook his head. She was cute. "Nice try. If you have any problems, or need anything, let me know."

They shook hands and he watched her walk out of his office and back toward the elevator. He stepped back behind his desk to hide the erection that was poking at the front of his trousers. As good as she was looking, he meant what he said. He was willing to help her with anything she needed. And he meant anything.

those are the breaks

Men had golf and Alexis had tae kwon do. A few of her office mates had looked at her a little funny when she left the office, but not one of them had the guts to say a word. She refused to feel guilty for allowing herself the one small pleasure of leaving her office at a decent time one day a week. In the middle of her newfound commitment to the firm, she still left room to do at least one thing a week for *her*. This class was it. Besides, it fit in with the new and improved, stronger Alexis.

She hated to be late. Her boss had summoned her to his little meeting for no other purpose than to poke his nose into her business, and now she was scurrying across town to get to her class on time. He had some nerve. Alexis could feel his eyes on her ass as she left the meeting.

Bee Caves Road was the pits as far as traffic was concerned. At one point, it had been a rural road, but had turned into a major thoroughfare for most of the new developments west of the city of Austin. Alexis felt her shoulders tighten and she adjusted the lumbar setting on her seat back. The drive always got her tensed up, actually a good thing, before her workout. She swore at the slower-than-usual driver in front of her. Ever since she'd turned onto the road, this car had been changing lanes with her and had been generally impossible to get around. More than five minutes late, and her tae kwon do instructor would have her doing pushups.

Martial arts was new to her repertoire. When she and Walter had first broken up, Alexis had read an ad that said the class would calm her and help her develop new discipline, and so far, it had. She smiled. It also had made her one bad ass. Her butt was firm, her abs were firm, and she could take care of herself when she needed to.

The car wheels made a loud crunching noise as they rolled across the unpaved lot in front of the martial arts school. Alexis wedged her MiniCar into a space that looked like it was made for a scooter. She wasn't even sure it was really a space. It wasn't like the dirt lot had lines. She knew it was the last piece of disorder she would encounter for the next hour and a half. She was a little close to the car next to her, but the space would do for now. She grabbed the bag with her uniform in it from her backseat and raced into the building.

The entryway was small with a tiled floor. The instructor's office and the rest of the small vestibule were separated from the main workout room by a glass wall. A set of old-fashioned white blinds covered the wall inside the office. These were drawn halfway up. The instructor, Master Um, stood in front of his desk, surveying the students in the workout room in front of him.

Thankfully, the class had not begun.

Master Um glanced at the large wall clock inside the *dojan* directly across from him and raised his eyebrows.

Alexis practically flew past the office, hoping she would be able to get dressed before he entered the workout space. The last one in would have to sweep up afterward, and she didn't want it to be her. She had promised her Aunt Athena that she would not be late for Paris's fitting.

The small changing room was dimly lit and smelled of old socks. Alexis rushed in and closed the door anyway, trying to hold her breath. A bargain-basement torchère cast a harsh glow on the poorly painted walls. She tried not to look at the dust that had settled into the corners of the makeshift room.

There was barely enough time to get herself together before the other members of the class got into their lines for the warm-ups. She snuck into the back line just as Master Um descended the three steps into the *dojan*. He bowed to the flags, both Korean and American, that hung on the front wall. The students immediately snapped to attention.

Instead of beginning the exercises as usual, the instructor walked to the front of the class. He was thin and muscular. All four of the women in the class kept their eyes glued to his sinewy body as they watched the fabric of his uniform moving with him. The view was certainly a plus. It took Alexis's mind off of the torture she had to endure every time she walked into this class.

"We have a new student," he said. Although he had been in the United States for many years, Master Um still had a very heavy accent and was sometimes difficult to understand.

He gestured toward the back of the class and everyone turned to look in Alexis's direction. "Remedy Brown is new to our sport. I trust you will all make him feel welcome. Alexis, Remedy will be your partner today."

She blushed, then nodded. *What kind of name was that?* she wondered. *His parents sure had a sense of humor.* Alexis had thought she was sneaking into the back line, but ended up standing right next to the man in the spotlight. They made eye contact and she nodded. He had a smug look on his face. With so many women in the class, he probably assumed that he would have an easy time of it or something. *Another ass-hole, just like the rest of them.* She tried not to hate him for just *being*, but it was hard.

They would have an extra-hard workout today. It was always that way when someone new joined the class. Master Um wanted to see what the new person was made of, if he could hang out with the current students or if he would end up running screaming from the building. Remedy, or whatever his name was, was certainly not easily scared off, it seemed. He seemed to be quite full of himself. She wanted to see what he would look like after the rest of the students finished kicking him around the room a bit.

He grinned, then winked at Alexis.

She narrowed her eyes, then turned away. What in the hell did he think this was? This wasn't some pickup bar. *He better ask somebody and not fuck with her. One wrong move and she would gladly kick him into tomorrow.* At five-foot-three, Alexis knew he was probably sizing her up as a "little woman." She got that a lot. Nothing like getting one's ass kicked by a small woman to adjust a macho attitude.

Alexis pushed him to the back of her mind as they made their way through the warm-up. She thought about the woman she'd interviewed today, anything to keep her mind off the number of jumping jacks she was doing. A bead or two of sweat rolled down her forehead. She wiped them away before they could make their way into her eyes. Finally, Master Um gave the signal to stop.

They moved to the heavy bag. Alexis showed Remedy how to hold the bag so it would not swing as they progressed through the kicking drills. He seemed to be a quick study. She concentrated her vision on one spot on the bag and pictured Walter's face, then delivered a roundhouse kick smack in the middle. The bag swung wildly.

Remedy was thrown off balance. He stumbled backward.

Alexis tried not to break her concentration. She waited for Remedy to get back to his place, ready to kick again.

He straightened his uniform, then put his hands back on the bag. "You are serious about this, aren't you?"

"You have no idea." Alexis didn't wait for him to respond. She immediately started kicking the bag again. She gave Walter's face a kick for working so hard and making almost no time for her. Another for not saying no to that damned massage lady when she offered him a *full*-body massage. And then many, many kicks for letting two months pass since he left and not even calling her to apologize.

The instructor called time. The mirrors that ran the circumference of the room were now clouded with steam. Although the room was not heated, the sweating students had generated so much heat it felt like a sauna.

Sparring would be next. This was Alexis's favorite part of

the class. A few students ran to the sides of the room and took big gulps of water from bottles lining the walls. They grabbed red, square pads and held them in their hands, then lined up facing their partners.

Alexis lined up with Remedy facing her. She quickly handed him the kicking pads and showed him how to put them on his hands to protect his arms.

She watched as he licked his lips and glanced around at the people on either side of him. He seemed to try his best to copy their stances and the way they held their hands. Alexis wondered if he had any hint at all that she would certainly not be cutting him any slack today. At just a hair above five-foot-three, she was tiny, but Alexis was proud of her legs. They were strong, solid, and had been compared to tree trunks. If she had her way, those same legs were about to make contact with his body in ways she was sure he'd never imagined. Alexis planned to kick as hard as she could, even if this was his first class. His inexperience was not her problem.

Alexis held her knee up to waist height and threw one test kick. It landed right in the middle of Remedy's pad, making a loud *thwack*. She smiled. He seemed to be concentrating really hard on not moving in response to her kicks. *Wrong answer*. She pursed her lips and concentrated, mentally drawing all of her energy up and out through her leg.

A loud crack ripped through the room as Alexis's kick met its target.

Remedy crumpled to the floor, his eyes wide with surprise.

The room became silent.

Alexis stood over Remedy and the rest of the students huddled around him, mouths agape.

Remedy was bent over on the floor, gripping his arm.

"C'mon. It wasn't that hard." Alexis tried not to smirk.

A guttural sound escaped his lips. "I think . . . you broke my arm."

just short of crazy

And so she had. In two places. Alexis stayed in the waiting room while the doctor treated Remedy. As soon as she'd realized what she had done, Alexis was immediately sorry and had boo-hooed all the way to the hospital, as if she was the one who had just had the shit kicked out of her. Alexis's stomach was tied up in knots. She hadn't meant to hurt him, not really. It wasn't his fault that she had become a pent-up, angry bitch. It was Walter's. He'd been the one to walk out on her without warning, leaving her waiting, alone and clueless in their favorite restaurant, then move across the country to get away from her and their relationship. She was embarrassed in front of her family and her friends, broke some guy's arm and now wouldn't be able to go back to the office tonight as she'd originally planned.

A nurse stuck her head over the desk that was across from where Alexis was sitting. She nodded at Alexis. "You can go back now."

Alexis grabbed two more tissues from the nearby box, and

once again, tried to wipe her face. A knot formed in the pit of her stomach. Just what did you say to a man whose arm you broke within the first twenty minutes of meeting him? *Good thing we all signed waivers or my next few words might be "please don't sue me."* She pushed through the doors that led into the main body of the emergency room.

The area she found was large, nothing more than a ware-house-like space with tons of people and activity in it. People scurried about and machines beeped loudly. Fluorescent lights cast a glow that made everything look dingy. Various areas were partitioned off by hospital gray curtains that hung from the ceiling. As Alexis walked among them, she could see that there were beds behind each curtain, and most of them were full. A shiver ran down her spine. She hated hospitals and had not been in one in a long, long time, almost ten years to be exact, since her mother had died.

She found Remedy off in a corner, reclined on a gurney. She poked her head through the curtain, then grimaced. "I am *so* sorry." With the way he was lying there, it looked horrible.

"Well, you said I had no idea." He half smiled at her.

His smile made Alexis even more uncomfortable. What type of man smiled after having his day ruined? Why wasn't he angry? "I didn't mean to——" She was suddenly conscious of the way she must look. Her uniform was soggy and hung off of her, her hair all sweated out and limp.

He held up his good arm. "I know. You don't need to apol-ogize. I was kinda cocky. Come in."

"I hope you will let me make it up to you." She bit her lip. *Why had she said that? It seemed like the right thing to say, but just how do you make it up to someone when you have quite possibly mangled them?*

"Just wait until my arm heals. We can have a rematch."

Alexis didn't know what to say to that. She was normally ready for most comments that made her uncomfortable with a quick comeback, but all words left her this time. It had been a while since a man had left her speechless. She shifted her weight nervously from one foot to the other. In other circumstances, she might have thought that Remedy's line was a come-on. She wasn't sure this time.

She didn't have a chance to think of anything else to say. The curtain separating them from the rest of the emergency-room treatment area suddenly swung open. Alexis jumped back and they were joined by a woman who looked vaguely familiar to her. She wore a hot-pink tracksuit made of thin material that hugged her body like a glove. The bottom was low-slung, and the top fitted to her chest and zipped only half-way up, exposing her ample breasts on one end and her pierced navel on the other. Alexis glanced at her feet and saw that she wore fuzzy knockoff mukluks that were exactly the same color as her sweat suit. She looked like an overgrown MTV video reject.

"Well, Rem," the pink diva said. "What have you gotten yourself into this time?" She stood with her weight shifted to the side and her hand on one hip. Her whole body seemed to smirk as she stood there, chewing loudly on her gum.

Remedy looked nervously from Alexis to the new woman, making Alexis feel as if she were the one who had suddenly arrived on the scene.

Alexis raised her eyebrows. It was obvious that these

two people had history. She could feel it flying around the room.

"Ayzah. You came fast." He swallowed hard. *Maybe a little too fast.* Remedy hated that he had to call his ex for anything. He kinda liked Alexis and knew it was better for Ayzah not to get any wind of that at all. She was known to be a little possessive. It didn't matter that they were not together anymore.

"What the hell did you expect? I didn't have a choice. You had someone call me, tell me it was an emergency. I thought you were dead or something. You ask me, this ain't no emergency. You are still breathing, dammit, so this better be good. I had a hella weekend planned." She paused and looked at her watch, then at Alexis.

Alexis cringed. The woman's eyes were like daggers.

"And who the hell is this? If you had a new bitch you could have asked her to take care of what you needed."

"Don't be stupid. I am nothing like you. You know I don't introduce our son to just anybody. And besides, she couldn't pick him up anyway, she isn't on the daycare list."

"So who is this?" She pointed at Alexis with two of her dragon lady fingernails.

Alexis cleared her throat.

"You don't have to worry. She isn't a girlfriend. Alexis, this is Ayzah Brown."

"I know you don't have strange women around my son—"

"Will you shut up and give me a chance?" He sighed. "This is Alexis. No relationship in any way. We just met. She is the one responsible for putting me here."

Ayzah was calmer now and a look of confusion crossed her face.

Alexis smiled sheepishly and tried to figure out how she could get out of the waiting area without walking too close to Ayzah. Alexis had no desire to get to know her better at all. "I broke his arm. In tae kwon do."

The three of them were silent as Ayzah looked from Alexis to Remedy and back again. Her mouth dropped open in disbelief, and then she burst out laughing. She laughed until tears rolled down her cheeks. "Tae kwon do? You know you too old for that fly-through-the-air Jackie Chan shit. It serves you right, Remedy. You are always trying some crazy mess." She extended her hand toward Alexis for a handshake. "I am so sorry. I'm his wife——"

"Ex-wife."

She rolled her eyes. "Whatever. I could be the queen of Sheba. Your ass needs me right now so don't piss me off."

Alexis shook her head. She *really* wanted no part of this. "I just came to check on him. I felt so badly about breaking his arm and all. But it doesn't look like I'm needed here now, so——"

"Girl, please. I should thank you. His ass probably deserved it. I should have broke something of his years ago." She turned to Remedy. "I told you you was soft."

Remedy's face flushed. He was used to Ayzah embarrassing him. "Don't worry about her. Ayzah, I just need you to pick up Jamal for me and make sure he gets to Soccertots."

"I told you I would, although I don't know why I should. You are wasting your money with that Soccertots and you insisted on having sole custody and all. And don't be apologizing to her, she is the one that broke your damn arm!"

"It was an accident." Alexis was having a hard time holding her tongue.

"Could you keep your voice down please, Ayzah?" Remedy's eyes were wide.

She ignored him and turned to Alexis. "You one of them proper bitches, huh?"

Alexis felt naked as Ayzah's eyes traveled the length of her body. She felt like she was back in the projects in Houston before she came to live with her aunt. She knew that Ayzah's anger at her actually had nothing to do with her at all.

Ayzah continued to glare at her. "You can go. I got this." Her voice was harsh and she seemed to spit her words across the small space.

Alexis fought to maintain her composure. Who was this woman to dismiss her like she was hired help? She hated it when people tried to make their inadequacies her fault. She counted to ten silently.

"Look, I'm sorry, Alexis. I appreciate you coming by to check on me. I'll see you in class."

"You really are coming back?"

"Of course. I was serious. How could I not?"

Ayzah interrupted them. "Wait, I know you. You are Alexis the lawyer. The divorce lawyer. I came to see you about two years ago, about my divorce."

Alexis shook her head. "I'm sorry. You do look familiar, but I don't think I handled your case. I would have remembered."

"Damn skippy you didn't. Your bourgie-ass firm wanted too damn much money. And your partner was snooty."

Remedy visibly exhaled. His arm hurt like hell and he was in no mood for a catfight.

Alexis was relieved, too. It would have been very bad if she had broken the arm of a client's ex-husband. That kind of thing was the stuff office legends were made of. "I assume you worked it out and found a lawyer who met your requirements?"

"Not exactly."

Remedy cleared his throat. "I actually ended up divorcing her and now I have full custody of our son." His face was dark and his mouth formed a tight line.

The air was thick with tension. Alexis wanted out more than ever. Their relationship was an obvious sore spot. "Okay, you know, I really do have to go now. I'm late for an appointment." The vibes between Ayzah and Remedy were way too strange for her taste. She would have never figured the two of them for a married couple. They seemed as different as two people could possibly be. Remedy was a little rough around the edges but he at least seemed semirefined; Ayzah, she was straight ghetto.

Alexis had enough going on in her life and certainly had no desire to be in the middle of other people's mess. Neither one of them was her concern. "I'm sorry again. Let me know if you need anything." She slid her card onto the small table by the side of Remedy's gurney.

Ayzah was angry again. "I told you I got this." She grabbed at the business card.

Talk about bad karma. Alexis's sixth, seventh, and eighth senses told her that it was well past time for her to go. She slid through the curtain and left the two of them glowering at each other. She shook her head and made a beeline for the exit. They were probably the most interesting couple she had met in quite some time. Or ex-couple. That woman seemed

just short of crazy, if anything, but Remedy, he seemed normal. Too bad he obviously had a lot of baggage. He wasn't
bad-looking; in fact, he was kinda fine. The little voice that
lived inside her head screamed at her. "Run! Run away fast,"
it said. He might be good-looking but she hadn't met a man
yet, no matter how intriguing, was worth that kind of drama.

♡   ♡   ♡

Ayzah shivered a little as she ran across the pavement to the
parked car. It wasn't cold, but the anxiety that had been building since she'd left Remedy's bedside still left her chilly.

Prince was waiting. He flipped his cell phone closed as she
neared.

She pulled on the car door just a little too hard, causing it
to open faster than she anticipated. Ayzah stumbled backward, giggled, then slid inside.

"Hey."

Prince grunted in reply. His eyes were cold. He turned his
cheek and the kiss that Ayzah intended for his face landed on
his ear.

"You going to fill me in or what?"

"He's fine. Some woman broke that fool's arm, is all. He
needs me to pick up Jamal for him."

Prince nodded deep and long as if he were contemplating
what this meant. "I hope you were nice to him. You know
how you can be. If I gotta drive your ass all over town whenever he calls, you make sure you are playing it right."

Ayzah's shoulders dropped. She was trying her best, but no
matter what, she seemed unable to please Prince. "You know
I'ma do what I gotta do. We got a plan, baby." She forced a

smile and tried again to kiss Prince. This time, her lips found their mark and Prince even kissed her back.

"That's what I'm talking 'bout. Your son needs to be growing up with you. With us. I ain't never heard nonsense like this shit here. You need your custody back so that he can pay you some child support. That is the way shit was supposed to be."

Prince started the car. His brows were knit into a tight line.

"Then we can be a family, right?" Ayzah's eyes searched his face. After years of living crazy, she missed that more than anything. She wanted to be part of a family. She and Remedy had only had that for a minute. She had just been too young and wild to recognize that as a good thing.

"Yeah, that's right." Prince cleared his throat. As much money as that asshole Remedy was making, the courts would make him pay big to support his child. And if Ayzah had custody, he would benefit, too.

ugly stepsisters

Athena was going to be pissed. Alexis weighed the options. She could tell the truth about why she was over an hour late for the dress fitting or she could lie about it. Although she knew she was certain to get less shit from her aunt if she did the former, Athena probably wouldn't believe the truth. But she sure did want to share her larger-than-life encounter with Miz Ayzah Brown with Paris and Sarah. They were her two best friends and they would most certainly have a field day with this one.

The parking lot of the bridal store was nearly empty. Only a few cars were left, and she recognized all but one of them. The gang was all here, waiting for her, of course. This wasn't good. Her stomach tightened. She was a grown woman and facing Athena still made her feel like a teenager. This was twice in one day that she was late, late, late.

The bells on the door jingled as Alexis pushed it open. Paris, Athena, and Sarah were in the front of the small store. Their stares bored through Alexis like tiny screws. You would think she had committed a crime punishable by death or something.

Alexis wanted to sink through the floor. "It couldn't be helped," she said, sounding as if she were asking a question rather than making a statement.

Paris looked to be near tears. But then again, she had looked that way ever since she and Tyson had set a date. Her cousin had been subject to more mood swings than a lithium-deprived manic-depressive.

"You did this on purpose," she moaned. "You could have at least put some clothes on instead of running around town in your pajamas. I would not have done this to you."

First crazy, now nasty, Alexis thought. *It could have been worse.* She sighed. "You know I am not doing anything to you. I had a small problem in my tae kwon do class. And these are not my pajamas so stop clowning."

"I hope you aren't too sweaty. These people are not going to want you funking up their clothes." Athena looked Paris up and down and gave her the best evil eye she could.

No way in hell I can win this one. "Have you picked a dress yet?" Changing the subject might be the smartest course of action. It was best not to be forced into a place where she was saying nasty things to Auntie.

"I hope whoever made you late to your favorite cousin's dress fitting, one of the most important occasions in any woman's life, was worth it." Paris dried the crocodile tears that had been running down her face.

Here come the fangs. "What makes you think that there was a *whoever*?"

"We know you. Not only is there a *whoever*, but I would

bet that the whoever is a man." Sarah grinned and fingered the fabric of a lacy dress hanging near her.

They were doing their best to make Alexis feel guilty, she knew that, and virtually every part of her was annoyed, right down to the Jimmy Choo flip-flops she wore on her feet. Still, she couldn't stop a smirk from creeping onto her face. "You are right," she said, "there was a man, but not in the way you think. I'm late because I broke a guy's arm. A guy in my class. I went to the hospital to check on him."

Paris rolled her eyes then turned around to talk with her mother.

"Ha. I guess if you knock him down then he can't run from you." She walked to the back of the store. "C'mon. Because you're late, your worst fear has transpired. I've picked a perfectly ugly dress for you." She held up a lime-colored dress.

"Didn't anyone hear me? I broke a man's arm. I kicked him and it snapped." Alexis could not believe it. None of them seemed in the least bit concerned or interested.

"You are never going to catch a husband like that." Athena came from the rear of the store where she had put on a dress. "Not that your opinions matter, ladies, but what do you think of this one for me?" She turned in a circle so they could admire her mother-of-the-bride special, a three-quarter-length blush-colored ensemble. The lapels were huge and encrusted with silver paillettes. "*You* should have kept Walter."

Sarah shook her head.

"Ma, Walter didn't want her. Alexis, your dress is in the room over there. Number four." Paris pointed to a small curtained-off area.

"Thanks for taking my side, Paris. Is anyone interested in hearing my story?"

"Not really. And I'm not taking your side. We all know that it is just a ploy to spoil my wedding. You are jealous. Passive aggressive. You know what I mean."

Alexis inhaled sharply. Her face began to get hot. She did know what Paris meant. Her cousin was as self-centered as she always had been, so Paris couldn't see past her perfect self. Alexis had spent her whole life feeling as if she were the ugly stepsister, trying to live up to Athena's unrealistic ideals. It was no family secret that she was always second to Paris, but she loved her anyway.

Her face crumpled and she counted to ten (again) to avoid crying. "What a hurtful thing to say. I would never do such a thing to you. You are insinuating that because of my breakup I would wish you something other than the best. I'm just not that small-minded."

Sarah cleared her throat and walked around a rack of dresses.

"And Aunt Athena, just so you know, I don't need a man to complete me. I have told you that before."

"You sure about that?" Athena appeared unfazed by Alexis's comments. She turned around to check for panty lines in the full-length mirror. "You young people are so confused about things, but you'll see."

"I'm positive."

"If you say so."

"Finish your story. I want to hear even if they don't." Sarah smiled. As usual, she was trying to keep the peace. The whole wedding business was stressful enough, at least the way they did it, without added bickering.

"Could you please finish in the dressing room, then? I'm sure these poor people want to go home sometime tonight," Paris said.

Alexis snatched the green dress and stepped into the room they indicated. She closed the curtain. "Well, like I said, I broke this guy's arm, then I felt bad. I ended up at the hospital the same time as his ex-wife. She was almost a client, but that is another story." She paused. "Anyway, she was ghetto, with a capital *G*, and a little belligerent. She didn't like my being there at all." Alexis struggled to pull the dress over her head and talk at the same time.

"Was she nasty? I would be mad if you broke my husband's arm." More interested now, Paris had moved closer to the curtain so she could hear better.

"Ex-husband."

"Whatever. Was he nice-looking? Do you know what he does for a living?"

"Auntie, I was working out, not taking boyfriend résumés. Besides, he has a crazy ex-wife and a small kid. You know I don't like to date men with kids, especially not little ones. Baby Mama Drama is a no-can-do for me.

"That makes your pickings slim. Are you in the dress yet?" Paris said.

"Just wait. Anyway, I came this close to getting black on the woman, she——"

"I really resent that people equate being black with being ghetto. They are not the same. I taught you better than that, Alexis." Athena's voice was sharp.

She sighed. "Yes, you did. That isn't what I meant." Finally in the dress, Alexis opened the curtain and stepped through.

The dress fitter rushed over with a tape measure.

"This doesn't look too bad, huh? Even in this horrible color." Alexis admired herself in the mirror.

"I like it," Sarah agreed.

"I find it hard to believe that you can make a perfectly ugly dress look good. Try the other one." Paris crossed her arms as she studied Alexis in the dress.

"You don't want me to look good?" Alexis replied.

"Don't be silly. I just want to make sure all eyes are on me at my wedding. *Try the other one.*"

Alexis stepped back into the curtained space. "Aunt Athena, what I meant was, people often think that I can't get down and dirty when they piss me off. I can roll my neck with the rest of them if I need to. I am proud to say I can hold my own."

"Can you hurry? You were always a little rough, even when you were a small girl." Athena paused. "You know what they say, you can take the girl out of the ghetto, but you can't take the ghetto out of the girl."

Alexis changed dresses and stepped outside again. "This better be it. I am not going to wear a butt-ugly dress for any-one, even you, Paris."

"I thought we already established that this isn't about you. When you get married, I will wear what you want, no matter how hideous. But right now, I am making the decision."

Alexis modeled the dress. It wasn't half bad, but she didn't want to act as if she liked it too much. If she did, then either Paris or Athena would not approve it.

"That isn't too different from mine. I like that one better." Sarah folded her arms.

"Yours is perfect for you." Paris contemplated her cousin in the dress. It really wasn't that bad at all. She could not under-stand why they were complaining about the choice of colors.

"So, did you tell her yet?" Athena was back again.

"I told you I would handle it, Mother."

Alexis looked from Paris to her Aunt Athena. That didn't sound good. "You know I don't like bad news. And I can tell it's bad by the way she said that. Don't let me have to get black on *you*."

Sarah cleared her throat and looked away. She was used to the way they talked to each other, flaunting their black talk. The three of them had been doing it in front of her for years, like they'd forgotten about her white skin or simply didn't see it anymore. They called her an honorary sistah, but she knew that there was only so far that honorary could take you and there were some conversations she just didn't participate in.

The room was filled with the awkward silence that hung between them.

"What?" Alexis asked. "I'm your maid of honor. I need to know all pertinent information." She tried to make light of the situation, but a terrible feeling was growing in the pit of her stomach. She was working her way toward an ulcer. Alexis put her hand on her stomach. "Paris——"

"Well, I was going to wait until later and it seems like you already had a bad day." She wrung her hands together. "Well, Walter is going to be in the wedding after all."

Alexis looked first at Paris, then at Sarah. "You knew this, didn't you?" Usually, whatever Paris hid, Alexis could cer-tainly find out from Sarah. She was not as good at covering up as her cousin could be. Her lips felt dry and cracked as she ran her tongue across them. "Okay. I can handle that."

Athena inhaled loud enough for all of them to hear.

"There's more. He is going to be the best man and your escort."

Tears welled up in Alexis's eyes. She had made it almost through the whole day without really feeling sorry for herself, but her day had just gone from bad to worse.

♡   ♡   ♡

The Yellow Rose seemed to be more crowded than usual. Ayzah peeked out from behind the curtain and surveyed the room. Lots of regulars right down front. She would make a mint tonight.

She stood behind the curtain. As her music started, she made one last check on the red-sequined pasties that covered her nipples. Her boss and bouncer, OJ, would have a cow if one of them came off. The tiny scraps of fabric were what kept the place respectable, he said. He was tripping. According to her mother, they were all going to hell, pasties or not. *Whatever.*

This was her favorite part of the night, the dancing. The lap dances were more lucrative, but this made her feel like a star, even if she wasn't a real dancer, not like the girls in the videos or in those shows. It was a start, though, and it paid the bills. She'd missed it while she was pregnant and for the time she'd been a married woman. That was over now and she was back in full effect.

Butterflies tickled her stomach as they always did before a show. The announcer called her name and the catcalls started, even before the curtain rolled back. Ayzah put on her best come-hither look, then started to strut her stuff. She loved the feeling of power she had when she was on the stage, and prided herself on looking as good as she did after she had popped out a baby, an almost ten-pounder at that.

Her music and her routine had just been updated, and she could feel the rhythm down deep as she gyrated and used her dance training in ways her dance teacher never imagined. She put her mind far away, visualizing the first time she had seen the movie *Flashdance* with her mother. She was very small, and that film had been her introduction to the world of exotic dancing. It was just a trip to the movies and the two of them never imagined that she would end up on the stage herself one day. It wasn't permanent, by any means, and it was only one step on the way, until something better came along, and it would. Ayzah could feel it in her bones.

The routine was almost over. Ayzah got close to some of the regulars who were seated around the raised stage. She let them put bills in her G-string and hoped that most of them were not singles. She licked her lips at one of the men and ran her hand across the top of another's head. They went wild, throwing bills at the stage. She made a point to scoop them all up as she exited.

The next girl was already lined up. She was a pretty bottle-redhead who did a routine in pink cowboy boots and matching thong and pasties. Ayzah tried not to stare. The woman had the biggest boobs she had ever seen in her life. She was almost deformed, especially when you compared them to her tiny waist and hips. It was like she was a cartoon, the top of one woman drawn onto the bottom of the other.

She nodded at Ayzah. "Good job."

"Thanks." Ayzah smiled. She knew she'd been good.

"OJ wants to see you right away."

She exhaled, then headed back toward his office, nothing more than a small closet behind the kitchen. OJ was pacing in his office and talking on the phone at the same time. He was big and bald with no facial hair, not even eyebrows. His office smelled of smoke.

OJ didn't even hang up the phone when Ayzah entered, just moved it a little to the side. His eyes raked over Ayzah's near-naked body. "I'm going to give you an advance. You need to go see this friend of mine. He will fix up those boobs for you."

"Fix up?"

"Yeah. They need to be bigger. We hired a specialist, a research man. He found out that customers drink more when the dancer's boobs are bigger."

She came down from the high that dancing had given her and her mood veered sharply toward anger. "I am not interested in having any damned surgery, OJ. Tell your specialist that he can kiss my ass."

He let the phone drop down by his side. "If you want to keep your job, you'll get it done." Beat. "You'll thank me later. Why don't you sleep on it for a week or so." He flashed her a patronizing smile.

Ayzah crossed her arms in front of her. She would sleep on it, but she didn't see her mind changing one bit.

kick him when he's down

Pain. Remedy swallowed the medication they had given him in the emergency room. Who knew that a broken arm would hurt so bad? Still, when you got over thinking about the pain the way he got injured had to be worth something. Alexis was fine as hell. If nothing else, he might be able to get to know her better. She looked like the type of woman who could change his luck. From the minute she had run into the *dojan*, he knew that he wanted to see her later.

He turned over her business card. It was a miracle he even had it. As crazy as Ayzah was, he was surprised that she didn't try to burn it or something. She'd snatched at it first and then forgot about it, dropping it back onto the table. She'd done worse things. In spite of the way Ayzah had clowned, Remedy could not seem to get Alexis off of his mind.

There was something about the way she carried herself that was intriguing. She'd come into the class wearing a conservative but expensive-looking pantsuit. The sort that said she was a no-nonsense kind of woman. It hugged her in all the right places. And in those few minutes, he could tell that she had a lot of right places.

Alexis was short, and her hair was cropped close and natural. He liked the natural part. Said a lot about a woman, mainly that she was comfortable with herself, or at least comfortable enough to let the real her hang out. More than that, the short hair made it easy to see her interesting features. He'd had enough of fake hair, extensions, and weaves to last him a lifetime. She was pixielike almost, disarming. And obviously mean as hell. He'd been so busy watching the determined way she had punched the bag, he forgot to be surprised when he ended up kissing the floor. The tae kwon do uniform she'd had on was square and formless, but watching her was like watching sex walking. Every now and then he met someone like that, someone so sexy she made other people stop and stare, but unaware of the effect she had on other people. Alexis was one of those people. Refreshing.

And then Ayzah had to spoil it all with her bad attitude. Remedy sighed and rubbed his cast. A one-night stand turned into years of misery. They had pity sex after a night out with friends. His. Not hers. She had just been a stripper along for the ride. An unspoken agreement, she would scratch his itch, he would scratch hers. Somewhere in the night the condom evaporated and they ended up married with a kid. It wasn't all bad; he got Jamal out of the deal.

He'd thought he was rid of her when he filed for divorce, but he had never been more wrong in his life. For eleven months, he'd had no idea where Ayzah even was, and now, she was everywhere, almost trying to be a model of motherhood.

At least she had shown up when he needed her. He had to admit that was a step in the right direction. Or so he thought.

The sound of a key turning in the front door lock startled Remedy and he jumped to his feet. *What in the hell . . . ?* he thought. His head swam. He steadied himself on the side of the sofa and rubbed his forehead. He must have bumped his head when he hit the floor. And that was one hard-ass floor. Most of his fall was a blur, but the memory of his body slamming into the painted concrete was as clear as could be.

Remedy kept a five-iron behind the sofa for opportunities just like this one. He grabbed it. He wasn't much of a golfer, but when you lived the life he had, he knew he could use it to put a hurting on anyone or anything.

He stepped behind the door with the club over his head just as it swung open. Remedy used his forearm to stop it from hitting him in the face. He realized that it was Ayzah just in time. One more second and she would have had a golf club planted up her ass.

She turned to close the door behind her and stopped. "You damn fool!" she shouted. "I know you wasn't going to even think about hitting me with that thing."

He cringed, almost wishing he'd hit her, but he had no desire to go to jail. Her voice was as shrill as ever. "What are you doing here, Ayzah?" He lowered the club and she snatched it out of his hands.

"You have no business coming up in here like this, lesser shit would get you killed. And where in the hell did you get my key?"

"I used to live here, remember? This was our apartment, you dumbass, or did you forget? If you'd hit me with that golf club I might have had to break your other arm."

If I had hit you, I guarantee you would no longer be stand-ing. Remedy walked behind her. Although she was trying to be a little normal, he still would not turn his back on her yet. In the last few years of their relationship, she had become more than a little unpredictable.

"It was only for a minute and you don't live here anymore, so next time, please be sure to use the doorbell. Where is my son?"

"*Our* son. Jamal is visiting his grandmother." Ayzah sat on the couch and made herself comfortable. She fluffed a pillow, then coughed as dust flew into the air. "I took him to my mother's house. She said you didn't get to bring him by much while I was gone."

As far as Remedy was concerned, they had barely earned the right to see Jamal at all. When Ayzah'd disappeared, no one in her damn family would even give him a clue as to where she was. She was just gone with no explanation, no nothing. He knew they knew something. Someone always did.

Remedy was still mad as hell at Ayzah for her disappearance. She'd just left like she was going to work one day and hadn't come back for months. "It's interesting the way you talk about that." He'd never gotten a full explanation, but decided to put it behind them for Jamal's sake. At least for now. But her parents shouldn't have to suffer for her mistakes. It was natural for them to want to protect their daughter. Besides, he had known what she was when he met her, so it really was his fault. Ayzah Brown was and always would be a hustler. Period. She did whatever she felt she had to to get by. He shook his head. She couldn't even tell how disgusted he was. Even if she could, he wasn't sure she cared. He had learned his lesson though and planned to call a locksmith as soon as she left. He was going to deactivate her security card, too. She wouldn't even be able to get past the first floor.

"I'm fine," he said. "You didn't have to come here at all, at least until you brought Jamal back on Monday."

Though he had full custody of their son, she didn't seem to get it. Ayzah had not been a bad mother, not really, and he had no problem with letting her see Jamal, as long as she didn't drag him into any of her shit.

"I was just checking on you, baby." Her husky voice was suddenly sugary and low. She slid closer to him and ran her hand along his shoulder.

He cringed. The phone rang, saving him. He grabbed it before her hand could wander any farther. He had no doubt that it would, and that would surely make them fight. Persistence always had been one of the things that made her attractive to him in the very beginning. He wasn't interested in a lap dance when she'd offered and she wouldn't take no for an answer. Ayzah'd danced for his friend, her eyes on him the whole time, then ended up joining them as they went bar to bar, for the night. Now it was no longer attractive. Instead, it made her a pain in the ass.

Remedy turned his face to the side to talk on the phone. If given the chance, Ayzah would be in his business. It was his doctor. He felt her slide up behind him, then walk away.

She headed toward the back of the apartment, probably to use the bathroom. The bedroom was back there, too. This was the first time she had been in the apartment since she'd left. Remedy knew that she would be going through the medicine cabinet and anything else she could if he didn't hurry, although he had no idea what she was looking for. He had never been the one with the secrets. He was like an open book. It was Ayzah who had the mysterious past.

Remedy assured the doctor that he was okay and quickly hung up the telephone. The last thing he needed was Ayzah going through his things. She'd done it when they were married and he had no doubt that she would do it now if given the chance.

The bedroom door was closed. Remedy snatched it open. Ayzah moved fast. She was already sprawled seductively across the bed, her clothes gone. Her wares were displayed in all their glory and she had a mischievous look on her face.

Remedy's words caught in his throat. He was done with her, for sure, but he was still a man. His body reacted without asking his brain permission.

He had to admit that she looked good. All he could see on top of his faux suede bedspread was black lace and sequins and more black lace, sensuously enveloping Ayzah's dancer's body. She knew how to hit him and she was certainly pulling out all the stops this time.

"Come here." She patted the bed next to her. Remedy shook his head. Sex with Ayzah was what had gotten him into this predicament in the first place. Too much wine and a broken condom had produced their son. Now they were linked forever whether they wanted to be or not.

"What are you doing?"

"Easing your pain. What I have is better than any narcotic that you could take. I can make it all better." Ayzah's voice had dropped down so low she did not sound unlike a purring cat about to pounce.

Remedy was no fool. There was no way in hell he was going near her. He shook his head.

"Ayzah, let's not complicate things."

"I try not to complicate anything. I want to make it as easy as possible." She purred like a kitten waiting to be scratched.

"What are you doing?" he asked again. "You told me you had a man, remember? Get dressed and go take care of him. Now."

Ayzah's face filled with disappointment. "I *do* have a man." She paused. "You kicked me to the curb."

"I didn't. You left me, happily and without any persuasion from me. There is no going back." Near the end, Ayzah had continually thrown her new relationship in his face, comparing him with Remedy. Only then she had claimed he was a hypothetical. And he was no fool. He'd seen through her the whole time. "I'm a get me a new man that knows how to handle his business," she'd said.

Remedy had a strong feeling that the two of them had been seeing each other secretly for quite some time. He just didn't know how long. He refused to be part of her triangle. Shit like that was dangerous nowadays.

Ayzah stood up and came closer. The strong musty smell of her perfume mixed with her natural body odor filled his nose. He used to love that smell. He'd been an idiot, thinking that the two of them could make things work. A dumbass romantic. He backed up, and she followed until he hit a wall. She pressed her body against his.

Ayzah's smile was slow. Coy. She was not smart about a lot of things but she knew men. "Your mouth may say you're not interested, but your body is speaking a whole 'nother language. He don't take care of me like you did. It's not the same."

Remedy pushed her away and Ayzah stumbled backward. She lost her footing, her head hitting the edge of the footboard as she went down.

"You threw that away forever when you cheated on me and then disappeared. We have been through this before. Ayzah, all I want from you is for you to be a mother to your son. You have ten minutes to get dressed and get the hell out of my house." Remedy's head throbbed as he spoke.

He left her on the floor, tears welling up in her eyes.

Ayzah dressed fast. When she finally came out of the bedroom, Remedy was pacing in the living room. Her face was streaked with makeup.

"I don't understand why I'm not good enough for you anymore." Tears streamed down her face.

Remedy looked at her in disbelief. He couldn't recall ever seeing her cry and wasn't sure if her tears were real. "There is nothing to understand. We are no longer together. Only thing we have in common now is Jamal."

Ayzah spotted the business card Remedy left on the coffee table. She reached over and picked it up. It was obviously easy for him to replace her when he'd found someone new already. "Oh, I see how it is now." She pursed her lips and waited for an explanation.

"That woman has nothing to do with it. I told you I just met her." He paused. His head was hurting like hell. "I don't have to explain myself to you, Ayzah."

"You got yourself all educated and shit and now you don't even wanna try and work things out. I wasn't good enough when I was working to bring in money so your ass could be up in school. Women like her would not have given you the time of day before."

"I did not tell you to do that. I had a job. I had a business, or did you forget that? And it was only one class."

"But I did it."

"Of your own choice." He lowered his voice. "Be rational, Ayzah. Or at least be civil with me. If we can't get along, then—"

"What? If we can't get along what? You won't let me see Jamal? I am taking your ass back to court, believe that!" She was furious as she folded her arms.

"Please leave now."

"You throwing me out?"

"I'm asking you to leave." Their eyes locked in a stalemate.

Ayzah acted as if she were walking toward the door, then, turning quickly, picked up a small heavy statue from the end table.

"What—"

She didn't wait for him to finish. Ayzah held the statue with both hands and used it to crack Remedy in the head.

For the second time in two days, he found himself facedown on the floor. Remedy felt his hair become wet. He reached up to touch where Ayzah had hit him. His fingers were covered with blood.

"Ayzah—"

"You dumbass." Her chest heaved. "There is no way in hell Ayzah Brown is going to be thrown away like a piece of trash."

Remedy got up and leaned back on his couch. His day had definitely gone from bad to worse. He pressed his hand to the back of his head to try and stop the bleeding. "I hope you're all done," he said, wincing.

Anger rolled through his body. He visualized grabbing Ayzah and throwing her around the room like a rag doll, but he refused to stoop to her level. He knew that would be what she wanted, anyway. If he came within five feet of her, there was a good chance he would be the one locked up for assault or domestic abuse. He couldn't afford a trip to the county lockup.

Ayzah's cell phone. "This is Ayzah," she said, turning away from Remedy and the couch. "Hey, honey. I needed a few things from the supermarket. I'll be right there. Okay, I love you, too."

She snapped her phone shut. Ayzah towered over Remedy. Her mouth was once again drawn into a tight line. She threw the business card at him. "Call your bitch."

She flashed a smile, then turned and left, letting the door slam behind her.

Remedy watched her go. If he knew nothing else, he knew that Ayzah would not be giving up that easily. She didn't really want him. Ayzah Brown just liked to win.

canned worms

The Whole Foods store had barely been open for a full month, but it bustled with activity as if it had graced this corner of downtown since Austin's horse-and-buggy days. The large parking lot was full, and Alexis and Sarah both had a hard time trying to find a place to park.

A City of Austin uniformed police officer stood near the door, and he nodded at Alexis as she walked through the café at the front of the store. She returned his nod, noticing the crispness of his short-sleeved uniform shirt and the muscled arms that extended from it, just as the smells from the bakery greeted her nose. Her stomach growled in response. She felt like she had adult ADD, the way she was jumping from one sensation to the next. It had been hard to concentrate on anything lately.

Sarah was already waiting at a small table near the front. Alexis joined her, sliding onto one of the sleek chrome-and-plastic chairs across from her. Sarah slid a small cup to Alexis. She knew that her favorite chocolate drink was in it and had been anticipating its decadent smoothness all morning. Sarah had already begun to nurse hers. They didn't speak at first. Both were pensive in between the sips, a heavy silence hanging between them. A worried look resided on Sarah's face. Alexis was used to her friend looking that way. Sarah was the type who always appeared deep in thought about something, even when she wasn't.

Alexis blew at the top of her cup, trying to cool the luxurious potion, then gently licked the rim. She took her time, making sure she got every drop. "So, how did we go from Walter not only being in the wedding but being my escort? What did I miss?"

"You know, I tried to tell Paris that I didn't think you'd like the idea."

"And you were right, I don't. I don't think I am ready to see him at all. But Paris is supposed to be my girl. I'm sure she knew how I would feel."

"Yes, but you forget that this is *her* wedding. Besides, you seem to have moved on. Walter's presence, or lack of, should be irrelevant to you by now."

Alexis cleared her throat. Sarah was making sense, but there was no explanation for the way her heart was behaving. Her head said it was definitely over, but she and Walter had unfinished business that haunted her every time she walked into her house. Essence of man hung in the air like cheap cologne no matter what she did. "And it is irrelevant." She paused. "Really."

Sarah didn't believe it. "Well, you knew you would have to face him sooner or later. He is partners now with Paris's fiancé."

Somewhere in the back of her mind, Alexis knew that it would only be a matter of time before she heard from Walter or, at the very least, their paths crossed. He and Sarah's husband, Barry, had bought into Paris's fiancé's start-up business a few months before and it had taken off like a rocket. Even though Walter had moved to California to be closer to suppliers, Austin was still the company's home base.

"I'll get through it. I would expect Paris to shut up and take whatever I sent her way if it were my wedding, so I guess I can do the same."

Sarah nodded. "I hope so. It will make this whole thing go so much smoother. And you know, please try and be on time for everything else. Things will only be more stressful between you, Athena, and Paris if you are not where you are supposed to be. You of all people should know how much that annoys Athena." She sipped her drink. "I *was* surprised anyway. Of the three of us, Paris is the one that is usually late for everything."

"These were extenuating circumstances."

"Unbelievable and extenuating. I really thought you made that up so that you would be able to avoid some of Athena's wrath."

"Shit. You say that like she gets on your case the way she does mine."

"Hey, I know nowadays Athena is an equal opportunity bitcher. If I didn't know better I would say that she has some Jewish grandmother in her."

Alexis shrugged. "You never know. She has a way of making you feel like no matter how right you are, you're always wrong. Even when I was a little kid, no matter how good I was I was never good enough. I spent my whole life feeling like I had to live up to what Paris was and did, even what Paris looks like."

"That's rough." The uneasy silence settled between them again. "So, did you make it up? The story about the man and the broken arm?"

"I'm a grown woman. And lying never works. I really did break that man's arm. It was awful. I feel real bad about that." The cracking sound that she heard when Remedy hit the ground resounded in her head again and she shuddered.

"Perhaps you need to look into some anger management in addition to that self-defense. You know, there are a lot easier ways to meet men. You don't have to club them over their heads to let them know you're interested."

Alexis chuckled. "I was with Walter for so long I feel like there might be no other way. You know that wasn't the plan, although I have to admit it seems like my hormones are out of control. I think sex every time I look at a man now."

"So, was he cute?"

"Very. No, make that handsome. He was a fine chocolate specimen. And now he's a chocolate specimen with a broken arm. But there is too much drama surrounding him for me. I told you he had a crazy ex-wife. She came to the hospital while I was there. She had a little attitude until she recognized me. Apparently, at one point she came to my office looking for representation for their divorce."

Sarah grimaced. "Um. Baby Mama Drama. That could be bad. But you can always get around her. It's not like it's a real conflict of interest or anything."

Alexis shook her head, thinking about Paris and Tyson.

Her cousin was the one who was usually the problem child, getting involved in relationships that had all kinds of crazy people and things going on. "Maybe not. But I'm just not interested in being mixed up in all kinds of drama. We had enough of that with Miss Perfect Paris. And even if it's not technically a conflict of interest, it is just too close for comfort. I mean, I certainly don't want to piss off a crazy woman, but definitely not a crazy woman who knows where I work. Besides, I get the impression things are going to get tough around there for me soon. I don't seem to be able to do much right."

"I remember those days. I'm so glad I don't have to put up with that anymore." Sarah was relieved that she was technically self-employed. When things annoyed her, she just didn't do them. She had left corporate America several years before, after cashing out stock options, when the company she worked for got swallowed up by IBM. On good days, she was the office manager for her husband's company, DBA Ventures.

"Yeah, apparently some of the powers that be in my office have decided that I am suddenly billing too many hours. Like that is possible."

"I didn't think that a lawyer could bill too many hours."

"I didn't either." Alexis was suddenly pensive. "But they are concerned with my work-life balance, if you can imagine that. I think that is an excuse though. I got the impression that they were trying hard to find something they could harass me about."

"Well, you should keep your eyes open. Speaking of work-life balance, I decided to do some things away from the office. You know, on my own."

Alexis's eyes narrowed. "But I thought you liked working with your husband. I thought you liked the business that you're in." There was definitely something that Sarah wasn't saying. There had not been a day over the past two years that she and Paris didn't have to hear about how great Sarah's job was.

"Well." Sarah paused. "You know, it's a lot of work. But there is definitely nothing more fulfilling than being in business for yourself. It's just that after all that fulfillment, I'm still not in business for myself. I am in business with my husband. We see each other at the office. We see each other at home. Didn't somebody tell us that no one needs a husband seven days a week? I mean, not only do I have a husband seven days a week, but I have mine twenty-four/seven. Between you and me, I need a break."

This was a surprise, but Alexis understood where Sarah was coming from. "So, what are you going to do? You're not the type to sit around."

A smile spread across Sarah's face. "No, I'm not. I found a little business that I'm interested in."

"You didn't waste any time. And what does your other half think about this? Doesn't he need you? He's always saying he couldn't do without you."

"I haven't exactly told him yet. But I will eventually. I have such a great idea and it won't take up much time and doesn't need a lot of investment."

"Right. That is what they all say."

"Really though. I am going to have trunk shows. Once a quarter. That's in the beginning. The plan is to eventually have my own place."

Alexis's mouth dropped open in surprise, then she quickly recovered. "Like a *store?* I didn't know you were interested in fashion." She knew that if she waited long enough Sarah would give her more details. She had to, because what she was hearing just didn't make sense yet.

Sarah sheepishly tried to hide behind her cup. "It's been a secret passion of mine. I just never had the guts to do it."

"But you have always been so *sensible.*" Alexis didn't want to tell her that she could never imagine her as a fashionista of any type.

"Exactly. Why are you looking at me like that?"

"I'm just surprised. You are usually the more logical one among us. The one we come to for advice." Alexis paused. "What happened to helping your husband build a future for you guys, a nest egg for your retirement and all that?"

"This won't affect that. Four weeks a year. As much as you are a wanna-be diva-shopping woman, I thought you would get this."

Alexis leaned back in her chair and crossed her legs. So far, the little that Sarah had told her left the idea sounding almost frivolous.

"You see, how can I tell my husband about this if my friends don't support me?" She sighed. "I was invited to one of these trunk shows, and let me tell you, I think you are going to be surprised. The stuff is nice."

"Okay." She shook her head. "I just didn't understand how it all works, but I trust your judgment and know that you have a good head on your shoulders. So, if you say that this is going to make you happy, then I am all for it. As long as I get a discount." Alexis tried her best to smile. If this was a phase, it would pass, just like everything else.

Sarah took the last sip of her chocolate. It was obvious that she had not yet convinced Alexis, but that was okay. Once she saw how it worked, she would come around. "Besides, the business will no doubt make the same amount of money with or without me, and one of us might as well find a way to enjoy it. I hate to sound like a cliché, but you can't take it with you. So, I basically decided to quit and spend some of my husband's money for a change."

They both laughed at that, so loud that Alexis was aware that other people in the café were staring at them. Neither of them cared.

Part of Alexis was very happy for her friend, the other part was wondering where this new Sarah had come from. Parts of what her friend was saying to her were laced with a little insecurity that she had never seen before, and this new choice highlighted the differences between them. Although her Aunt Athena tried to be a poster child for marrying a man who could support you if he needed to, Alexis was more modern than that. She believed that women *needed* to be able to support themselves at all times. The power of the regular paycheck was without equal.

Sarah on the other hand, was laughing in relief, glad that someone was so accepting of her idea. She had been friends with Alexis a long time. If anyone would support her, Alexis would.

♡   ♡   ♡

Fluorescent light was hell on makeup. Ayzah looked at her reflection in the mirror of her compact and dabbed at her face harder. She pulled the small mirror closer and grimaced. In this light, it was impossible to tell if she had missed a spot or not. She sat in a worn cloth chair outside the endocrinology clinic, waiting for her mother. Why in the hell couldn't she find someone else to bring her to this godforsaken place? The hospital gave her the creeps and it wasn't like her brother had anything better to do anyway. But her mother never called him. She didn't want to inconvenience her baby. Whenever she needed to be ferried around town, Ma'dear always called her.

The oversize, institutional-looking clock told her that she had been waiting over an hour already. A shock of annoyance ran through her body. Ayzah threw her compact back into her bag and crossed her legs, bouncing one of them the way she always did. She looked at her foot as it jumped up and down, admiring her shoes. *Damn good-looking.* She looked up, realizing that an elderly man sitting across from her was staring at her. Ayzah made a face, then tugged at her purple suede skirt, pulling it down an imaginary inch. No use giving him a heart attack or anything. She couldn't tell how old he was, but it had obviously been a long time since he had seen any ass, or at least any ass that looked like hers.

The one good thing about waiting for her mother in this place was that they always had the gossip magazines in the waiting room. Ayzah picked up a magazine to flip through just as her mother shuffled through the door. She looked up, then folded the magazine and tucked it under her arm. There was no use in her missing out.

Ma'dear was neatly dressed, very sharp for a woman with so many medical problems. Her hair was tastefully pulled back into a chignon, and her purse matched her brown shoes exactly. Too exactly for Ayzah. Everyone knew that matchy-matchy was passé.

Everywhere Ayzah was daring, her mother was not. She was an old-fashioned, god-fearing, church-lady–type Southern woman. Funny thing was, she just wasn't that old.

"Hey, Mama," she said. "Everything all right? What did the doctor say?" Ayzah uncrossed her legs and stood up.

"Please. You know I told you to call me Ma'dear. It shows more respect. The least you can do is respect me even if you can't respect yourself."

Here we go. Ayzah took a deep breath. Her mother wasn't old enough to be called Ma'dear, considering that barely seventeen years separated them. She was immediately sorry she had asked her anything. "Okay. Ma'dear then. I gotta get you home. I have to meet Prince."

"Oh. Excuse me for expecting my only daughter to help me out just a little every now and then. Good thing I didn't have to get nowhere when I was busy birthing you or raising you by myself. Good thing I had no problem making sacrifices for you, huh?"

They started walking toward the door, Ayzah falling into her routine of staying half a step behind her mother. She had heard this same argument many times and knew she couldn't win. Her mother may have made some sacrifices for her, that's true, but she was making sure that Ayzah paid for those sacrifices for a long time. And Ayzah hated it when she turned on the "old lady" that she imagined she was. To hear her tell it, Ma'dear had been old all of her life. It was just better not to fight her.

"You still shackin' with that no-count man of yours? I liked Remedy better."

"Ma'dear, no one says shackin' anymore."

"That's not the point. They might call it something else

but it's all still the same, ain't it? You left a good, honest man for what? You messed up on that one, if you ask me. I almost didn't help you with that one at all. I can't believe I ever gave in to your crazy ideas. I should have told that man where you were first thing. I had to pray on it a long time, I tell you."

"So you have said. I don't want to argue with you, Ma'dear. Prince is a good man too. I can't help who I love."

"Hmmph." Ma'dear smoothed her skirt. "Yeah, you can."

Yeah, like you helped who you loved, right? How many times have you told me that my own father was the love of your life and then turned around and said he was good for nothing? "Prince is where my heart is right now, okay?"

"Just make sure his heart is with you, too. If you ask me, he doesn't seem to always have your best interests in mind. I'm not sure I like the way he treats you." Ma'dear narrowed her eyes.

They had reached the car door. Ayzah pressed the button on the remote and opened the door for her mother. "Yes, Ma'dear. Let me get you home now."

"You ain't even listening to me, are you?"

Ayzah didn't answer. *Not really.* Instead she slid into the car and started the ignition.

"I need to go by Fiesta. I want to get me some spices. It shouldn't take too long, it's right on the way."

It wasn't on the way, but Ayzah didn't dare say so. Instead she sighed and looked down as she waited for her car to turn fully on. "You know, my car is kinda broken down. I think I got the worst one in the family."

"Genesis, Exodus, Leviticus, Numbers." Ma'dear recited her trademark phrase. She chanted the books of the Bible instead of swearing. How far she got was directly related to how mad she was. "You should be glad to help me out, Ayzah Marie. And if that man of yours was any good, he would see to your car." She glanced down at Ayzah's exposed knees. "And your clothes, too. You only seem to be wearing half of them."

If it were anyone else besides her mother, Ayzah might have clocked her for dissing her clothes the way she had. At the very least, she would have gotten a big piece of her mind. Besides, her mother might get on her nerves, but if nothing else, she had taught her to respect her elders. She was a grown woman, but there was only so far she would go with talking back to her mother. When she was a child, her mother would often give her the famous "I brought you in, I'll take you out" comment. The fact that she had lived to adulthood was almost a miracle given the number of times her mother had threatened to end her life, but Ayzah was not about to test Ma'dear. Instead of responding, she concentrated on the road, and before she knew it, they were in the parking lot of Fiesta Supermarket, even though it was all the way across town from where they started out.

The small parking lot was overshadowed by the interstate that passed overhead and littered with debris. Scraps of paper blew in the wind. Ayzah navigated her small car through the lot, avoiding the dented shopping carts that seemed to have been left in every other parking spot. She could hear the noise from the highway above her through her closed windows. People of varying ethnic backgrounds were herding into the store. Some of them had come from all over town, maybe even outside of Austin. Fiesta was the only supermarket that sold many of the ethnic goods that they needed for their cook-ing. Hog maws? Fiesta had that. Tripe? That, too, and more.

She pulled into a small space, virtually wedging her car between two equally dented pickup trucks. She felt squeezed, but couldn't really tell if it was because the parking space was so small or because her mother had managed to make her tense in the twenty minutes she had been in the car.

Ayzah reached down and slid back her car seat as Ma'dear undid her seat belt. She could read her stolen magazine while she waited for her mother to finish her grocery shopping.

"You coming in?" Her mother paused with one leg outside the door.

"Huh?" she said. Although she had heard her mother clearly, Ayzah acted as if she were surprised at her mother's question.

"You know I need you to come on in with me. It will go much faster that way."

She gritted her teeth and turned off the car, then got out to follow her mother. Just as her mother had expectations for her, there were some things she expected from her mother, and treating her like this was one of them. It was as if Ma'dear enjoyed figuring out just what to say, do, or ask for in order to push Ayzah's buttons. It was all good, though. Ayzah knew that her mother would do anything for her that she asked, and she had asked on more than one occasion. The last time, her mother had promised not to reveal her whereabouts to Remedy when she had run off with Prince. Ma'dear had made it clear that she didn't agree with her motivations, but in the end, she'd proven that blood was thicker than water. Ayzah smiled. Prince had put a hurting on her pussy that was so good, it was like she was under a spell or something. There had been nothing that she wouldn't do if he'd asked.

The cold air of the supermarket sent a chill through Ayzah. She shivered, then crossed her arms in front of her as they walked through the door. All of the smells of various ethnic ingredients mixed together, but somehow Ayzah was still able to identify onions mixed with ginger floating on top.

"Hey, girl!"

Ayzah recognized the voice immediately. She had known Erica since they were little girls, and her voice grated on her nerves now as it always had. It was shrill and high, almost sounding false. Ayzah turned around slowly, dreading the conversation she was about to have.

"Hey, Erica," she said. "What you doing here?"

"Hello, Ma'dear." Erica's voice was as sweet as it could possibly be as she greeted Ma'dear. *Wolf in sheep's clothing.*

Ayzah cringed. Was she the only one who could see how phony Erica was? Erica had proven time and again that she could smile in your face and then stab you in the back.

Erica gave Ayzah's mother a hug, a big smile plastered on her face.

Ayzah stood behind them and looked on. *Friends close, enemies closer.* Grandmother wisdom echoed in her head. Erica's jeans were tight and so low-cut that her thong underwear peeked out of the top. She wore a thick brown belt with a jeweled buckle. The belt sat low on her hips and the front had the word *sweet* emblazoned in pink rhinestones.

If Ma'dear could see the view that Ayzah did, she would not approve of Erica's intentional flashing in public. She even had the nerve to have a single jewel in the middle of the waistband of her panties. If Ayzah dressed like that, her mother would condemn her for sure. To hear her tell it, Ayzah's outfit was no better anyway.

Erica released Ma'dear, and for a quick second, Ayzah got a view of the beautiful woman her mother used to be. It was hard to see the real her through all the scowling she seemed to do.

"I'ma go head and start without you, Ayzah. I know you young folks got things to talk about."

Ayzah nodded without taking her eyes off of Erica.

"Don't be too long now," she said.

"I won't. I'll catch up to you in just a minute, okay? Let me holla at Miss Erica a minute." Ayzah tried to copy Erica's smile since it seemed to work so well a minute before.

Ma'dear was barely out of earshot when Erica started in on Ayzah.

"So, what is really up, heifer? Why you didn't tell me about Prince?"

Ayzah measured her words. "Tell you what? You know I ain't the type to put my business in the streets."

Erica moved closer. "Maybe. But I thought you was my girl."

The smell of Erica's J.Lo perfume met her nose. It was overpowering, as if she had used the whole bottle instead of bathing. Ayzah had no idea what Erica was talking about, but she was not about to let her know that. *What in the hell was Prince up to now?* Her eyes narrowed, but she tried to stay calm. She hated nothing more than everyone else knowing things that she didn't. "You know you are."

A wide, open smile spread across Erica's face. "I knew all that shit you were talking about trying to live a clean life, et cetera, et cetera, was just bullshit." She gestured in the air while she spoke. "I didn't think you would go for the two of them working together, so I was *real* surprised when I found out that Prince was going to be coming in on the business. We are going to be like sisters."

What in the hell? Was Prince planning on working with Deon? He'd never mentioned anything to her. This was certainly news, but Ayzah managed to hide her surprise.

"Sisters?" Deon was Erica's man, a real hustler. Ayzah was never sure what business he was in at the moment. Sometimes it was legal, but most of the time it was not. Word was that he had his hand in anything and everything that would make him some money, ranging from drugs to fencing stolen goods. He was smart though. He was well loved in the neighborhood because of the way he always made sure some of his money leaked into the "right" hands.

"We was practically that before, but Deon said they were going to be working on some deal together. It's a good thing, too, 'cause I was worrying about you a little. Your gear was looking crazy, if you know what I mean." Erica grinned. "I know everyone does the best they can, but Deon always makes sure that my ride is together and I have a little cash when I need it. Prince can do that for you, too, now. We—"

Ayzah stopped her. "You know, I don't think we should discuss this now." Her mind whirled. Here she was, trying to do the best she could to be a good woman for a change, and what in the world was she hearing? Her mother was always talking about how important it was for a woman to support her man in whatever he was doing, especially a black man. How could she do that if she didn't know what he was into?

"You are so right. I will see you. We should get together."

"Yeah," she said. "Sure. I have to catch up to my mother before she kills me." She let Erica walk away first, then purposely went in the other direction. She could feel a headache coming on. Why was it that she couldn't win for losing? She was trying her best to be committed to Prince, had been for a long time. Even when she was with someone else, Prince was where her heart had been. She had screwed up her relationship with Remedy, and just when she decided that she was going to try and do things right for a change, things got all crazy.

What was Prince thinking? How in the hell was she ever going to get custody of Jamal if he was involved in some obviously illegal shit? Ayzah shook her head. They would have a talk when she got home. There was a certain example she wanted to set for her son. If she didn't show him what a good woman was like, how would he ever find one for himself when the time came? Prince had to understand that he had a part in this, too. He claimed he wanted to have custody of her son as much as she did, so he was going to have to act right.

oil and water

The buzzer interrupted the silence in Alexis's office. She jumped, then sucked her teeth, annoyed. She wasn't expecting anyone and she really had to finish reviewing her paperwork. And a nail broke as she pressed the intercom button on her phone. Not a good sign.

"Your client is here."

Alexis didn't answer. She quickly glanced at her calendar, then the clock to make sure she had not screwed up or anything. It was not beyond her to get the days mixed up.

She closed the file she was looking at, then stood up and smoothed her skirt. She would have to talk to that woman. How hard was it to check the computer to see if she had anything scheduled?

Alexis walked in a no-nonsense manner, head down, arms swinging. She meant to give the woman her best "you will pay for this later" glare, but was instead stopped in her tracks. Remedy was standing in the waiting area. His eyes captured hers and the lethal calmness in her face slid away.

"What? How?" Alexis had to remember to close her mouth. Remedy was more good-looking than she remembered. There was something about the way his clothes hung on him that could not be taken away by the cast that was now on his arm. His jaw was square and manly, giving him a rugged look, and his cheek held a dimple that showed even when he wasn't smiling. A single diamond earring glinted in his ear.

"It's my fault. Not hers. I told her I was a client."

Alexis leaned on the half desk in the reception area, not taking her eyes off of Remedy. She talked out of the side of her mouth, half to him and half to her. "She could have checked."

The receptionist raised her eyebrows, then lowered them. She did not make eye contact with Alexis.

"You gave me your business card. I decided to use it."

Alexis was suddenly aware that people inside the glass doors she had just come through were pointing, and not being very nonchalant about it either. From the corner of her eye, she saw one of her coworkers walk past, almost too slowly. She blushed, then cleared her throat. Maybe he had decided to sue her for something after all. "How can I help you?" she asked as calmly as possible. "Is there something else you need?"

Remedy didn't say what was on his mind. He wanted to say "you" in response to her question, but he didn't, partly because he would sound corny, like some kind of weirdo, and partly because he didn't want to sound desperate. "Do you think we could talk in private?" he asked instead. "Do you have an office or something?"

Alexis considered her options. She could stand here in the vestibule, with the leader of the office grapevine looking on,

she could escort Remedy back to her office, or she could ask
him to leave. Any one of the options would probably start office lips flapping. And after her last meeting with her boss,
she wasn't too sure she wanted the folks around there to know
too much more of her business. "I guess we can go on back,"
she said.

As soon as she moved, Remedy moved, too, and he beat her
to the glass doors, broken arm and all. He moved so fast that
his arm seemed to flash in front of Alexis and she jumped in
surprise. He pulled on the door with his good arm and it
swung open as if it were made of paper.

He noticed her reaction. "Just being a gentleman." A tat-
too peeked out from the cuff of his white shirt.

Alexis didn't answer. She stepped through the door and
avoided making eye contact with any of the other people in
the office. She was sure they could see the conflicting emotions on her face. Remedy was the last person she expected to
see ever again, much less at her office. She closed her office
door behind them, then stepped behind her desk to purposely
put some distance between them. She motioned for Remedy
to have a seat.

She waited for him to sit, then did the same. Alexis tried
hard to breathe easy. Inside, she cursed at herself. Her stomach was all tied up in knots and her palms were sweating. And
the man had barely said anything to her. Her hormones were
doing a Riverdance all up and down her body. Just how long
had it been since—

"I'm not going to take up too much more of your time," he
said. "I can tell you are a busy woman." Remedy glanced
around the office nervously.

Oh, here it comes. Her mind once again burned with the

memory of the sound his body had made when it hit the floor.

"Look, I was wondering if you had time to get together, maybe go out for coffee or something."

Alexis sat stock-still. His words numbed her. *Go out for coffee for what?* "I. Don't. Understand."

Remedy wet his lips with his tongue, then leaned forward in his chair. His voice was scratchy. "I know this is awkward, considering how we met. But, what I'm trying to say is, if I had met you any other way I would have tried to get to know you better. I want to take you out for coffee, maybe—"

There was a bruise on his forehead. Alexis exhaled. "I'm *really* busy during the day. I usually don't make time for coffee and things like that." She lowered her voice. "I can't make time. . . ." She didn't want to insult him any further than she had already by breaking his arm, but she had a pretty full calendar over the next couple of days.

He nodded in understanding. "I see. How about dinner then?"

The room was silent again.

The chair squeaked as Alexis leaned back. She hadn't really thought about dating anyone since Walter. Hadn't wanted to. But Remedy, he was interesting. Not only was he attractive, but he was not afraid of a fight. Literally. Not if his ex was any indication. Tension began to drain from Alexis's body.

A warning voice spoke up in her head. *He has major issues, one bigger than most—about five-foot-five with a Texas-sized attitude.* What did she want with someone else's baggage? She had enough of her own.

"Just when did you have in mind?" she asked. A smile danced about her mouth for the first time. Her hormones were obviously speaking to her louder than her brain.

"I have busy weekends sometimes. My cousin is getting married soon and I am her maid of honor. I have been really preoccupied with that. And work. There's always work." She stopped herself from rambling further. Some people thought that thinking aloud was, well, strange.

A smile spread across Remedy's face, deepening his dimple. "This Saturday?"

Remedy's smile was arresting. He'd caught her off guard. He was not asking her to get married. Just have dinner. Certainly not what she expected him to say, but then, what exactly had she expected?

He looked at her questioningly, waiting for an answer. It would be nice to date someone normal again. He'd been spending so much time concentrating on Jamal lately, there had been little time for dating. When Alexis knocked him on his ass, it was clear to him that what he was really doing was hiding his head in the sand and licking his wounds.

Alexis nodded, then smiled. She wanted to go. Why the hell shouldn't she?

He stood up then. "Good. I'll plan on picking you up." Remedy felt relief spread through his body. For a minute, he thought she might turn him down. What else could he expect after she met Ayzah? Most people could sense her craziness from a football field's length away. He was the only one who had been fooled.

On standing, Alexis realized she was nervous, something that she had not been for quite some time. Not in a situation like this. Hell, she hadn't been asked out on a date for quite some time either. "Okay," she said. "Let me write my information down for you. Are you sure it's okay? I mean, can you drive with one arm and all? I can pick you up, if you need me to." She was rambling again. Alexis stopped talking and scribbled nervously on a piece of scrap paper.

"No, I think I can manage. I can drive, I just can't write much. Thank goodness I don't need to." He smiled again, and Alexis's stomach went back to rumbling.

Her hand went nervously to her shoulder, where her hair used to be, then up to her head. She gently ran it across her scalp.

He glanced at the paper she handed him, then slipped it into his shirt pocket.

Her Aunt Athena's face flashed in front of Alexis and her senses returned. Although she knew she was jumping the gun, Alexis could hear Athena asking her what it was he did for a living. She'd had a cow when Paris took up with her then-unemployed boyfriend over someone she'd thought was more suitable. "So, you don't need to use your hand in your job? That's lucky."

Remedy knew what she was doing, but it was okay. He was proud of what he did, although Alexis didn't look like the type who would be impressed. "Some. I own nightclubs, so it's not much of a necessity. I can input most things into the computer with one hand."

They walked to the door. Alexis was much more in control now. "I feel so bad about this."

"I'll manage. Just think, I might be asking someone else out if this hadn't happened."

"Are the clubs here in Austin?" Austin had a famous nightclub district, known for its live music. Alexis had lived here most of her life and she wasn't aware of any nightclubs owned by African-Americans.

"Not yet. I own two in Dallas though. My partners and I are looking at expanding down here."

Alexis's eyebrows rose. That was interesting. "We *had* one black-owned club. It was almost a community institution."

"I heard about that. Midtown Live, right? The one that just burned down?"

"That's the one." Alexis knew the place well. She and Walter had gone there for many a happy hour. "There is still a lot of controversy around that one."

They paused in front of the elevator. "You'll tell me all about it on Saturday, then?" His smile was disarming and caused his dimple to show more than ever.

Alexis nodded, just as the doors opened. She rested her hand on her stomach to try and make it calm down.

Remedy stepped in and she waved good-bye, standing there to watch the doors close behind him. She turned away from the doors and headed back to her office, ignoring the questioning glances her office mates threw her way.

Lost in her own world, Alexis almost ran into her boss as he was leaving her office. Her mouth dropped open in surprise.

"Just the woman I was looking for." His expressionless face gave no indication of the reason for his visit.

"Am I?" Alexis recalled their conversation from earlier in the week. Her mouth tightened. It seemed that her instincts were right. She was certainly getting a lot more attention in the office lately. "What can I do for you?"

He looked around her. "Was that a new client that I'm not

aware of?" He pointed in the direction of the elevator. "I saw he had a cast on his arm. We really don't do personal injury if that is what he was here for."

"It wasn't." Alexis lifted her chin questioningly. No use in answering the question he wanted her to. "His visit wasn't work-related."

His blue eyes were piercing as the silent challenge grew between them. "New boyfriend already?"

"No." *Some nerve.* "You say what's on your mind, huh?" Alexis was not used to being on the receiving end of questions like these, at least not at work. "What can I help you with?"

"I'm sorry. I didn't mean to offend you. I have a tendency to be a little . . . brash. That isn't why I came down here anyway."

Condescending and arrogant is more like it, she thought. Alexis paused to stop herself from being rude and to let him fill in his own blanks.

He crossed his arms. "I need you to go to a meeting with me. A dinner with some clients."

Alexis held her breath. Just as long as he didn't say Saturday, things were okay.

"I know we don't generally stay too late on Fridays, at least I don't, but in this case, the dinner is Friday night. How are you with Tex-Mex?"

She exhaled. Friday was doable. "I'm good. I can work that."

He nodded and walked toward her office door.

"Um, can I ask you why me?"

He paused, then said, "I knew you would be available." There was a trace of laughter in his voice as he left the room.

Alexis tensed, then relaxed again. She was angry at herself for the embarrassment she felt, but was not about to let him spoil her day or the good feeling she'd had after Remedy left. For the life of her, she couldn't see why she had even thought that the asshole who'd just left her office was attractive.

She ran her hand through her hair again, enjoying the feeling of its soft fuzziness on her hand. She refused to even give her boss a second thought as she sat at her desk and put the customer dinner on her calendar.

Short hair was easy, but it occurred to her that she was going to have to get her hair done much more often now. She glanced at her watch. There was just enough time for her to get Angel on the phone to make an appointment. She was going to have to look her best for her date. *Me on a date. What a funny thought.* Hopefully Angel would be able to fit her in before Saturday night. For the first time in a long time, she was looking forward to her weekend.

ride or die

There were two ways Ayzah could handle the situation. Ma'dear always said that you catch more flies with honey than with vinegar. And Prince loved her honey. Or so he said, especially when his head was buried deep between her legs. She could use that to her advantage and be sweet to get the truth out of him about his new business dealings, or she could act crazy and try her best to kill him for withholding information from her.

She would try the sweet road this time. Prince had made it clear that he didn't like to be questioned and could be unpredictable if he thought he wasn't in control. Anger was what fucked her up before, and he never let her forget it. Back when she was still with Remedy, the original plan had been for her to stay married for much longer than she had. That way, she and Prince would have easier access to cash when they needed it, from Remedy's pockets, of course.

Prince had come up with a good plan, and if she had done what he'd asked, they would have been set for life. Ayzah was the one who had messed up. She was the one who hadn't trusted and run off, leaving both Jamal and Remedy. She was the one who couldn't hold her temper afterward when Prince had questioned her about how she'd left. He thought that if she said the right things, Remedy would take her back, but she just couldn't stand being there anymore. And she was the one who couldn't stick it out long enough to get custody of Jamal like she was supposed to. Up until then, Prince had done everything he'd promised her. And when she and Remedy were finally making good ground she'd messed it all up again when she hit him with that damned statue. Ayzah shook her head as she thought about how dumb she had been. She was just so jealous at the thought of him moving on. It wasn't like she really wanted him or anything; she did have Prince after all. But she and Prince just hadn't planned on any other people coming into the picture. He was not supposed to suddenly get a girlfriend or anything like that.

It was even her temper that had gotten her involved with Remedy in the first place. He had been nothing more than a revenge fuck when she was mad at Prince for stepping out on her, and look what that had gotten her. She sighed. She'd just wanted to never see him again, and Prince convinced her to push up to him, that Remedy could be their cash cow and she could stop stripping. All she ever wanted was to do just one thing right, but she just couldn't seem to get there.

All that aside, why in the hell did Prince have to go and get involved with that good-for-nothing Deon? She wondered. They could do things on their own. And why had he been so secretive about it? Ayzah planned to make him think that telling her what new "business" he was involved in was his idea.

His favorite color was red, so she dug through her drawer and found her sexiest red underwear. She rubbed her body with scented sparkle lotion, paying extra attention to her toes (just in case he wanted to suck them), and then slipped a simple but sexy dress over the top, one that he had bought her. She finished it off with the highest CFM shoes in her arsenal. Ayzah was ready for battle.

Two hours later, when Prince came through the door, she was still ready. She tried her best to ignore that he was later than he'd said he would be. Ayzah sat on the couch, flipping through a *Jet* magazine when she heard his key in the lock. Where the hell had he been?

The door swung open and Prince stepped through the door into their small living room. The house had no entryway, so he stood less than four feet from where Ayzah was sitting. The only light in the room came from the flickering of the television. It was tuned to nothing in particular; Ayzah had it on merely for background noise.

"Hey, woman." Prince stood in the doorway to let his eyes adjust to the darkness. He swayed a little and his oversize pants were dusty.

Ayzah could smell the alcohol on his body before he was even in the house good. She scowled, then tried to hide her reaction. She sat back on the couch and took all of him in, as she did every day. She always could smell where he'd been, knew immediately if he had been out drinking or sweating too heavily from being in the club or whatever. She inhaled deeply, checking to make sure she didn't smell any woman on him. "You drunk?"

"Don't be nagging me before I'm even in the door, first

thing. Second, you know better than to ask me questions like that." He slammed the door behind him, and she remembered her vow to be nice. There was something she wanted to know. Honey, not vinegar. Ayzah exhaled to shake her anger off, then got up. She didn't say anything else while she followed him as he walked through the house into the kitchen. She knew exactly how to get what she wanted from a man from years of watching her mother, back before she had turned into the church lady she was nowadays. Ma'dear had been something else then; she'd been someone else, too. Up until ten years ago, she was not even allowed to call her Mommy, Mother, or anything like it, unless they were at school. Her name was Stacia. She didn't want too many people to know she had a daughter so old. She was a single mother, but they always had everything they needed, because her mother had been a hustler who knew how to get what they needed, whatever it was. From anybody. All she had to do was to bat her eyelashes and men would come out of the woodwork, noses and wallets wide open.

Prince opened the refrigerator, and Ayzah put her hands on his shoulders, massaging them gently.

He twisted his back in response, leaning back into her fingers. "You cook?" he asked as he peered inside.

Ayzah was not going to be deterred that easily. He could act like he didn't see her standing there all dressed up for him if he wanted to, but she planned to make sure he noticed, one way or another. "Uh-huh," she said. "I got something for you. Why don't you eat and then let me tighten up your braids. I can oil your scalp and get you looking new again."

Prince stiffened. "Okay, what are you up to? You want to

go shopping with your girls or something?" The last time Ayzah sounded that sweet she put some kind of hurting on his wallet.

Ayzah felt a jolt of anger. She pushed at Prince. "I was try-ing to be nice and you always think I want something." She sucked her teeth, not knowing if she was mad because he was right, she did want something, or because she had to find out things the way she had. She crossed her arms in front of her and leaned back on the sink. She gritted her teeth. *Honey is getting thin.* Ayzah decided to get right to the point. "As a matter of fact, I *do* want something. I was in Fiesta with Ma'dear, and I ran into Erica. She said—"

He didn't let her finish. "That girl is such a bitch. Always in folks' business. What did she tell you?"

"Why don't *you* tell me?"

Prince's face darkened. He hadn't missed the flare of her temper.

Ayzah was immediately sorry. Prince could be almost un-controllable when he was angry. She bent her head and stud-ied her hands.

"You wanna watch how you talk to me. I told you before, I am a man and I expect you to respect me as one in my house." His voice had a hardness to it that was frightening. "I didn't even have time to tell you about things. I had a plan and that bitch has gone and messed it up."

Ayzah tapped her foot on the floor impatiently but didn't move. *He always had a plan.* "Why didn't you tell me about you and your boy Deon?" Her voice was lower this time, and she made it as reasonable as she could manage.

"There wasn't nothing to tell. I was trying to get my shit

together so I could surprise you. A man got to take care of his business, you know what I mean?"

"Surprise me? With what? Ending up in jail?"

"Baby, I ain't going to jail. I'm smarter than that."

She raised her eyebrows. "You might be, but he ain't. And don't you think that if he goes to jail, *again*, that he won't be singing like a bird?"

Prince put his arms around Ayzah. She turned her head away, keeping her arms folded. "C'mon, baby. Just calm down." He breathed his words into her ear. "I might come up with some crazy schemes, but have I ever done anything to put you in any danger at all? Trust me."

Without answering, Ayzah bit her lip. Sometimes she didn't know what Prince was thinking at all. Tears stung her eyes and she fumed inside. Prince obviously did not understand how much she cared abut him. "I ain't afraid of no danger. I'm with you always. I just don't want anything to happen to you. That's all." She buried her face in his shoulder.

Prince wrapped his arms around her tighter, then kissed her on her neck. "Don't worry about that. Believe I am taking care of business. For us, okay? You just take care of your end and work on Remedy for me. Our plan is still the same, this is just going to speed things up a bit, that's all. The sooner we get the money we need, the sooner our asses are out of here. You know as well as I do that we just can't move out to L.A. on a wing and a prayer. It takes cash." He wound his hands in the back of her hair.

Ayzah stiffened, then sniffled. She raised her head and nodded. "I just don't like finding shit out on the street. How would you feel, Prince?"

Prince kissed her slowly and thoughtfully, and Ayzah felt shivers of excitement run through her the same as they had when they first met. Her reservations melted away as she basked in the connection she'd always felt between them.

He reached into his back pocket. "I have something for you. I was supposed to give it to you when I told you about me and Deon working together, but now is as good a time as any." His timing was amazing. Something had told him that Ayzah wouldn't understand.

"You do?"

Prince dug deeper into his pocket and pulled out a small gold chain. He held it up for her to see. A diamond pendant glinted in the air as the chain swung back and forth.

Ayzah gasped, then reached for it. "Damn, baby. What did I do to get this?"

A sly grin spread across Prince's face. "You didn't have to do anything. Nothing at all. This is just for standing by me."

Her eyes narrowed. "This ain't a bribe, is it? You know I can't be bought. I don't want it if it is from Deon's money."

Prince's face darkened. "Deon's money? I'ma earn that, and more. You betta believe it. I don't know why you have to question me like that. Don't worry about where shit comes from, just take the damn thing. Most heifers would just be happy that I thought of them."

Ayzah looked at the floor. "I'm sorry." She played with the pendant. It was the nicest thing he had given her in a long time. "It just looks so expensive."

A smile crept back onto Prince's face. "I want my woman to have all the finest shit. That's why we are moving up out of this small-ass town." He paused. "Now, what were you saying you had for me?"

"Food." She crossed her arms in front of her and pretended to pout.

"I'm not hungry for that." His deep-timbred voice sent a shiver through her.

Gently, Ayzah ran her hands around the top of his loose-fitting jeans, then stopped at the front. He was just barely wearing a belt, more for show than to hold up his pants. She unbuckled it and his already large jeans dropped to the floor easily. She pushed his underwear down on top of his pants.

Prince leaned up off of her to give her room. His eyes rolled up in his head as he used his hands to guide her shoulders downward. His girl knew exactly what he wanted. He smiled as her lips found their way to his penis. He'd thought it was going to be harder than that. She was no fool, she knew that he was going to take her places that no one else could. She needed him. She was the one who wanted to go to L.A. to try and be a dancer or something. He just wanted to get out of Austin.

one man's trash

Lamar Boulevard was perhaps the longest street in Austin, running from south of the city to the far north, so long that the name changed from North Lamar to South Lamar midway through the city. It ran in only two lanes in both directions for most of the way, and traffic was heavy enough that occasional road rage was unavoidable along the endless stream of unsynchronized stoplights.

Alexis was headed for Angel's Place, down off the older, south end of the road. It was on a street lined with small wooden buildings that at one point had been residential and over time had turned into businesses without too many outward physical changes. She swore under her breath as she turned off the main road and into Angel's small parking lot. It seemed as if every stoplight had caught her and she was two minutes late for her appointment. *Breathe*, she thought.

It was almost always impossible to find a spot easily. There was a spot on the street, so Alexis pulled in there instead, in front of the building next door. It was another former house turned bohemian boutique and had been painted an electric shade of lime green. A clothesline full of colorful women's underwear flew outside like the vibrant flag of an emancipated nation whose citizens were disciples of the thong queen.

Angel had been doing Alexis's hair for years. This was the third spot he'd been in and she had followed him to each one. It was by far the most unusual and out of the way, but Angel was good at what he did. He was as flamboyant as they came, but he knew how to hook each client up so that her hair fit her personality perfectly. He always offered you something to drink, but the thing that Alexis liked best was that he never kept you waiting like other hairdressers might. He usually worked on one person at a time and finished and started when he said he would. And you never had to sit on a metal folding chair if you did have to wait.

Alexis glanced at her watch, then turned off her car and grabbed her bag. Angel's one-at-a-time policy was sure to leave him pissed off even if you were just a minute late, and no one wanted a pissed-off artist working on her head.

Angel had only been in this particular spot a few short months, and although it was a nice place, she was the only one of her group that came there. Both Paris and Sarah would never set foot in a place like Angel's. They preferred the sleekness of the salon at Saks or that fancy place downtown that everyone crowed about. At Angel's, all of the operators rented space and seemed an unlikely mix. Any kind of person could get any kind of beauty treatment there.

Alexis had seen all kinds of people come through that door in the past few months. Black, white, blue—it didn't matter, you never knew who would be sitting in the chair next to you.

The front of the shop was shielded from the working area by a wall, the same type of screen that separated each operator's station from the next. A young white man with long, blond hair looked up as she entered, then nodded. Alexis nodded in return, then took a seat next to him in her usual spot.

"How are you?" she said, not really wanting an answer.

"Fine, thanks." He looked back down at the magazine he held in his hands.

Alexis hadn't been sure she liked the setup at this place at first. It was very different from the last place Angel had been. Even though the walls between the booths didn't go all the way up to the ceiling, they made everything seem claustrophic. The separation took away the feeling of community the old place had, but it also gave Alexis a sense of privacy she didn't have before. The cushioned benches in the waiting area were a nice touch, too. Alexis settled back in her seat, remembering how her butt used to fall asleep before if she had to wait too long.

Angel called out to her from the back almost as soon as she had sat down. "Is that you, Miss Alexis?"

Alexis smiled, listening to his distinctive shuffling as he sashayed his way to the front. "You know it is."

Angel had a better-looking ass than she did. As usual, his jeans were way too tight. Alexis pursed her lips as she looked at him, checking him out. He was usually trendy, but matched perfectly. Today was no exception. His jeans were topped by a white wife-beater tank top, exposing the long, lean muscles in his arms. He wore designer-looking flip-flops on his feet that Alexis was sure had cost him well over one hundred dollars, exposing his obviously manicured toes. His hair was long and curly today and hung down almost to his shoulders. The total package brought to mind a much younger and much gayer Fabio dipped in a caramel coating.

They kissed the air on the side of each other's cheeks, then hugged. "This is a new look for you," she said.

He patted his hair lightly. "Well, you now how I do," he said. "I gotta go with what I feel for the day. And this is how I was feeling. Wild and free." He tossed his head and his sewn-on tresses tumbled about his shoulders.

Alexis smiled, then followed Angel as he turned back into the shop. She couldn't help but watch his ass as he switched it from side to side. A smile crept onto her face. *He is so stereotypically gay,* she thought. *But he can do him some hair.*

Angel's chair was the third one in. He spun his chair around, letting Alexis slide into it without too much effort. She jumped as he snapped a black silk cape in front of her, then fastened it around her neck.

"I told you that cutting all your hair short like that was a bad idea. You are going to be up in here every other day, making me a mint."

"You did, but I ain't complaining."

He spun her back around to face the mirror, then stood behind her, his hands on his hips. "You women always give me a hard time, act like I don't know what I'm talking about. I been doing this a long time—"

"You are only thirty-five. Stop tripping and just do my hair."

"See? That is what I'm talking about." Angel pouted but grabbed his comb and his scissors anyway. "What you want me to do? You was just up in here the other day."

"What do you mean? My edges are raggedy. I need you to tighten me up. Shave down by my neck, okay?"

"If this bothers you, you know you are going to have to come in here every week for a while. You want something to drink before I start?"

Alexis shook her head. She still had ten thousand things to do before her evening could even get started. There was no need to make her visit any longer.

"Why are you looking all perky? I didn't think I would hear from you until next week."

Alexis couldn't help the grin that crept onto her face. "I'm not perky. I needed my hair done. You told me yourself that the short haircut would need more maintenance."

Angel clipped at the top of her hair with his scissors. "Uh-huh. You got a date, right? It's about time, girl. For a while there I thought you was in mourning or something."

"Not mourning. I was just taking my time." Alexis didn't want to say more. She hadn't talked about her breakup with Walter too much in the shop, but she knew that Angel had probably talked about it for her. It was no secret that customers were often the topic of conversation among the stylists and other customers, too.

Angel cleared his throat. "So, what's his name? How did you meet? Don't keep me in the dark."

"I didn't say I was going to tell you anything." She lowered her voice, grinning. "Besides, it's not really a date."

Angel nodded. "What the hell does that mean, not really a date?" He snipped lightly at the top of her head with his scissors. "Are you going out to eat?"

"Yes."

"Is he your brother or some other close relative? Note I

said close 'cause folks around here have been known to date their cousins."

Her lips curved into a smile.

"That's a date, sweetheart. Now stop stalling. What are you not telling Angel? Is he ugly or a good friend's ex or something? As long as you ain't trying to date my man, it's all good. Why are you holding out?"

"You know you are stupid, right?"

"Shoot, he *has* been known to play on both sides of the fence. I gotta check."

"Nothing like that." Lowering her voice, Alexis related the story of how she and Remedy had met.

Angel spun her around. "Okay, let me get this straight." His left eyebrow lifted a fraction. "The first time you meet this guy you kick his behind, and then he shows up and wants to go on a date? You must got some kind of gold up in that pussy of yours that he can smell or something. Either that or he is a little crazy. You need to be careful." He waved his comb in the air. "Those S and M types are dangerous, girl. Trust me on that one."

Alexis chuckled. "I don't doubt that."

"You betta ask somebody, okay? I repeat: What. Is. Wrong. With. Him?"

She thought a minute. Remedy was rugged, good-looking and had just enough of a touch of roughneck in him to make him attractive. "Nothing that I can see, but keep in mind that I haven't really seen much of him at all."

"Back up. You have got to go slow for me. You have only seen this man down on the floor, and in a hospital bed, right? That doesn't leave much time for questions."

She nodded. "And then a few minutes in my office. I know

he's divorced. And he has a kid." Alexis had a gnawing feeling in the pit of her stomach. She didn't even want to mention her encounter in the hospital. From the way Angel was reacting, he might pass out if she told him about meeting Remedy's ex.

Angel clucked. "This isn't sounding good. I told you something was wrong with him. Someone has already thrown him away. And can you say drama? Men with kids always have drama—"

"He has custody of his son, so I can't imagine—"

He threw up his hands. "Oh, Lord," he shouted. "I thought you were a smart woman." He fanned himself. "I need a drink of something."

"What? I think it is great that he is man enough to step up to his responsibilities. So many men don't."

"But that means you will *always,* and I do mean always, have to deal with his ex. I don't know his circumstances, but I can tell you that if the woman is walking around, she will forever be where her kid is, okay? Stop kidding yourself. You. Know. This. Dating him and his kid is one thing. But you are going to be dating his ex, too. You better find out what kind of person she is before you get too far down the road or your life might be hell." Angel twisted up his mouth, but said nothing further.

Alexis sensed a new hush that had fallen over the shop. She imagined other stylists and customers getting an earful on the other sides of the dividing walls. The sad thing was, she knew he was right. Meeting Ayzah had given her a bad feeling, but not bad enough where she planned to cancel her date. *Why was she even thinking about taking advice from a gay hairstylist anyway?*

"I'm about done." Angel still had a look of skepticism on his face. "You want me to fix up your eyebrows, too?"

She nodded.

Angel turned on a brighter facial light and maneuvered it toward her face.

"I would be careful. What happens when she decides she wants custody of her child, that you are now attached to as well? Custody that he doesn't want to give up?"

"Rein in that imagination. You are getting way ahead of yourself. Not everything is a conspiracy."

He plucked at her eyebrows. "Okay. Whatever. I'm just saying."

Angel said nothing else as he finished her eyebrows and then wrote her a receipt. Alexis was tense until he was done. His teasing had crossed over into meddling and she damn sure didn't appreciate it. It annoyed her even more that parts of what he said were true. Some fact-finding did need to be done before she got too invested in Remedy and his life.

worlds apart

During the week, evenings and early mornings were Remedy's favorite times of the day, so much so that one would often segue into the other. He peeked in on Jamal. His chest rose and fell gently as he slept soundless on his bed. Remedy marveled at how much his son had grown in such a short time. They would have to move soon; his too-small room was quickly becoming overcrowded.

Remedy's routine was the same as it often was this time of night. He planned to sit in his favorite overstuffed reading chair, enjoy whatever book had caught his attention and nurse a glass of wine. The old chair squeaked as he settled back into it.

He had become his father. Remedy shook his head. His father had not been an educated man, and before the drugs robbed him of everything, he would end most evenings just as Remedy did, learning whatever he could from a book or newspaper. Remedy's fondest memories of his childhood had been of him reading, or of them doing the newspaper crossword puzzle together. He enjoyed those things himself now, but that was where his similarity with his father ended.

Remedy reminded himself that he was still on painkillers and would have to forgo his glass of wine this time. The big skull-and-crossbones on the label of his medicine was all it took to convince him. Even so, Remedy always stopped at one glass, something his father could never do.

Just as he reached for his book, a big thick novel, a knock at the door startled him. Remedy glanced at the clock across the room. He was not expecting anyone and he wasn't the type folks just dropped in on, especially near ten o'clock at night. He frowned, then walked over to the door and peeked through the peephole without opening it.

Ayzah's face stared back at him and she was not alone. Remedy's mouth set in annoyance. This dropping in that she did was becoming a pattern. What in the world could she want this time of night? He took a deep breath, paused, then opened the door.

Remedy expected Ayzah to be her usually sullen and smart-mouthed self. Instead, she tittered nervously and shuffled from foot to foot. She was wearing yet another close-fitting sweat suit with wedge-heeled open-toed shoes. Her hair was braided and drawn up into a high ponytail. He cocked one eyebrow and looked from her to the man he knew was Prince, although they had never formally met.

"Um, hi, Remedy." She cleared her throat awkwardly. "I, we need to talk with you."

"Jamal is asleep. It's kind of late." His eyes locked on Prince, who nodded but didn't speak. He looked exactly like Remedy knew he would. He was a thick man, not fat but stocky, and a scar ran from the bottom of his right eye back toward his ear. His hair was cornrowed straight back from the front of his head to the nape of his neck, and he wore oversize but expensive-looking jeans and shirt. His eyes locked onto Remedy's. There was nothing but coldness in them. He would bet that Prince had no idea that Ayzah was naked in his bed a few days before. But he had known then that it wasn't really about sex. Remedy knew Ayzah better than she would like to admit. Over time, he'd come to learn that she often used sex as a tool of manipulation. He suspected she'd wanted something. Their presence at his door was now proof of that.

"Aren't you going to invite us in?" Ayzah laughed again nervously, and reluctantly, Remedy stepped aside so they could enter.

Prince followed Ayzah in. She sat on the same sofa where she had hit Remedy earlier in the week. Prince stood behind the couch, directly behind her, and thrust his hands into his pockets. His face was blank and hard.

The tension in the room grew as Remedy waited for someone to tell him something about why they were there. He looked to Ayzah for a clue but she wouldn't make eye contact, choosing instead to play with her slender hands and look at the floor.

Finally he cleared his throat. "Okay . . ." It was more of a statement than a question.

"Well, Prince thinks that I should have more time with Jamal."

Remedy cocked his head to the side. He'd known this was coming. "Prince thinks?" This was almost comical.

"He does." She paused. "And I agree."

"Do you?"

"Don't make this hard, Remedy."

"I don't have to do anything. You made it hard on yourself." He felt his amusement changing into anger. "You have a lot of nerve even bringing him into my house."

"Don't sleep. Just because I ain't said anything yet don't mean I ain't listening." The sound of Prince's voice angered Remedy more and he found himself clenching his fists. He gave Prince a hostile glare, then took a deep breath.

"You want to tell me why you should spend more time with Jamal? I already give you more than I have to."

"Because she's his mother. We didn't have to come over here to ask. She could have just taken him. You best man up and just do the right thing."

Remedy paced the living room. He measured his words carefully. "The right thing? The court says I was doing the right thing when I stepped up to my responsibility as his father. What do you know about the right thing? Ayzah obviously doesn't know a damn thing about it. How many mothers just abandon their kids at the drop of a hat?"

Prince strode around the couch. "I know that you could end up with some more shit broken if—"

Ayzah jumped up and stood in between the two men. "That isn't what we came here for." She turned to Remedy. "We just want overnight visits." Tears streamed down her face.

"Since when, Ayzah? I have not had a problem letting you see him, even when I didn't have to. Why the urgency all of a sudden?" Remedy was surprised to see this new, more timid Ayzah, asking for things instead of demanding them. "And what does he have to do with it? Unless there is something you haven't told me, you aren't married."

The two men stepped away from each other. Their eyes stayed locked together in silent challenge.

"It's the right thing." Her voice quivered.

"She's his mother. She could just take him."

Remedy shook his head, his face rock-hard. Prince wasn't too smart, it seemed. "She couldn't. Not if she wants to stay out of jail. Her parental rights have been relinquished. Do you know what that means? And no court in the world is going to let him come live with you." His voice dropped to a harsh whisper. "She abandoned him. And me. And the two of you don't exactly present a stable home. Neither one of you has a job. Do you want to take that gamble?" He paused. "Should I go on?"

Prince looked perplexed for a minute, as if he were pondering what he had been told. Ayzah still stood between the two of them, her arms folded now. Her tear-streaked face looked confused.

Remedy walked toward the door. He doubted they had any money to spend on a court battle. "I don't have a problem with doing the right thing. I know we can work out a suitable agreement, but I have to do what's right for Jamal. He is my main concern. Now, if you aren't happy with my decisions, Ayzah knows how to find my lawyer."

The three of them stood at the door, not speaking. Ayzah's crestfallen face looked strained as she stood slightly behind Prince, almost shrinking.

"You ain't heard the last of this." Prince ran his thumb and forefinger around his thin goatee.

"Maybe not," Remedy said. "Ayzah, Jamal is not a doll. He has feelings, too. You don't want him to end up hating you because you pulled him into the middle of your drama."

"Stop it. The only drama is in your head. This is real shit, something you don't know nothing about, with your fancy business and address and shit. You are just confusing her. A mother needs her child. Ayzah, meet me in the car." Prince stormed off, leaving the two of them in the hallway.

Remedy shook his head. "You got yourself a winner, Ayzah."

"Don't hate. Prince is a good man. He wants us to be happy together. Be a family."

"If you don't recall, you had that. All I have heard you say is what you want and what's best for you. Don't forget about Jamal. He is the innocent in all of this. How is he going to be affected if his parents can't get along?"

Tears started to stream down Ayzah's face again. "Why do you have to make this hard? I just want to be a good woman for Prince."

Remedy could not believe what he was hearing. She still hadn't heard a word he'd said. He felt pity for her, then more anger. He wanted to tell her that she needed to be a good woman for herself first, but decided that some things were best left unsaid. He sighed. "You don't want to keep Prince waiting," he said, then stepped back inside his apartment. He closed the door, and hoped that she would get a lawyer. They obviously needed someone between them.

down for the count

On Friday nights, Z Tejas was usually busy, and Alexis saw just what she expected as she walked up from the parking lot. The small terrace in front was full as people waited, huddled in small groups, clutching the round restaurant paging disks in their hands. She waded through the crowd, glad that the night was not chilly. Alexis hoped that Monty had had the foresight to make a reservation, or at the very least, get there early enough to put them on the often lengthy waiting list. It wouldn't be good to keep whatever client they were meeting waiting, and she was in no mood to join the group of folks waiting outside.

Alexis had gotten over her irritation hours ago, but still wondered why Monty needed her here. It wasn't as if her idea of a fun Friday night was having dinner with clients and a boss whom she rarely saw and who barely even knew her last name. They'd never tried to include her this much before, so it was interesting that he asked her to join him now. She was usually relegated to the straightforward cases, ones that were not too high-profile and didn't really require too much hand-holding. It was all good though, it wasn't like she had plans or anything. She would have most likely ended up staying home and caressing her TiVo remote since both Paris and Sarah had lives now.

Inside the small vestibule, people were standing just about shoulder to shoulder. A wave of annoyance hit her as Alexis maneuvered through them. It just didn't make sense why anyone would pick this place for a client meeting. It wasn't convenient. Also many of their clients liked to be discreet, and Z Tejas was anything but that. It was a hot spot, a place to see and be seen, that was usually noisy, and got noisier as the evening wore on and the margaritas poured.

The hostess looked at her questioningly. She was on the phone and her pen was poised in one hand. Alexis peered over the small table that was in front of her. The waiting list seemed to be quite lengthy, and from what she could tell, very close to being at least forty minutes long. "I'm meeting someone." She scanned the list for a familiar name. "Here." She pointed at Monty's name, frowning. It only said two people. That was strange, she thought.

"He's in the back, on the terrace."

She nodded her thanks, then made her way through the maze of fancy wrought-iron and wooden tables. The restaurant was half inside, half out, with a picture-perfect terrace that jutted out over the hilly countryside. Texas through and through. Even on chilly days, the terrace was always warm and beautiful, usually heated by standing heaters that gave off just enough warmth to allow you to enjoy your meal without shivering.

Memories of visiting this same restaurant with Walter flooded her mind. Alexis shuddered. She and Walter had frequented this place quite a bit. Z Tejas was one of their favorite places to come, especially for late-night food during the week. The place was never as crowded then as it was right now; later it was more homey. They could sit together and eat and talk in almost complete privacy. Alexis shook off the thought. She needed to create some new memories, that was for sure.

Monty was sitting in the far corner of the terrace, at a table that had one of the best views in the restaurant. Alexis spotted him first. He was staring off into space, seemingly mesmerized by the scenery. His blond hair fluttered lightly in the soft breeze that was coming in through the open patio. He turned around suddenly as if he sensed Alexis approaching, smiling sheepishly at first and then more broadly. He stood up and stepped around the table to pull out her chair.

"I was hoping you got here early to get a table. This place can be nuts sometimes," she said. "Especially on a Friday."

"I know what you mean. But you must know that I am not the type to let details slip through the cracks." He held the chair for Alexis to sit down, then returned to his own seat.

They both settled back into their chairs. Alexis took a sip from her water glass and tried to be cool about her thoughts. She cleared her throat, then looked at her watch. Any minute now he would tell her what the game plan was. She waited as long as she could bear. "So who is this client we are meeting?"

"Well," he said. "They aren't coming. They canceled about an hour ago." Monty's eyes darted around nervously. "I would have called you earlier but I figured you were probably already on your way and that was no reason for us to waste a perfectly good reservation." A nervous laugh came from his lips.

"Excuse me?" The alarm bells that had been going off in her head since she came through the doorway got slightly louder. "I'm . . ." She didn't finish. Austin wasn't that big. An hour would have been time enough.

"Don't worry. I promise not to bite." Monty sipped his wine. "We can discuss work if it will make you more comfortable. Matter of fact, it could only be good for work if we got to know each other better. We know almost nothing about you, Alexis." He sat back in his chair and picked up his plastic-covered menu. "Your new boyfriend won't mind that, right?" Hr grinned at Alexis as if he had just made the joke of the century.

Alexis's eyes narrowed but she didn't answer immediately. She refused to let her good mood of the past few days be ruined and his comment was obviously one of those things best ignored, even if he was more than a little obnoxious. She already knew from his comments in the office that he was curious.

"I guess you are right," she said. *This was going to be agony.*

And it was. Alexis studied her menu in silence. She forced herself to look down. The heat from Monty's eyes burned a hole in the top of her skull, but she still refused to look up. He was dying to ask her something, she could feel it, but there was no way she would let him know how uncomfortable she was. The waitress came and took their orders, and finally he gave in.

"So," he said. "You are obviously not back together with Walter, I guess. That was his name, right?"

Alexis half smiled. More of a statement than a question. With her menu gone, there was no way she could continue to avoid eye contact. She cleared her throat. "You can tell me something." She paused. "I don't understand why I am suddenly so interesting to you or anyone else at the office. It's not like I am the new girl in town or anything." It was her turn to laugh nervously.

He cocked his head to the side. "Well, you always kept pretty much to yourself before, didn't really seem too interested in what was going on. The increase in time spent sent up a flag and made some people take notice. We want to get to know you better, find out who you really are. Especially since it seems like you have set some goals for yourself. We want to know what those goals are." He talked in his "official" voice.

She'd never thought of it that way, but it was true. When she was with Walter, Alexis had let her life revolve around his, often pushing hers and her work to the back burner. Those days were over. "Well, you could say I made a promise to myself to make sure I take care of my needs a little better. And that includes work, too."

He nodded. "I would guess that is related to your breakup?"

"That's right, it is." *No need to give him information unnecessarily*, she thought.

"And so was the man I saw in the office—"

"Just someone I know." She played with her napkin. "If you don't mind, I would rather not discuss things not work-related." Her thin-lipped smile was unconvincing.

"I understand." He paused. "But can I ask who left whom? I can't imagine why anyone would want to let you get away." There was something seductive in his look.

Her cheeks warmed. Was Monty giving her an offhanded compliment? "He broke up with me. But our relationship was over long before it was officially over, if you know what I mean."

"I do know," he said. "Sometimes it's easier to stay together than it is to put up with the drama a breakup brings with it. And just so you know, being newly single is one of the things that makes you more interesting, at least to me."

"You know, can you please excuse me?" She stood up. The conversation was becoming much too personal for her and Alexis was uncomfortable.

"I hope I didn't offend you." He rose, too.

She shook her head. "Not at all," she lied. He obviously couldn't take a hint. "Just give me a minute." Alexis backed away from the table, then turned and headed a little too quickly toward the neon sign just inside the restaurant that screamed out where the rest rooms were. She needed time to regroup. Dinner with the boss had not been a part of her plan and the conversation was getting strange.

The narrow hallway that led to the rest rooms snaked back through the restaurant, then headed down a small flight of stairs, as if the rest rooms had been an afterthought. Alexis recalled many a night when there was a bottleneck here, even when the place was relatively empty. Tonight, just the reverse was true. She didn't pass a soul on the way.

Even the rest room itself was empty.

The one-person room was lit by light from several small

candles and the air smelled heavily of lavender. Alexis stood just inside the doorway and took a deep breath. When he had first announced that it would be the two of them for dinner, she'd thought she could handle it. She was wrong. Just a few days before, thanks to her lack of a sex life, she'd thought he was handsome, but then again, she'd thought every man was handsome. Knowing she had a date had taken the edge off and reality had set in. He. Was. Her. Boss. Her white boss. Married. And somewhat obvious in his inappropriate hitting on her. The best thing for her to do was to make up an excuse, say her good-byes and go home. If she left now, she could excuse his remarks and glares, chalking it up to the wine.

Alexis peered into the mirror, avoiding leaning on the wet sink. She pulled her compact from her bag and dabbed at her nose. She would say she had to go home and review a new case or something. He would understand that, surely. She freshened her lipstick, then juggled it and the compact back into her too-small bag and prepared to face the challenge ahead of her. It was perfectly okay not to want to have dinner with your boss, she told her reflection, then opened the door to the hallway.

Monty was right outside the rest room door. Alexis was looking down and almost stepped right into him. They came so close they were almost touching. Alexis's every pore was at attention; Monty was so close that she could feel him breathe.

"Sorry." She looked away. Talk about uncomfortable. She glanced helplessly up the steps, hoping someone would join them, then tried to step to the side.

He moved, too. "I thought I would use the rest room, too."

They stepped back and forth as Alexis tried to get around him, almost as if they were dancing.

She stopped moving and her jaw tensed. "You go," she said.

Monty stared at her, then licked his lips. "What's happening here?" He took an abrupt step, moving in closer to Alexis. He was between her and the stairway now, her back almost to a wall, so close that she could smell the sharp aroma of the red wine he had been drinking.

Her mouth dropped open in surprise. "Move, please," she said. The hard edge in her voice seemed to surprise him. It surprised her.

He hesitated, then crushed his lips to hers. Monty forced his tongue into her mouth. The air was being forced out of her as he held her there. Her mind clicked as she realized what was happening.

The response was automatic. Alexis drew back as best she could, then grabbed and held in the vicinity of where Monty's penis would be. Using a twisting motion, she pulled, then squeezed as hard as she possibly could through his thick khaki pants. As expected, he released his kiss, then doubled over in pain.

"What did you think? That I would be easy? That you could get what you want?" Alexis boiled over with anger. She hated when people assumed things about her. He had thought that because she had broken up with Walter, she must be desperate. "You dumb motherfucker." He obviously had no idea how tough she was.

"Please——" he panted.

Alexis was unable to stop herself. Her pulse beat erratically. She squeezed harder, guiding Monty down to his knees. His mouth stayed open and his face twisted in agony. Finally, Alexis released her grip and he lay there, knees pulled into his stomach almost in a fetal position. Fear and anger left her stomach in knots.

And then it hit her, a quick and disturbing thought. "I'm sorry," she stammered. This was the second time in as many weeks that she'd brought a man to his knees, and not in a good way, either. And she had serious doubts that he would take this as easily as Remedy had. If she wasn't so angry at him, she might cry. In this case, Alexis decided it was best to leave well enough alone. She took a few steps back, and then turned and ran up the steps back toward the main part of the restaurant. She dug in her bag for her keys as she ran.

The lobby area was still crammed full of people and Alexis kept her eyes on the floor as she pushed through the crowd, garnering more than a few dirty looks. The reality of her situation hit her hard, and she fought to hold back tears, unable even to mutter an apology to anyone she offended. She was just a few steps shy of the door when she felt a hand grabbing her arm. She was instantly ready to fight again.

"Hey, what are you doing here?" The normal friendliness in Sarah's voice trailed off as she noticed the distraught look on Alexis's face.

She didn't answer.

"We are having dinner. Didn't know you were going to be here, too." She looked concerned as she stepped around to get a better look at Alexis. She was shocked at what she saw.

Of the three friends, Alexis was the one usually making jokes about the others. Sarah could not remember a time when she had ever seen her look so upset. She made eye contact with her husband over Alexis's shoulder as she slid her arms around her friend. She nodded to him, knowing he would know exactly what she meant. It was obvious that Alexis was distraught. Dinner was going to have to wait.

taking care of business

"I don't know, Prince. Maybe Remedy was right. Jamal might be better off with him than me." It was a weak attempt, but Ayzah wanted to give it a try. Maybe she could change Prince's mind about them getting custody of Jamal. It wasn't a good idea and she was beginning to have second thoughts about it. Prince was more interested in the child-support money than he was in her son and she knew that. They lay in bed, their legs intertwined. Ayzah hugged him tighter, her head on his naked chest.

He pushed back and looked her in the face. "It ain't about the custody. Do you realize how much money we could get if you have custody? It would make it a helluva lot easier for us. We would have a cushion for our move."

Ayzah tensed. She didn't want to make an already bad situation worse. "He can give him things that I can't."

"Not with my new gig. We will be raking in the cash. Remedy Brown won't be the only baller in town."

A thought whispered in her head. If that were true

they wouldn't need Remedy's money, right? "And I ain't sure we could just move away like that. That wouldn't be fair to Remedy."

"I ain't said shit about being fair. He wasn't fair to you when he got sole custody. I want that boy in this house, period. You were my girl first. Always been. I didn't tell your ass to go get pregnant by someone else, and then marry him, too, although after I thought about it, I have to admit it wasn't such a bad idea. If you want to be with me, then this is how it's gonna be."

She swallowed hard. She didn't want to lose Prince. He loved her no matter what, didn't he? He'd even come back like he'd said he would after she'd married Remedy. Shit, truth be told he'd really only been mad at her for two weeks and then they were back to kicking it like they always had.

His voice softened. "I don't know about all that shit he was talking about, but you know what, you need to find out today. I got an appointment anyway." He slid out of the bed and grabbed his pants.

"What? It's Friday. I thought we were going to spend the day together."

"Business is business. I got to go over to your girl's house. We got some business to take care of." He kissed her on the forehead, then bent closer to her ear. "You want to make me happy, don't you?"

His masculine smell filled her nose and she inhaled, immediately becoming wet. "You know I do," she panted. "But you got business here." She ran her fingers down his sinewy arm, circling the tattoos.

"We can take care of that later," he growled. "You call up

a lawyer so we can figure things out." Prince stood up, pulling on his jeans.

She pouted. "But it's Friday," she said again. He'd promised her some time.

"Look in the phone book." Prince talked to her over his shoulder without looking back.

♡   ♡   ♡

Who knew that you couldn't find a lawyer on a Friday afternoon? Ayzah had called almost every number she could find in the phone book. At most of the numbers, she'd reached a recording, but one or two had just rung. It was bad enough her mother had been looking over her shoulder the whole time. Finally, Ayzah let the heavy book drop to the floor with a bang and then kicked it.

"Genesis, Exodus, Ayzah," her mother had said. "What is wrong with you, girl? You just wasted your energy on that book."

"Ma'dear, please." She rubbed her temples.

"Whatever is troubling you, you need to just let it go. Give it to Jesus."

"Jesus obviously don't care about my problems." She was sorry as soon as she'd said it. All of the air seemed to be sucked out of the room. Ma'dear looked as if she might explode.

"You're right, Ayzah. Why should he care about you and your life if you don't?"

And for the first time in a long time, what her mother said made sense to her. She didn't need a lawyer to find out what she needed to know. She wanted something from Remedy. She might as well talk to him directly, without Prince pushing her.

After the fourth call, she stopped leaving messages. Remedy was home, she could feel it. When they were married he had a way of not answering the phone that she could not understand, but he claimed that the phone belonged to him, not the other way around. If he was busy, he'd say he was busy. And Ayzah could tell that was what was happening now. Either that or he was checking the caller ID and choosing to ignore her calls. Who could blame him? She'd told Prince that they shouldn't have gone over there in the first place. They had given him too much information about their plans on that visit. Prince had been the impatient one this time. She had been doing just fine, going along with the plan. Ayzah sucked her teeth, then sank back into her chair. She would give him three hours to call her back, then she was going over there. She wanted some answers. Tonight.

♥   ♥   ♥

The shrill ringing of the phone jolted Alexis from a deep sleep. She wiped her eyes, then answered it. There were only a few people who would dare call her before eight on a weekend. Athena, Paris, or Sarah.

Athena would be calling to remind her about Sunday dinner, a family tradition which no one person dared to forget. Paris would be calling to chatter on endlessly about her wedding, as if anyone was allowed to forget that she was getting married. Or Sarah would be calling to check on her and tell her she needed to seriously consider taking her advice. Like she really needed anger management class. She could forget that. Okay, she thought, maybe for the first time, but anyone would have reacted the way she had with her boss. He'd gotten exactly what he'd deserved.

"Hello?"

"I hope I didn't wake you."

Alexis paused, trying to figure out if Paris was calling her because Sarah had told her about last night or not. They'd talked a long time and Sarah had been a good friend, listening and letting her cry on her shoulder. That didn't mean she hadn't called up Paris as soon as she'd gotten the chance. "You lie. It's early, Paris, and you knew I was asleep. What do you need?"

"I'm sorry. You need to get you some coffee quick so you can soften up."

"I don't want to soften." Alexis swung her feet out of bed and padded to the bathroom. There was an awkward pause in their conversation.

"Sarah told me about yesterday and I think her suggestion was a good one. And anger management might be covered by your health insurance. Under mental health."

"My anger doesn't need to be *managed*, thank you very much." Alexis paused, wondering how much Sarah had told Paris. "I'm fine." She didn't want to add that she probably wouldn't have health insurance much longer and she doubted if that skeleton coverage you got when you left a job covered much of anything. If you got that when you quit.

"Okay then. I'm going to taste cakes this morning. Are you coming with me?"

She was back to the wedding again. Alexis bit her lip, then grunted. "I don't think so."

"But you are my maid of honor. You are supposed to do things like this with me. Help me decide." Her voice took on a decidedly whining tone, one with which Alexis had become quite familiar.

"I have to take care of some things. Besides," she said, "Tyson should go with you to do that." Alexis had the distinct feeling that this was some plot Paris and Sarah had hatched to get her out of the house. "I really do have some things I have to do. Important things."

Paris was silent for a minute, and Alexis could almost hear her mind clicking through the phone. She would be offering to come with her next. That would be the last thing she needed. There were some things that had to be done alone.

"What could you possibly have to do on a Saturday morning?"

"Not your business." Alexis tried to ignore what she knew Paris meant. That it was Saturday and since she was unattached she couldn't possibly have any plans of her own.

Paris stammered. "I just thought—"

"I know what you thought. Don't worry about me. Besides, I have a date tonight." That should hold her off, even if it was only half of the truth. She did have a date, one that she planned to keep, later that evening.

"Oh. Really? Don't answer that. That's good. I guess we will hear all about it then. Tomorrow at dinner, right?"

"Maybe. Look I gotta get going." She grabbed her toothbrush. "Got a lot to do, you know."

They hung up and Alexis was relieved that Paris seemed to be satisfied with her half-truth. She wasn't ready to tell her that she had to go to her office this morning. To clean out her desk. Last night's dinner had made it clear to her that it was time to move on. After her boss's behavior, it was going to be impossible for her to continue to work at her firm. Her big plans for this morning included going to her office to clean out her desk. It was time to take action, file a sexual harassment claim, and quit her job.

grand larceny

Saturday morning was Ayzah's time. It was barely light out when she slid out of bed, leaving Prince sleeping. She washed up quickly. Ma'dear called what she did a Whore's Bath, claiming that whores washed up in the sink between clients like she did, but she could not be late for her appointment. She slipped on a baseball cap and matching Baby Phat sweats, admiring the way they made her ass look, and hopped in the car. Normally, she would be Angel's first appointment at 6:45 A.M. every week. He'd asked her to come early today because he had something or the other to do, and since she could not fix her hair herself, she hadn't complained.

It took less than ten minutes to get to Angel's Place. Ayzah smiled and pulled her car into the small parking lot. This sure was an improvement over the old place, she thought. Angel hadn't been there long and he was already talking about moving again, this time to the east side, where he had started. Lots of business seemed to want to move there lately. She locked her car and half hoped that someone would steal it or something, but she knew that her insurance would barely pay off this one and she would be left walking.

Angel was still flipping on lights when she opened the door. Ayzah walked right in, letting the door close behind her with a bang. She bypassed the small waiting area and slipped into Angel's chair as if she belonged there.

He peeked his head out from the back of the shop. "My girl." There was an obvious smile in his voice. "I'll be right there. I'm putting the coffee on."

Ayzah could hear the sound of running water coming from his direction. She spun herself around in the chair and looked at her reflection. Her hair was sticking up in a couple of different directions. She hadn't done much to it other than take the braids down. Angel came up behind her.

"You look a mess."

"And I love you, too. That's why I came here. So fix me my do."

He grabbed a small comb and played at arranging her hair. She had more wrong with her than he could take care of in a minute. A good hairstyle could only go so far. "What are we doing today?"

Ayzah sighed. "Ain't that your job? *You* need to figure out how to hook me up."

It was too early to take shit from anyone, even a regular customer like Ayzah. He made a face at her in the mirror. "You don't have to be so testy. You know I haven't had my coffee."

"I'm sorry. I got a lot of things on my mind."

"Honey, we all do. Men are a pain in the ass, ain't they?"

Ayzah turned around sharply, causing Angel to pull on her

head. "Ow," she said. "I didn't say it had anything to do with a man."

"I wasn't talking about you. I was talking about me." He laughed a little too loudly for Ayzah's taste. "When do the troubles *not* have to do with men? You didn't have to say a word. You have all the symptoms."

"What the hell are you talking about?"

"You ain't got on no makeup."

"Please. It's the middle of the night."

"Uh-huh. As I was saying, your eyes are puffy and you have dark circles. I don't think I have ever seen you look like this no matter what time of day it was and I been knowing you a long time."

"Stop trippin'. I musta missed where you went to psychology school." They laughed at that, Ayzah uncomfortably, and Angel to humor her. He kept a sideways half smile on his face.

"So? Tell me. Prince ain't running around on you or anything, is he? You know that most of the drama that happens around here comes through this beauty shop in one form or another." He opened a jar and started applying cream relaxer to Ayzah's hair.

"Prince ain't the problem. He wants the best for me. It's Remedy that's giving me hell. About Jamal."

"What? I always thought he was so nice. Though not your type really." He laughed again, but narrowed his eyes. "Just kidding."

"You ain't right. He's cool, or at least he *was* cool. Doing things he didn't even have to. And then Prince suggested—"

"I thought you said this doesn't have to do with Prince—"

"Let me finish. We want to spend more time with Jamal, and up to now, you know, Remedy has been cool with me about it. But I thought I would try to get joint custody again——"

"But you left, remember? You had to go back to Prince for some reason."

"I don't see how that's a problem. I'm still his mother."

Angel pursed his lips. "Maybe biologically, but not in the eyes of the court. You. Abandoned. Him." He gestured in the air with the small comb he was using.

"You don't have to be so harsh." Her stomach churned with frustration just from talking about it.

"Just stating the facts as I know them to be."

"I was getting myself together. Remedy moved faster than I did. Prince thought it was best for me to take some time."

"That's bullshit. You didn't answer when you were served so what you have now is the result."

"What?" Ayzah didn't like the way Angel was challenging her. Who'd asked him anyway?

"I said that's bullshit. You were off somewhere with that man screwing him and the dick was so good you didn't give a damn about anything else, even Jamal. You knew that he would be all right with Remedy, so you just did whatever you felt like. Or whatever Prince told you to."

"I didn't ask you for your advice. You ain't no damned expert anyway."

Angel shrugged. "Maybe not. But I have heard my share of Baby Mama Drama to know what the courts would decide. You are going to have to prove that you can take care of that child and if you ask me, your track record ain't too good. How are you even going to feed him without asking your mother?

Your work history is what? You claim you work at Wal-Mart but we all know you are really a stripper."

"Exotic dancer."

"Whatever. Same difference. You don't even have any W-2s from that strip club gig, so forget that. And Prince? I don't think he has ever worked a day in his life. Not doing something he could admit to in a court of law. You might be mad at me for saying so but I have been here through the whole thing, even put your head back together after you let some strange, no-talent hairdresser hook you up in your travels."

His voice dropped in volume as the front door chimed. Angel leaned back to see who had come through the door.

Erica tipped in, her heels clicking on the linoleum. Although it was barely seven-thirty in the morning, she was fully made-up. Ayzah checked her out as she and Angel exchanged air kisses. Her short jeans were rolled up to midcalf and so distressed in some places that she could see flesh peeking through. On her feet, she wore badass purple shoes that Ayzah knew were the real thing, no cheap flea-market knock-offs. She still had no idea what her man was into now, but whatever it was, Erica had given up the Ma-No-Nos for good. She was sporting authentic six-hundred-dollar shoes and although Ayzah hated to admit it, they looked damned good. Looking at Erica made her wish she'd put more thought into her outfit instead of just throwing something on the way she had.

"Hey, Ayzah." She turned to Angel. "I know I don't have an appointment, but do you think you could fit me in? I got a hot night planned."

Ayzah's chest immediately began to tighten. Although she

had known Erica virtually all her life, there was something about her that set a bell ringing in her head, like she couldn't be trusted. She returned Erica's greeting and sat tight-lipped. She had no desire to have that one in her business, that was for sure.

"Oh, Miss Thang, look at you. You stepping out on your man or what?" He winked.

Her eyebrows rose, and then Erica giggled. "Shit. My stuff is good at home. And if I was, I damned sure wouldn't tell you."

"Can you give me twenty minutes? I just gotta get her washed and under the dryer." Angel continued to smooth the white cream through Ayzah's hair. Her scalp began to tingle.

Erica went to the front of the shop to wait.

"Have you talked to Remedy?" Angel asked.

Ayzah clenched and unclenched her right hand under the cape. Her voice dropped to barely above a whisper. "I was. I tried. I even ran to the hospital when he called me. But as soon as we mentioned it to him, he changed."

Something in what she said hit a nerve in Angel, something in the back of his mind. "What did you expect him to do? With you, he really had to do the right thing, but Prince? Now that's another story. Prince stole from him."

"What are you talking about? You been inhaling too many of these fumes around here. Prince is a lot of things, but he ain't a thief."

"Says who? You think about it? Adultery is really stealing. The two of you robbed Remedy of the chance at a happy family life."

"Get out. It's too early for you to have been smokin' that shit."

"It was in a book I read, for real. You should try it some-times. Reading, that is." He paused. "A lot of sins boil down to stealing. And a thief is the worst kind of criminal."

Indignant, she crossed her arms under the cape. Pieces of broken hair fluttered to the floor. "Whatever, Angel, ain't no such thing as a happy family life. This ain't TV. You need to be concentrating on my head and stop trying to be some kind of beauty-shop scholar."

"I'm trying to tell ya. *Grand larceny.*" Beat. "I need to move you to the sink." He guided Ayzah back to the washing area. "You can think what you want to, but back to the other thing. Jamal? If Remedy ain't willing, the only way I see your rights being restored is if you can prove to the court that you were under duress when you left, not in your right mind. You are also going to have to show a stable lifestyle."

Ayzah slid back into the chair and then laid back as Angel reclined it to put her head in the sink. Her head was burning by now and she was ready to get the relaxer out of her hair.

"So, my best bet is to talk to him. Alone, though, 'cause I made the mistake of taking Prince over there——"

"Not smart. You threw it in his face." He pumped on the shampoo bottles behind the sink.

"Not a good scene. He's just too busy since he broke his arm."

And then it clicked. The hospital. Ayzah's Remedy was Alexis's man with the broken arm. Angel's mouth dropped open. "I know why you can't reach Remedy."

"You do?" Her eyebrows drew into a tight line.

"Yes, girl. The man has a date."

peace pipe

Six P.M. was early for a date, but Alexis was ready as she'd promised she would be. She'd spent the morning taking care of her business, all the while angry at herself and at her boss, mulling over what she was going to do next. A night out would be a welcome thing and she was determined not to let anything that had happened get her down. The old Alexis would have moped around. The new Alexis was stronger than that. She refused to sweat any of that stuff, not even wanting to discuss it any further than she already had with Sarah. Alexis sighed, thinking about that now. She had been so frazzled and hoped that telling her friend about it would not prove to be a mistake. The new Alexis would come up with a plan and go on with her life. She could see Paris looking at her in pity and Athena having a heart attack and lecturing her for hours about her rash decisions.

Butterflies tickled her stomach as she waited; she didn't remember dating feeling this way. Perhaps it was the suspense. Remedy had refused to tell her where they were going, only that it would take them a little while to get there and that they would be back late. Anticipation felt good for a change. Since Walter had broken up with her, she spent so much time trying to be in control that the suspense of her impending date was a relief. She'd forgotten that a surprise every now and then was a good thing.

When she opened the door for Remedy, she had to take in her breath. He was gorgeous. Walter had been handsome, but Remedy was something else. Rugged. Alexis had to will herself to look away from him. It was hard for her to stop making a comparison even though she knew that every relationship therapist in the world would probably tell her she shouldn't. Walter had always been so put-together, neat and clean. Not that Remedy wasn't, but his clothing was more eclectic than Walter's would ever dare to be. He had that new metrosexual look going on. The tingling in her belly told her that it worked.

He wore a blue velvet jacket even though it was warm. The buttons were closed. She suspected that he didn't have a shirt on underneath, but couldn't tell because he also wore an ascot. The jacket hinted at the muscular chest and arms that lay underneath, and she noticed the cast on his arm was now almost entirely hidden. His faded jeans were fashionably distressed, even frayed at the bottom, stopping just below the ankles of his Texas cowboy boots. Alexis instantly felt like she had dressed too conservatively in her simple jersey wrap dress.

He smiled and she nearly fainted. "Are you going to invite me in or say hello?"

"I'm sorry. I was just . . . I don't know. Come in." She

hadn't noticed that he wore two earrings before. He hadn't had any on in the *dojan;* jewelry wasn't allowed. He'd switched from the simple stud he'd worn to her office. There was one in each ear, small horseshoe-shaped hoops. They didn't dangle exactly, but they seemed to frame his square jaw perfectly and set off his deep eyes. Alexis noticed a brilliant intelligence in them, like a much older person than she'd guessed he was.

"You about ready?" He glanced at his watch. "We have got to hustle."

Her curiosity returned and she paused, one eyebrow raised.

"Yes, we do. We are flying to Dallas for dinner."

"What? I hadn't planned—"

"I'm not kidnapping you or anything. You'll be back tonight."

"But what about your son? You must have one helluva sitter."

Remedy smiled. "He's taken care of. His grandmother is looking after him overnight."

"But we have thousands of places to eat here. In Austin."

"That's true, but this one is different. And you'll like it. Scout's honor." There was a hint of humor in his eyes.

Alexis was skeptical. "Were you ever a scout?"

"Nope. Not my thing. You coming?" He held the door open for her.

She didn't know what to say. This was so un-ordinary. Remedy was un-ordinary. A tingling was happening in her stomach that she hadn't felt in a very long time. She could see Aunt Athena's face in the back of her mind, giving her disapproving looks. Again. Mentally, she batted the image away. She would want to know what Alexis really knew about this man. She frowned. Who cared? Her gut said he was a good person. Sexy. Fun. She was a big girl and had a strong sense of people. Remedy Brown was not a bad person. And she would enjoy herself. Hell, as rough as her week had been, she needed to. The old Alexis cared about what her aunt would think. The new Alexis didn't. She was daring and spontaneous and in charge of her life. She picked up her bag, then nodded.

Remedy held the door open for her, then waited as she locked it. She followed him down the hallway and noticed that he was actually wearing spurs on his boots.

"I'm not sure they will let you fly with those things."

He smiled, revealing one of the sexiest smiles Alexis had seen in a long time. He looked like he had fallen out of a toothpaste commercial. "Well, we're about to find out."

♡ ♡ ♡

The flight lasted a little over thirty minutes. It was so short, Alexis had little time to wonder about the intelligence of their mission. A simple black car greeted them. By eight, they were pulling onto a block Alexis knew was famous for being a trendy hot spot. She had only been to Deep Ellum once before, and that had been in daylight. It looked somehow different as the town car sliced its way through the Texas night. They didn't talk, just stared at the eclectic mix of people who were milling around the streets. Her stomach quivered; she couldn't remember the last time she had done anything as spontaneous as go to another city on a date or even just on a whim. Walter wouldn't have dared to do anything like this, especially not a trip to Deep Ellum, the Greenwich Village of Texas. Everything would have had to be so planned. If the place wasn't four-star and didn't take reservations, they would not have been going. He would have been uncomfortable. Alexis liked this though. It felt good to her.

The car slid to a stop in front of a small, dark-looking place on Elm, right on the corner. Remedy had a half smile on his face and didn't move as Alexis tried to gauge his expression for some tiny hint of where they were. He didn't give a thing away. On the trip up, he'd danced around her curiosity quite well, giving her very little information as they made small talk.

The driver held the door open and Alexis got out first. Maybe spontaneity was not such a good idea. Half of her hoped that they were not going into the place they were standing in front of. There didn't seem to be a door. The entryway was wide open. A thin-looking man sat in front of the building on a low stool. There was a scarf wrapped around his head and like Remedy, he wore earrings in both ears. He stood, smiling as they approached. The two men hugged without speaking and Alexis followed Remedy inside.

Dallas was not as familiar to Alexis as some of the rest of Texas, and this place was like nothing she had seen in Austin. The walls were red, covered with what looked like velvet wallpaper. Although the lights were low, Alexis could tell that almost every table was filled. She inhaled, and realized that the air was filled with a light smoke. It reminded her of cigar smoke, but mellow. Remedy grabbed her hand and she followed as he led her through a maze of tables to the back of the room. They walked through curtains the same color as the walls into another, smaller room. This one was empty, and the tables here were low to the ground like in a Japanese restaurant, surrounded by large pillows.

"I hope this is okay."

Alexis was glad that her dress wasn't tight. She nodded, then followed his lead as he fluffed the pillows for her. She felt a twinge of guilt as he struggled to move the large velvet and silk pillows with one arm and slid down into them. They were surprisingly comfortable. She chuckled to herself, realizing that she couldn't remember the last time she'd sat on the floor outside of an exercise class.

"This is unusual."

"Just different." He smiled up at her, flashing his dimple.

She glanced around. It was both of those things. A waitress joined them without speaking, sliding a large contraption onto the table. It looked like Aladdin's lamp with some type of plunger bulb on top.

"Is this my favorite blend?"

"You know it is, Rem." She smiled and Alexis spotted a flash of a tongue ring. She pulled a long-nosed fireplace lighter from her pocket and pressed the igniter button. Alexis jumped as a flame leapt from the end of it. The waitress touched it to the top of the contraption, cupping it with her hand to keep the flame from going out.

Remedy waited for her to leave, then adjusted some of the tubing that was coming from it. "I don't guess you have ever smoked a hookah before."

Hookah. The name on the building. Alexis was relieved. She'd thought the name of the place was the Velvet Hooka. "I can't tell you I even know what a hookah is."

He laughed. "This is a hookah. Here. A water pipe."

"Why didn't they call it that? Is it legal?"

"The Velvet Place to Smoke Water Pipes wouldn't have sounded as cool. And yes, it is legal. Besides, do I look like the criminal type to you?" He paused. "Don't answer that."

"I have never smoked anything before."

The waitress returned, this time sliding two glasses in front of them, then slid away again. They hadn't ordered a thing yet. Alexis tried to act unsurprised. She might have been annoyed if Walter had ordered for her, but it was somehow charming on Remedy. She just couldn't tell how or when he'd did it.

"I hope you like that."

"So, you obviously know your way around this place. You get here a lot?"

"You could say that. Not as much as I used to before I moved to Austin. I used to live here. There is another one of these north of here in Addison."

"You must really like this spot if you know where all of them are."

He chuckled. "I do. And I should. Considering that I am one of the owners." He leaned in toward her. "I have to confess that this was a dual-purpose date. I needed to check on the place, so here we are. Besides, considering our short but colorful history, I thought we might need to smoke a little peace pipe before I ended up with any more broken parts."

"Okay. One point for you." Alexis thought about Remedy, realizing that he seemed to be right at home here. More of a Dallas type than Austin. She hadn't taken him to be a nightclub owner though, at least not one that looked like this. She realized that she hadn't had much time to take him for anything. "What brought you to Austin anyway?"

Remedy took a long drag before answering. "It'll relax you."

"I can't do illegal shit. It goes—"

Remedy smiled again. "I promise. Legal all the way. This is one of the few legal places to smoke anything in Dallas. Scout's honor."

"Again?"

He grinned.

Alexis hesitated, then sucked on the tubing the way Remedy had.

"Nothing brought me there." A beat. "I ran there. Did I mention I have fourteen brothers and sisters?"

Alexis choked and some of the wine she was sipping escaped from her mouth. "Get out. Fourteen?" She dabbed at her chin with her napkin.

"Fourteen. I know. It's shocking."

"Wow. I can't imagine. All from the same parents?"

He shook his head. "Different mothers. We all have the same daddy. No more than two of us have the same mother."

"That is amazing. I didn't think people had that many kids anymore. Papa was a rollin' stone, huh?"

Remedy laughed, shaking his head. "No, he wasn't. Papa was a ho'." He paused. "I have two brothers that were born in the same year that I was and we all lived within a ten-mile radius of each other."

"Amazing," she said again. "You must have had an interesting life then." That made Alexis think of her own life. That could have been her but for Aunt Athena. She would have grown up in what her aunt affectionately called The Bottom if they hadn't brought her to Austin. She might have been a different person, too. Who knows how many brothers and sisters she had. Her daddy had her and never looked back.

Remedy laughed again. "What is amazing is that any of us are sane at all. We walked around for years with baggage that wasn't even ours. Our parents' baggage."

Alexis really couldn't imagine. Even though she had been born to a teenaged mother herself, her aunt and uncle worked hard to provide an environment that at least appeared to be stable. She knew she had her own issues because of that, but what Remedy was talking about, that was more than issues. His type of drama, she could only surmise, would be cataclysmic on her scale. Maybe she was ungrateful like Athena kept saying. She had only come to realize that she resented her aunt. Sometimes Athena acted as if she had done the good deed of the year.

"You turned out fine though." And he was fine, in more ways than one. Remedy seemed as normal as they came. Driven. Pulled together. And fine as hell.

He reached across the table and rubbed the back of her hand. "Fine now. I wasn't always like this."

Alexis watched as the light that had been dancing in his eyes dimmed a little. He licked his lips and she sat on the edge of her chair, waiting.

"Before 1992, I was *always* high. I smoked four, maybe five joints a day."

This was surprising. She couldn't imagine him high. Remedy barely touched his wine. "Really?"

He nodded. "Really. I stopped one day because I bet my bio-dad."

"Bio-dad?" Alexis had never heard this term before.

"Don't look confused. He fathered me, but he wasn't much of a daddy. You wouldn't know anything about that though."

"In a way I would. I never knew my father either." It slipped from her lips before she could stop herself. "The only daddy I know is really my Uncle Brian. He's married to my Aunt Athena. They raised me along with their own daughter." She blushed. "But you finish. Tell me."

Remedy raised an eyebrow. There was more to Alexis than he'd thought. He'd taken her for one of those blue-blooded types with the perfect life. "As I was saying, I bet my father that if he would stop using for two weeks, I wouldn't smoke another joint the rest of my life."

"And—"

"And nothing. He couldn't make it. He would probably still be a junkie if he weren't incarcerated. We got some jokes out of it though. My sisters were placing bets on who would win. It was quite the circus."

Alexis didn't know what to say. Compared to what Remedy was talking about, she had practically grown up with a silver spoon in her mouth.

"I'm sorry, I didn't mean to make you sad. Look at the good side. I came out ahead. I kept my promise and now I am successful. I'm not rich, but I can eat."

"I'm not sad."

"No? I hope you aren't feeling sorry for me or anything like that. I assure you, I do well."

"No, I was thinking." Remedy had lived the kind of life

that she had always been told would keep her from being anything. She was supposedly better off. "What were you running from? I still didn't get that. How did you get from high all the time to where you are now?"

"I was all cleaned up and I didn't want to live in the cycle. Things were going good. I didn't go to Austin first. I left here though. I went on vacation. Like that skater who tried to break her competition's kneecaps. What was her name?"

"Tonya Harding."

"Yeah. Her. When it was all over, she went to Disney World. I went to Club Med. Only I didn't come back. I went there, liked it so much I got a job as a bartender. I had no intention of ever coming back to the States."

Silence.

Remedy sipped his drink, then continued. "I met some guys there. They liked what they saw and made me an offer. What resulted was managing partnership in The Velvet Hookah."

"This place?" Self-employed. That *could* go over well with her aunt.

He nodded. "You got it."

"That sounds like a great story. A fairy tale."

"I guess you could say that. And for some reason unbeknownst to me, I was the prince. Except when things were going well in the kingdom, relatives started to come out of the woodwork, if you know what I mean."

"Tell me about it. Everyone always thinks that you have more than they do because you appear to be making ends meet, like your grass is always greener than theirs. And of course you are obligated to give them a piece of it."

"We were looking at expanding, and I wanted to get away from here. You know what they say. Out of sight, out of mind. I needed to get away from Cousin Ray-Ray anem."

"That's not his name."

"Their names. No, it's not, but it didn't matter. I was looking like a meal ticket to everybody and their mama. So, the plan was that I would move and scout out Austin for a third Hookah."

There was no such place in Austin as far as Alexis knew. "But you have been there awhile—"

"I have. True. But that is when things got sidetracked. Hanging out with some friends, I met Ayzah." His face darkened. "And I guess you could say I am just getting back on track."

"Now *that* I understand. I was engaged for a while. Lived with someone. He was a nice guy, too. He just wasn't for me."

"Bad breakup?" Her scene could not have possibly been anything like his.

She swallowed. "I guess you could say that. We never really broke up. He just left. Moved." She looked down at her hands. This was the first time she'd ever told anyone the truth about her and Walter, and for some reason, it didn't hurt as much as she thought it would.

"You seem pretty calm about it. Did you get some help or do you just deal with things like that well? I had a whirlwind marriage with really no romance in the beginning and the counseling I got really helped me."

Alexis chuckled. "My counseling was talking to my friends. I am not really the counseling type. I guess you could say I dealt with it myself. Made my own life changes. That is how I ended up in tae kwon do. Therapy."

He nodded. "It's not for everybody. I didn't think it was for me either. So, you were trying to channel your anger. I guess I owe my broken arm to your ex then?" Remedy raised one eyebrow.

She'd thought she was handling her feelings well. Channeling her anger. Claiming her power as Oprah would have said. It would probably be a bad idea to mention her boss right now.

"Maybe you ought to consider anger management instead of counseling." He rubbed his arm.

Again with the anger management. "I'm not angry. Not anymore."

"You don't say?" A beat. "Okay, at least you haven't sworn off all mankind. Or decided to take it out on all the other men in your life. I've heard that some women do things like that after a bad breakup. You haven't decided to make me suffer, have you?"

"Nothing like that. And my breakup wasn't bad." They really hadn't had the time for it to be bad. Walter avoided any confrontation by leaving the way he had. "It was more like sudden. We were going along, business as usual and he just didn't show up for dinner one day. I guess you could say I decided to work on me instead." She sipped her drink. She was itching to ask him questions about his ex, but resisted. "I guess I could say the same about you then?"

Remedy thought about Ayzah. Prince. The ludicrous scene at his apartment. "Yeah. I guess you could." He wouldn't talk about her now. She didn't need to know about all of his drama. Yet.

patiently waiting

Business. Ayzah hated Prince's business and she had no idea, really, what it was. All she knew was that since he started it, he was staying out later and later. She changed the radio station on her car. His business left her going through the drive-through at Wendy's on a Saturday night instead of out with her man somewhere. She would settle for *home* with her man.

She glided into the take-out lane and placed her order, jumping when the voice squawked at her through the intercom. She ordered for her mother, too. Might as well take her something since that was where she would be spending her evening. She shook her head. She was barely thirty-five and she was spending her Saturday evening at her mother's, with her and her church friends probably. Like she was one of those ugly single girls with no male companionship in their lives. She had a man. Sort of.

There were no surprises at her mother's house. Ma'dear was where she always was on Saturday. Her television was tuned to Lifetime and she sat in her favorite chair with her favorite blanket across her lap even though it wasn't cold. Her Bible was open on the table next to her. Ayzah peeped through the front window, and then opened the door without knocking. She tried to come up with a smile for her mother.

Ma'dear barely moved from her seat when she opened the door. "Surprised to see you."

Ayzah measured her words. She didn't feel like fighting with her mother and she certainly didn't want to be picked at. "Hello, Ma'dear. You really should double lock the door."

"Why? Ain't nobody interested in me, girl."

So far, so good. "I bought you some food. I stopped by Wendy's and picked up your favorite."

Ma'dear smiled. "Well, praise the Lord. Where's that man of yours tonight? You two should be out painting the town."

Ayzah cringed. The drama was about to start. "He had to work, Ma."

"Ma'dear. Ain't nothing wrong with honest work. I was just about to watch me a movie. You got time to stay and watch with me? Whatever you do, just be quiet. I just got your son down for the night."

"What's Jamal doing here? Remedy didn't mention anything to me. He broke something else?" Her heart raced. It looked like Angel was right. Remedy might really have a date after all. If Jamal was here, Remedy would have to pick him up. That could be her chance to talk to him.

She shook her head. "You see, that's why you let the good man get away from you. Your mouth is always so smart. He could be nasty about the situation, but thank goodness he is a good person. He doesn't have to let me see the boy, but he let water flow under the bridge and now makes time for me and my grandbaby every chance he gets." She paused. "He had somewhere to go tonight. He'll pick him up in the morning. Sit on down."

Ayzah eased onto the slip-covered couch near her mother. There went that idea. No Prince. No Remedy. She had nothing but time.

♡   ♡   ♡

Ayzah was restless. She couldn't concentrate on the movie and couldn't think about anything but Prince. She'd called him three times already and each time it had just gone right to his voice mail. What was so important that he couldn't take her calls? It was almost midnight and every bone in her body had a bad feeling. She hoped to God that she was wrong.

"I'll be back, Ma'dear."

"You need to see a doctor if you have to keep running to the bathroom like this." Ma'dear gave her daughter a knowing smile. From the worry lines that had creased Ayzah's face since she had arrived, it was obvious that she wasn't really running to the bathroom at all, but running after a man. Prince meant her no good and Ayzah was the only one who couldn't see it.

The bathroom in her mother's house was small and all the way at the back of the house. It was farthest away from where they had been sitting, and that made it the best place to go so her mother couldn't hear her conversation. Ayzah closed then locked the door. When she was a teenager, she would do the very same thing, only then the phone cord used to trail under the door and would give her whereabouts away. Thank goodness for cell phones.

Ayzah didn't call Prince again, not this time. She'd already left too many messages for him. If someone asked her what had happened in the past half hour of the movie she had been watching with her mother, Ayzah would not be able to tell them. She had missed it, and was instead engrossed in a debate with herself over the wisdom of what she was about to do.

Calling Erica was inviting trouble. That woman had a way of either broadcasting your business when you didn't want her to, or keeping the things she knew until she could use them to her benefit. Erica had a history of being loyal to no one but herself. Still, she was the only person who might possibly be able to shed some light on what was going on with Prince. Ever since the whole business of her getting custody of Jamal had started, Ayzah'd had a bad feeling. She had been willing to take baby steps, but he seemed to be in much more of a rush than she was, ever since he'd calculated how much money Remedy actually made. When Prince had heard about the clubs, he did some digging around and came up with a ballpark figure of Remedy's net worth.

He kept claiming that he was thinking of her and loved her. She loved him, too, but a part of her felt that the money was really all he was thinking about. He said he was making plans for them to move to California where she could start over. She wanted to go, heaven knows, she did. Her life in Austin had been too much, and it seemed that no matter where she went, her legacy as an exotic dancer would follow her. The city was just too small. No one would ever take her seriously here.

The phone rang six times before Erica answered it, and Ayzah was caught off guard. She was positive she would get voice mail and had to think a minute about what she wanted to say.

She cleared her throat. "You busy?"

"Is this Ayzah? This is a surprise." Erica hesitated.

"You don't have to be a smart-ass."

"*You* called me."

Ayzah chewed on her lip and took a deep breath. She didn't want to seem desperate.

"You have something on your mind?" Erica's voice was husky, winded.

"Not really. Were you exercising or something?" Ayzah looked at her watch. It was late at night. Who in the hell would be working out now?

"No. I wasn't. I'm good." She paused. "Okay. I know this isn't really a social call."

"This was a mistake. You wouldn't understand." There were muffled voices on Erica's end. "Look, I can just talk to you later if you are busy. I didn't mean to disturb you. I thought that you would be alone since Prince is working."

"Wait. No problem. He is working." A giggle. "I just have a little company. Me and my girl kickin' it. What do you need?"

Ayzah hesitated. "I don't really *need* anything. I was just trying to understand what all Prince was doing. He didn't really give me any details."

"Uh-huh." Beat. "And you thought I could help you?"

"This is normal for you. Not me."

"I see. Wait."

Erica's muffled voice came through the phone. It sounded as if she had put her hand over the phone, but Ayzah wasn't sure.

"Okay," Erica said. "I'm back. I don't understand what you want to know. I probably know as much as you do. I'm really not concerned with what he does, as long as he keeps his ass out of jail and takes care of what he is supposed to take care of."

"I don't understand how you can do that. I need to feel like I am a partner."

Erica's laughter hurt her ear. "I *am* a partner. A well taken care of one."

"So you aren't concerned about them getting locked up or something like that? Ya'll ain't married. If something happens to him what do you have? Probably the same thing I do, which is nothing."

"No, I'm not concerned and you shouldn't be either. But I do have some shit, that's where you're wrong. I told you your man needs to be hooking you up and I ain't talking 'bout in the bed either, but I don't guess Prince has any problems there. Hold on."

More muffled talking. Laughter. Ayzah could almost make out the words "look, this is my conversation."

"Okay, sorry." Erica was back. "Make sure he buys you shit you can sell come hard times, if you know what I mean. Other than that, you got a roof over your head? Ain't no man gonna be living with me for free."

"Yeah. I got a place. He takes care."

"Then I don't see what the problem is. As long as he don't bring no drama or diseases home, you got it made. Don't be a dummy. You don't want to push him away because you are nagging him about dumb shit. You just need to concentrate on being what he wants. Trust me when I tell you there are a lot of skanks out there just waiting for a man like yours to come around. Don't nobody like to be alone. Stop doing that."

"What?"

"Not you. Look, I gotta go take care of some business. You holla at me lata, okay?"

Ayzah shut her phone and contemplated what Erica had said. Erica's "business" didn't sound like no girlfriend, but that was her shit to deal with. Ayzah, on the other hand, had real things to take care of. Erica was right; she needed to concentrate on making Prince happy. She really didn't want to be alone, that much was true. So she was going to go back to smoothing things over with Remedy while Prince was doing whatever he was doing.

♥ ♥ ♥

"I don't see why you had to keep messing with me while I was on the phone. So childish." Erica giggled. She perched a hand on her left hip, turning fully around to face the man on her bed.

Candlelight flickered and illuminated her. Erica wore nothing but knee-high boots. Her stance had the effect she wanted; he was able to admire all of her. "You bring out the kid in me. I couldn't help myself. Besides, I had to stop the two of you and your silly woman talk anyway, remind you I was here so you would stop saying all that crazy shit you was talking."

Erica straddled Prince. "It wasn't crazy. It ain't like she going to pay any attention to me anyway. Ayzah don't even like me."

"Would you like you? She is just a little needy sometimes, that's all."

"She was really calling here looking for you, you know that, right?"

"You don't need to be starting any trouble." He put his hands on her hips, then pulled her forward enough to put his tongue in her belly button. She smelled good and raw. If he had anything to do with it, she would smell that way for several more hours.

"She obviously don't got you trained right. You need to handle your business so we can keep this between you and me."

"Oh, and you got me trained?"

"Whipped." Erica's laugh was devilish. She slid herself down the length of Prince's body with the skill of an acrobat. Proud of the power she had over him, Erica took his penis in her hand.

He moaned in anticipation, then tried to guide her head. Erica hummed as her mouth covered his penis. He couldn't move if he wanted to. Prince closed his eyes, straining to talk. Thoughts of Ayzah were the furthest thing from his mind.

foreplay

Remedy lived in Deep Ellum, around the corner from the Velvet Hookah. After dinner, he suggested they take a walk to wait out the effects of the wine and Alexis didn't hesitate. It was getting late, but it was obvious by the swarms of people still on the street that the night was young here. From the looks of things, there would be people here well into morning.

Alexis listened intently as he pointed out places of interest. He knew small things that she didn't. Things that made a difference. She enjoyed the warmth in his voice as he told her about the history of the area.

"I have a place in this building. A loft." Remedy looked down at his feet. He didn't want to seem too forward, but he would like nothing more than for her to see his place.

"I thought you lived in Austin."

"I do. Most of the time. I lived here before and I just never sold my place. I have been meaning to lease it, but in the meantime I use it to crash whenever I am in town."

"This looks like an office building." Alexis let him slip his arm around her, wishing she could melt into him. The soft smell of his cologne wafted through the smoke left in his clothes.

"It was. Actually an historic building. Restored. You can come up to see it if you want." Remedy caught her eyes with his. "Just until your head feels better. I don't want you to think—"

"I didn't." Alexis wasn't blind to the attraction he felt for her. She felt it, too. "I would love to see where you live." Her heart skipped. Remedy would be the first man she had been alone with since breaking up with Walter. He was in trouble and didn't even know it.

He nodded. "Only part of the time, remember? It's kind of sparse. I hope you don't mind. I keep my things spread between here and Austin."

"I'm sure it's fine."

The loft was more than fine, it was beautiful. Alexis stood in the doorway and admired the hardwood floors that stretched like a ribbon to the floor-to-ceiling windows. Remedy stood quietly behind her as she entered.

She was drawn to the windows. The click of her heels on the floor echoed throughout the dim apartment as she walked over and gasped at the breathtaking view of the city.

"I had that same reaction." Remedy slipped his arms around her waist, savoring the way her body felt against his.

"How could you give this up? You live downtown but still, we have nothing like this."

"I haven't given it up. Life happened so fast, and before I knew it, I was just spending more time in Austin than here. I like to think of myself as a dual-city man." Remedy's phone chimed and he silenced it.

"Don't you want to get that?"

"Whoever it is, they can wait." He leaned over and gently kissed the place where her shoulders joined with her neck.

Her senses jumped to life and a shiver ran through her body. Alexis froze. His kiss was gentle, but it sent a sharp spark throughout her body. She gasped again.

"Can I offer you some wine?" His sensuous and husky voice caressed the place he kissed.

"I thought we came here to get rid of the buzz. Don't you think that wine would add more?"

He laughed softly. "I never said the buzz was caused by the wine. I think it was my special blend in the hookah that got you going. It has that effect on first-timers."

"Really?"

He nodded. "It was called 'foreplay'."

Alexis gulped. "You see—"

Remedy held up his hand. "That was the name of the blend. Really. Didn't you see the other menu there? It was a menu of blends for the pipes."

"Sure it was." Alexis joked, but she was relieved. "For a minute I thought I was catching a glimpse of the arrogant guy I saw in tae kwon do the other day." She turned around to face Remedy.

"I wasn't arrogant. Why would you say that?"

"Yeah, you were. The way you looked at me that day. If you weren't full of yourself then I don't know what that was."

"Is that why you tried to kick me into tomorrow? I was just being friendly."

"Riiight—" Alexis's words caught in her throat as she searched for a smart retort. It had been a long time since she was at a loss for words.

They made eye contact and the amused look that had been dancing in Remedy's eyes suddenly left. His mouth went dry and he was almost entranced by the deep brown of Alexis's eyes.

Her heart throbbed in her ears as Remedy drew her to him, one arm on the small of her back. They didn't speak. Alexis couldn't have moved if she wanted to. She enjoyed the warmth of his one-armed embrace. He kissed her slowly and thoughtfully.

"I think we should skip the wine," he said.

She nodded. All of the questions in her head about being with him on the first date vanished. Without a second thought, Alexis followed his lead back to the bedroom.

the hurting truth

The absence of sound woke her up. Dim light peeked through the blinds and Ayzah shielded her eyes. At first she was disoriented, and then she remembered where she was. On her mother's couch. And she had been there all night. The last thing she remembered was stewing after talking to Erica, then leaving a message or two for Remedy while waiting for Prince to call her back. He hadn't. Ayzah wiped her face with the back of her hand and then reached down to grab her phone.

"You didn't get any calls." Ma'dear's voiced boomed at her.

She jumped. "Did you move or have you been sitting there all night?"

Ma'dear stood up, then walked over to the window. "Girl, I went to bed after my movie went off and been up for hours." She pulled the string to open the blinds. Sun came streaming through, blinding Ayzah. "You know, the early bird gets the worm and all that."

"Ma'dear. I can't see." She shielded her eyes with her arm. "Do you have to do that now? Where's Jamal?"

"Still asleep. Remedy will get him after church. You been blinded for months by that Prince. I'll get him up soon."

It had been too good to be true. Ayzah sat up. It was obvious that she and Ma'dear had gotten through one night without fighting, but from the sound of things, that was about to end.

"Yeah. I know you don't think I was born yesterday. Prince didn't come home last night, did he? I know you were waiting on him to call you. It was obvious the way you kept looking at your phone, like you were willing it to ring or something."

"I wasn't." Ayzah crossed her arms in front of her. Why did her mother always have to be so harsh to her?

"Okay. But ain't no man worth what he puts you through. If I said it once I said it a thousand times. Prince don't care about nobody but himself. I don't understand what it is going to take——"

Ayzah couldn't hold back anymore. She burst into tears.

Ma'dear stood in silence, stunned. She'd thought that Ayzah was tougher than that. It was strange that a few loud words would make her cave in this way. Her face softened.

"I don't know what to do. I try to do the right things. Be a good woman for my man like you always talk about."

Ma'dear sat on the couch next to her daughter. She had no idea that she felt this way. "Ayzah, I'm sorry." She rubbed Ayzah's back. "All I want for you is to be happy. A good woman has to take care of herself first before she can take care of anyone else. Prince, Jamal. Anybody."

She wiped her face with the back of her hand. "But you said——"

"I know what I said. But you have to remember the context. I am your mother. It is my job to give you advice. Especially since I haven't always set the best example. I don't know if you noticed, but I ain't never been married. I have never been in a long-term relationship with anyone other than your daddy. And that wasn't really long, if you know what I mean."

"You sure give me advice like you know about how it's supposed to go all the time." Ayzah pouted. Sometimes her mother told her what to do so much she had to tune her out to stay sane.

"Yes, I do. I'm sorry for that. But I see him taking advantage of you. He never puts your needs first. He told you to leave, and you did, without looking back. You left Jamal and a man who would have been good to you. Hell, after all that, Remedy is still good to you."

Ayzah sniffed, then nodded. He *was* being good to her, even after everything they had been through.

"But I love Prince, Ma. And he loves me, too."

Ma'dear didn't correct her. She looked at her daughter and shook her head. "You just think you do. I know you better than you know yourself, and I have to tell you, you are afraid to be alone, that's all. And Prince don't no more love you than anybody else." She paused. "Think about it. His actions don't say he loves you. His actions don't even say that he is even your friend." A beat. "Would you treat a friend the way that he treats you? And now he is pushing you to get custody of Jamal, for what? I find it hard to believe that he had you or Jamal's best interests in mind."

Ayzah's mouth dropped open. How in the world did her mother know about that?

"Don't look so surprised. Remedy told me everything.

Prince is claiming it's what *you* want and need, but let me ask you this: Did you and he ever discuss what was best for Jamal? Neither one of you have a job, not really. And Jamal is little now, but how are you going to feel when he is going to school and his school friends are teasing him because their daddies remember his mama shaking her ass for money?"

"I don't see what that has to do with anything."

"You don't? You need to get yourself together, Ayzah. You could be a smart woman if you opened your eyes and stopped walking around here eyes closed, nose open, angry at the world. Remedy doesn't want to keep you from your child, but legally he can, and no court in the world is going to tell him any different. Not from where I am standing."

"Prince said I would probably get custody, full custody if I wanted. Then we could be a family and move out to LA. I could start over." Ayzah bounced her leg up and down. Tears were streaming down her face again and she didn't try to stop them.

"Did he? Genesis, Exodus, Leviticus, Numbers. . . ." She took a deep, cleansing breath. "Deuteronomy, Joshua, Judges, Ruth."

Ayzah cringed. Her mother had gone almost to the New Testament that time.

Ma'dear willed herself to calm down. There was no way she was going to get through to Ayzah if she was angry. "Okay. Did I miss him going to law school like I missed him going to college? It's a miracle they let that boy get out of high school." Ma'dear stood up and began pacing the room. "That's your problem, Ayzah. You have got to start thinking for yourself. There are a few problems with that logic. First, you aban-

doned your child and you don't really have gainful employment. I did my research. The only way you have a chance in
hell of getting custody away from Remedy, who, by the way is
not only gainfully employed but also quite enterprising, is to
get a stable job and home life. But that is only half of it. No
judge in the world is going to understand why any woman,
any person, would abandon their baby. You would probably
have to damn near convince them that you were kidnapped or
coerced. That would be kind of hard to do since you are still
fooling around with the man you left with, right?"

"I didn't think—"

Ma'dear shook her head. She lowered her voice. "No, you
didn't."

Her surprise was fading away. Ayzah had almost had
enough of her mother's tirade. "I didn't ask you—"

"No, you didn't. But let me finish. See, Remedy has been
good to you. And to me. He goes out of his way to make sure I
have some relationship with my only grandson. So why would
you try to wrench his son away from him by moving away,
even if you could do that? Ayzah Marie, that is not right and
you know it. The way I see it, you are messing up a real chance
to get yourself together and do what is best for your son. Nothing would benefit him better than having two loving parents,
even if they are not married to each other. Besides, what in
the hell is in LA? You think there is a fairy tale out there waiting for you or something?"

"How would you know, Ma? You said yourself, you ain't
never been in my shoes."

"You watch your tone. I never said that. I said I have never
been married, and you aren't now. But I been in your shoes,

believe that. You're scared, confused, and looking for an easy way out of the mess you created. You better believe I been there. Let me be the first to tell you. The fairy tale you looking for? It doesn't exist. Don't think you can run away from your problems and things will miraculously get better. There is no Prince Charming that can save you from yourself, Ayzah."

Ayzah leaned back on the couch, sobbing. "So, what should I do?"

Ma'dear shook her head. Ayzah still didn't understand. "That you are going to have to figure out for yourself."

A few deep breaths calmed her crying. Her mother was right; she needed a plan. Her life was a disaster and she could not remember a time when her mother had been so angry at her. She picked at her all the time, but this was different. Harsh. The sad part was that she was right.

♥   ♥   ♥

She could deal with Prince later, whenever he chose to surface. Part of her wanted to believe he had some legitimate reason for staying out all night. Part of her didn't care.

Ayzah got into her small car and headed over to Remedy's. Her mother was right. He had been good to her and now was as good a time as any to try and smooth things over with him. He really hadn't asked for all this drama.

Downtown Austin was deserted, as usual for Sunday morning. It was too early for the shoppers and most folks would be getting ready for church, as her mother had been when she'd left her. If she'd stayed there another minute, Ma'dear would have been trying to guilt her into going to church with her, and she just wasn't up to that. Last time she went they treated her like a prodigal daughter come home. Ma'dear was not known to be the most closemouthed saint in the church so they probably all knew her business already and would greet her at the door, ready to surround her and pray for her lost soul or something or the other. There was too much on her mind to be dealing with that, too.

The entrance to the parking garage under Remedy's building was on a side street. Ayzah pulled down into the gated driveway and stopped just shy of the large metal driveway door that blocked the entry like a prison. She keyed in the code at the small black access pad and held her breath. Just because it worked last time did not mean it would work again. It took a minute, but the door finally roared to life and lifted. Thank God for small miracles, Ayzah thought. The code obviously hadn't been changed. Yet.

Ayzah guided her car into the dark garage. She and Remedy needed to have a long heart-to-heart, without Prince looking over her shoulder. And whatever Prince's excuse would be for where he had been all night, she was going to put her foot down. It would be hard, but she made a deal with herself that she would not let things go as she usually did. He was good at apologizing and then charming his way right into her panties.

She and Remedy, without Prince, would decide what was good for their son. There might be good money in the child support, but some things didn't have a price. She shuddered. Even she had to admit that her behavior over the past few days had been terrible, and it was all to try to please some man who didn't even have the courtesy to call her.

Remedy got two parking spaces with his fancy downtown address. His car was in one of them. Ayzah was glad to see that. At least that meant there was a possibility that he was home. She fit her car into the other, just like she used to, and killed her engine. Remedy was a man of habit. Sunday mornings, if he went anywhere, he would find his way over to Whole Foods to read the paper and have some of that fancy coffee he liked so much. During the short time she lived there, he would bring some back for her, too, letting her sleep late. Remedy had been thoughtful that way, even if she really didn't deserve it. Prince never did shit like that. Something down deep told her that maybe her mother was right about him only caring about himself.

Large glass doors led to the lobby of Remedy's building. It was new, built to attract the younger, single type to downtown living. What seemed like miles of stone floor stretched across the lobby of the building, flanked on one side by a tall, rounded counter where security sat and monitored the building and the entryways. The guard smiled as soon as she walked through the door.

Ayzah hesitated. She had not seen this woman before.

"Can I help you?" She smiled warmly up at Ayzah from her seat behind the counter.

"No, I'll just let myself in." Ayzah could feel the woman's eyes on her back, watching her intently. She fumbled in her bag for the keys and access card. Minutes moved by too slowly but she eventually found them and flashed a smile at the woman, now standing behind her desk.

"I don't think we've met. I'm new."

Ayzah could hear the anticipation in her voice, but she

didn't acknowledge it. There was no reason for her to give the woman any more information than was necessary. She was not in the mood for small talk. She still needed some coffee and certainly didn't need this woman in her business. "No, we haven't."

The answer threw the guard off. Her face held a perplexed look, as if Ayzah's comment left her speechless. It was obvious that her mind was working as she tried to figure out what her next step would be. Ayzah ignored her, continuing to fumble with the access key.

She dropped it, swore under her breath, then picked it up again and inserted it repeatedly into the reader. After a few minutes, it became obvious that she was not going to have the same luck she'd had with the garage door. The tightening of her jaw betrayed her frustration. Remedy was not the type to get caught twice. He would be an idiot if he hadn't had her card deactivated after her last surprise visit. The sound the statue had made when it clocked him in the head echoed in Ayzah's memory. Another one of her smart moves come back to bite her in the ass. Damn. The way she had acted it was a wonder he hadn't put her on the "no access under any circumstances" list.

"I think my magnetic strip is not working. Do you think you could let me up?" She tried to sound friendlier, somehow nicer than she had a minute ago, and managed a tremulous smile.

The look on the guard's face appeared as if she might scream, "Hell no," at any minute. She blinked, then looked as if she was pondering what to do.

The smile that Ayzah had plastered on her face dimmed a

little as their eyes met. *Stay calm*, she thought. Every time she let her anger get the best of her, she made stupid decisions. There was still a chance this woman would have pity on her.

"No problem. Tell me your name and I can look you up in my computer. I'm sorry that I don't know everyone yet."

"Um . . ." There was no way that was going to work. She was not listed as a resident and never had been. The guard caught on fast, but was polite, although Ayzah could detect a hint of a chill in her voice.

"You can use the intercom system over there to have someone buzz you up, or if you'd like, I can call upstairs for you."

Ayzah clenched her teeth. She shook her head, then stormed over to the intercom and pushed Remedy's button. There was a good chance that he would answer and then not let her up anyway.

She paced the floor in between buzzes, tapping her foot nervously when she was standing still. Her shoes made a clicking sound that echoed loudly through the marble-floored entryway. Ayzah glanced at her watch. Where in the hell was Remedy? If he'd gone to Whole Foods, he would have been back by now.

The guard had returned to her seat back behind the high desk. Ayzah walked over and she looked up, meeting her eyes. The same pleasant look that had been there when she had arrived had found its way back onto her face.

"I am looking for my husband—"

"Husband?"

"Ex-husband." She felt irritable and unhappy with herself. Ayzah drummed her fingers on the desk. "Remedy Brown. On four?"

There was a twinkle of understanding in her eyes. "I wish you had told me that. I haven't seen him this morning. Matter of fact, I think he went out yesterday and hasn't come back yet. I've been here all night. Ten to ten. And he took that cute little boy with him. Is that your son?" She smiled. "He is a handsome young one." She paused, her smile dimming. "You're really not his wife, are you? 'Cause if I remember correctly, I asked him why he had such a smile on his face. Did he have a hot date? He smiled at me and said that as a matter of fact, he did."

Ayzah barely heard what the woman said. Remedy had not come back since he'd gone out. And he had a date. She knew this, but he stayed out all night, too? Waves of jealousy washed over her and she shuddered. She went hot, then cold, then hot again. What was going on? She walked back to the garage in a cloud, wondering all the way where Remedy was last night. What was it with men who couldn't answer their phones? She knew that he often went to Dallas to check on his clubs there, but even then, he'd always answered the phone when she called. Unless he really had met someone new, someone whom he really liked. She was sure it was that proper lawyer bitch. She knew it was.

Ayzah was unprepared for the mixture of emotions she felt. She was angry, then sad, then jealous several times. Her throat tightened up, making it hard to swallow. A date. Remedy had some nerve. He'd moved on quick enough. Too quickly. She must have really meant nothing to him. What if he was thinking about getting married? What if he was the one who made the perfect family for Jamal while she still didn't even really know where she lived and had no career prospects? Ayzah gritted her teeth. In her mind she saw colored lights, then heard a deep scratching sound, the sound of metal grating on metal. She began to perspire, then tried to count to ten to get herself back under control. There was no use having a heart attack over speculation.

Ayzah counted to ten again, calming down enough to be able to see. She looked around. She'd made her way back to the garage where her car was parked, but couldn't remember the steps in between. She gasped. A large gash decorated the side of Remedy's car. And her keys were in her hand, held between her fingers like a weapon, one that had just keyed the paint on her ex-husband's car.

breaking the rules

The surface of Lake Travis glistened in the fading sunlight. Alexis sat out on the stone deck of her Aunt Athena's house. The deck ran around two sides of the building, built out over the lake, giving a spectacular view of Graveyard Point that was only visible when the water levels were low. Inside the house, Alexis could hear the murmur of the crowd of guests; it blended with the hum of a single boat engine far below. Alexis took in the view while she could. This was her favorite place to be at sunset, especially one as peaceful as this one. She doubted it would stay that way. It was only a matter of time before someone discovered her here.

Athena's dinners were both tradition and occasion. It was akin to family blasphemy to miss one, and Alexis usually liked to attend them.

The thought of being discovered had just run through her head and Alexis could hear voices on the other end of the deck, the part that bent around the house. She sat still, hoping that they would stay over there. She was not ready to be disturbed yet. The voices grew louder and Alexis recognized one of them as belonging to Sarah.

"I don't understand why this is a problem for you." Sarah sounded agitated.

"It's no problem. I'm just confused. If you leave us, we have to find someone else to do what you do, that's all. Your work is valuable to us."

"Stop it. I'm a glorified gofer. Besides, it makes the sex better if we don't work together. Gives you time to miss me."

They were silent for a second. Alexis blushed, then cleared her throat. Might as well let them know she was there before they embarrassed themselves any further. She heard a door open and close, and then Sarah appeared at the corner of the deck, a coy smile on her face. A light wind tousled her dirty-blond hair.

"Were you eavesdropping on me?"

"I wasn't. I think I was here first." Alexis paused. "But you can tell me what that was all about if you like. Sounded like there is some trouble in paradise."

"I don't like. Not now. And it's not trouble, more like par for the course. We were discussing my business ideas on the way over here. Just like I thought, he didn't like them." She shrugged. "He just makes me so angry sometimes." She changed the subject. She didn't want to talk about her problems. "So, where were *you* last night?"

Alexis stood up, surprised, then blushed. "What are—"

The door to the house opened and Athena stepped out. She had a wineglass in her hand and wore a pink apron over her dress. "Hey, you two come on in here and eat something. You can't hide out here all night."

They both turned to look at her. Relief washed over Alexis.

She would tell Sarah what she wanted her to know in her own time. "Aunty, what are you wearing?" Alexis walked toward her aunt. "You look like you climbed out of *Leave It to Beaver.*"

"Don't talk about my antique apron. It was a gift. And how can you even speak to me when you snuck into my house and didn't even say hello?" She grabbed Alexis and hugged her, then Sarah. "You have quite the glow about you today, Alexis. You need to come inside and share that with everybody."

She and Sarah exchanged glances. Sarah raised an eyebrow, but didn't say a word. It was obvious that Miss Alexis had a secret. It was written all over her face.

Athena held the door open for them. "And Sarah, you ought to be ashamed of yourself. That man of yours is wandering around the house looking lost. You'd better get in here."

"He can't be too lost, Mrs. Montague. He was just on the patio with me. He'll get over it. He's a little mad, that's all. He needs to be by himself for a while."

"Whaat? I don't know what is going on, but you need to act right. Just because he pissed you off a little is no reason to just throw him away like a piece of common trash. You don't know how lucky you are. So many young women today have half a man or no man at all. You need to appreciate what you do have. You understand me?"

Alexis was sure her aunt was referring to her. She could be so old-fashioned at times. Sarah nodded. She had known Athena a long time and didn't expect her to see her side of things. She had worked behind the scenes at her husband's small lobbying firm until recently when Paris had taken it over.

"Auntie, they have been married awhile." The words rumbled out of her mouth before she could stop them. Alexis knew she was making a mistake by disagreeing with her aunt before her sentence was even finished. "I'm sure whatever it is they will handle it. He needs to see her side, too, even if he doesn't agree. It's not like she's his property or anything. A marriage should be a partnership."

"And how would you know?" A flash of amusement crossed Athena's face. "I think I am the only one with a longterm marriage in this room. Some of us can't even stay in a relationship for long, even when a perfectly good candidate is willing." She cleared her throat. "You could learn a lesson or two from Paris, my dear."

Alexis's mouth dropped open.

Athena went off into the kitchen, leaving the two alone. She'd obviously given them enough of her "wisdom" for now.

"She doesn't pull any punches, huh?" Sarah's voice was barely above a whisper. She was afraid to speak any louder just in case Athena wanted to come back and start in on her.

"She's always been that way. I don't know why it surprises me every time. As soon as I think I have an opinion, she cuts me down." Alexis was determined not to let her aunt or anyone else spoil her good mood.

The front room suddenly got noisy. Alexis knew what that meant. Paris, the woman of the hour, had arrived. "Let's sit," she said to Sarah.

"But Paris—"

"She'll find us." She flopped down in an overstuffed chair.

"What is this? Jealousy? I can't believe it. For the longest time you and Paris have been as close as sisters. You can't be—"

"I'm not."

"If you say so. Don't bite my head off about it."

She didn't care if Sarah did not believe her. There was a small part of her that did feel a twinge of jealousy, but it wasn't because Paris was getting all of the family's attention. She should be. She was getting married in a big fancy wedding in just a short time. Alexis missed their friendship. The wedding planning and Tyson were taking up all of her time and Paris seemed to have less and less time for her and Sarah.

It took Paris about ten minutes to find them. Alexis could hear her, laughing as she greeted everyone. She blew into the room like a storm. It was so obvious that she was happy. She gave off a glow that lit up the room. Her freshly cut hair shined in the sunlight streaming through the windows, and her outfit, a pair of thin-striped gray-green pants with matching solid jacket, was perfect.

"Why are you two hiding back here?" She flopped down opposite Alexis. "I take that back. We all need to hide from these crazy folk." Paris let out a peal of laughter.

"Both of us already got taken down by Aunt Athena," Alexis said.

"Well, you know that's going to happen around here every time you come. But you don't look too sad, Alexis. Matter of fact, you look like you're glowing. If I didn't know any better I would say you look like you got you some."

Sarah leaned over and looked closer at Alexis. "You know what? You're right. I knew something looked different."

"What? How can you?" She couldn't stop herself from blushing.

Paris leaned back in her chair and picked her nails. "So, are you going to tell us?"

"There's nothing to tell. Let's just say I had a busy week."

"How busy?" Sarah's eyes twinkled. "You know, the funny thing is, I remember last year this time, it was Paris who had a secret and you were the one teasing her about her mysterious lover."

When Paris had first met Tyson, they were lovers for several months before she had revealed him to her friends and family. Alexis had been the only one to know when she had sneaked off to meet him in some clandestine spot. Then, he wasn't exactly what Athena would have considered marriage material. They didn't know him *or* his people, and he was just some guy with a high-tech idea and no money or real job. Almost unforgivable in the family's eyes. The funny thing was, the man that Athena had for Paris turned out to be a criminal, a swindler, and in the end, he ended up dead. Killed and burned up in his car. Now Paris was set to marry Tyson with more than everyone's blessing, but the best thing was, she didn't give a damn if they blessed her choice or not. Alexis admired that about her. The whole mess caused a big uproar in the family, but once again, Paris was perfect and Alexis just didn't know how she did it.

Alexis sat up straight. "Let's just say I had a hot date with an unexpected candidate and I woke up this morning in Dallas."

Sarah and Paris spoke at the same time. "Dallas!"

"You are definitely going to have to fill us in then," Paris said.

They were going to find out sooner or later. She planned to go out with Remedy again. She had a wonderful night and then some. Alexis couldn't remember the last time she'd had sex that good. She licked her lips. "Well, remember when I was late to the fitting and I told you about the man whose arm I broke? Well, we——"

Paris held up her hand and shook her head in astonishment. Her light brown hair, straightened to within an inch of its life, flowed around her shoulders as she moved. She couldn't believe what she was hearing. "Okay, wait," she said. "Let's go back a minute. You met this guy when you broke his arm, damn near kicked him into tomorrow, and you ended up on a date with him? On a date that lasted overnight? What am I missing? I didn't understand how you got from point A to point B."

"To tell the truth, I don't either. I was in my office minding my own business and next thing I knew, he was there asking me on a date."

"That must have been one hell of a kick," Sarah said. "I hope he wasn't kinky or anything. I'd be worried that he might be into S and M or something if he came running back after that."

"How do you know *she* isn't into S and M?"

"Okay, stop." *Why was it that Sarah knew just when to add her two cents?* "I don't know why I bothered to tell you two anything at all. And he didn't exactly come running back."

"No," Paris said. "It was probably more like he limped back."

"That's what I'm talking about. You got jokes."

Paris grinned. "Turnabout is fair play."

"But the million-dollar question is, was it good?" Both Sarah and Paris laughed until their eyes watered.

Alexis tried hard to suppress a smile. "I'm not answering. You are having far too much fun at my expense."

"Okay, okay," Paris said. "Didn't you say that he had Baby Mama Drama? And you went away with him? You barely know him."

Alexis rolled her eyes. "Dallas isn't exactly away. It's more like up the road a piece."

"Did you fly or drive?" Sarah said.

"We flew."

"Then that is away. You know better. You seem to be forgetting the rules. Though shalt not date men with children or crazy ex-wives. And you can't go away on an overnight trip with men you barely know."

"I know him. At least I'm *getting* to know him."

"Alexis, she isn't talking about biblically. Remember her drama with JaBari." They were silent for a minute and Paris shifted uncomfortably, as if Sarah had done a forbidden thing by mentioning the name. JaBari had been Tyson's competition, the one who turned out to be a criminal. Sarah and her connections had been instrumental in finding out the truth about him.

"Those rules went out the window back when we hit thirty. How many men our age do you know that don't have a crazy ex or a child?"

"Tyson. And you can speak for yourself. I am only just about to have my thirtieth birthday." At the mention of her fiancé's name, Paris gushed with pride.

"Okay, stop. Tyson has his issues, too, we just haven't discovered them yet. And you can stop kidding yourself. You can't count *down*. You must be having an anniversary of that thirtieth birthday, 'cause it has long since come and gone."

"Ladies, be nice." Sarah was always the peacekeeper between them, the one to see the reason in the madness. She cleared her throat. "So, have you told your aunt about your new man?"

"It was one date. That's all. And you know how she is. She would be checking his Dun and Bradstreet rating and planning a wedding if she could, or she would be telling me that he isn't professional enough. Let's not get ahead of ourselves. Just because we had a good time doesn't mean I am in it for the long haul. You know what? I think I need a drink." Alexis rose and left Sarah and Paris, both still chattering on. There was no way she was going to win in this discussion and she refused to feed into their nonsense any longer. The two of them were having too much fun at her expense. It was all good, though. Everyone got their turn at the teasing and this must be hers.

Alexis walked toward the kitchen. She wound through the rooms to make her way to the back of the house, following the spicy smell of gumbo that was caressing her nose. It was where most of the noise seemed to be coming from, and from the look of things, it was where most of the people were, too. She could hear laughter and loud talking and a smile came to her face. People were talking shit all over the house, as usual. There was not one of Aunt Athena's dinners that she could remember that didn't come with lots and lots of people talking trash. Anywhere else in the house would be good at this point anyway. There was a pretty good chance she would not be as interesting if there were more folks around. Hopefully they all could find another relative on which to concentrate.

Her ears were right. The island counter was surrounded by at least seven people, all with wineglasses in hand. Athena was stirring a big pot. Her stomach grumbled. Athena's gumbo was famous, and she was famished.

Athena looked up as Alexis entered the kitchen. She cast her eyes downward. "I was just about to come find you." She removed her spoon, then knocked on the pot to remove the excess gumbo. "There's someone here to talk to you." Athena glanced back over her shoulder toward the windows behind her. Alexis followed her gaze.

Her breath caught in her throat. Walter was on the patio. She hadn't seen him in months. Matter of fact, the last time she had seen him was before she'd known he was breaking up with her. Her eyes narrowed. "What is he doing here?"

"I invited him." Athena wiped her hands on her apron, then removed it. "He has some things to say to you."

"I have nothing to say to him." She grabbed an open bottle of wine from the counter and searched for a glass.

"Go talk to the man, Alexis." Athena gave Alexis her best "I know what is best for you" look. "He just wants to talk."

Alexis put the bottle back on the counter. *Fine.* She could talk. She didn't feel like it but she would, to avoid a scene. Every person in the room stood silent, staring at her. Walter caught her gaze through the open window and waved. She ran her hand across the top of her hair. Even from that distance, she could tell that he was as fine as he ever was, even more so. Alexis sighed, then crossed the few steps to the patio door. Every eye in the room was on her as she slipped outside.

It was getting late in the evening and there was a slight breeze blowing. Normally, Alexis would enjoy the feeling of the wind in her hair, something she had just begun to appreciate since Walter left. She'd been too concerned with keeping things in place before. Now she was just annoyed.

He licked his lips and Alexis followed the trail his tongue made with her eyes. "You don't have to say anything."

Alexis didn't know what she expected. The earth wasn't moving, her heart wasn't even beating loudly in her ears. Where was her anger? All the rage that was still supposed to be pent up inside her? Instead of feeling angry, she felt nothing. The last time she'd spoken to Walter, he'd called her, said he had something to discuss, then asked her to meet for dinner. Only she'd shown up, and he hadn't. His lame behind had begged Sarah to come instead, to explain to her how he was moving to California without consulting her at all, even if they had been engaged and, at one point, living together. He wasn't able to face her then. Why did he have the courage or the balls to now? "I don't have anything to say to you."

He nodded, then rubbed his hand across his face. "Okay. Wow. You look fantastic. And I like the hair. But that is what you women do, isn't it? Get better after it's over?"

"What do you want, Walter? Why are you here?"

He rested on the black wrought-iron railing and crossed his arms in front of his body. "I wanted to see you. To apologize."

Alexis laughed. "That is so funny. And what makes you think I would accept an apology from you? Why should I absolve you for your sins so you can feel better about yourself?"

She wanted to tell him that he didn't deserve it, not after making her feel miserable all that time, so miserable she had to re-create herself.

"I thought you might react that way, but can you please hear me out?"

Alexis glared at him but didn't speak.

"I'm really sorry. You deserved better than what I did, even if we were on the downhill side of our relationship. But I was a coward and didn't know what to say to you."

"So you ran away like a child? Walter, we have known each other since we were children."

He nodded. "I know, but I didn't know what else to do."

"Ignorance is no excuse." Alexis folded her arms in front of her.

"I don't expect you to forgive me, I guess. And that is not what this is about anyway. You want to get through Paris and Tyson's wedding as much as I do. I just thought we could do it as friends."

And then it hit her. She was feeling no emotion because there was nothing to feel. Whatever feeling she'd had for Walter was gone. She'd filled up the space he used to occupy with other things and other people. Or maybe she just had too much on her mind to be bothered. More than likely it was a bit of both. The sudden realization made her feel good. Powerful in some way. A tiny smile crossed her face.

"I think I am adult enough to stand next to you for half an hour without beating you up or anything."

"That's a relief." He paused. "So, maybe we can get together for drinks later?"

Alexis froze. He couldn't have mistaken her smile to mean

that she wanted to reconcile? What an idiot. "I'm busy. I have a date."

♡   ♡   ♡

He stayed, but in another room. Every time Alexis walked into a room, he seemed to slip out, right on cue. It felt good to be the powerful one for a change. They were all in the den, the only room in the house that had any hint of a masculine influence. This was the one place Athena had not made over the last time she had redone the house. By no coincidence, it was Alexis's favorite room, and probably everybody else's, too.

The den was in the corner of the house, looking out over the water to the cliffs across the lake. A limestone fireplace lined one wall; the rest were covered by light seventies paneling, and the room perpetually smelled of sweet cigar smoke.

Alexis and Sarah sat on the floor in the corner like they were teenagers, and a group of men crowded around her Uncle Brian, Paris's stepfather, at the other side of the room. He was sitting in his easy chair instead of standing at the center of the crowd as he might have been six months before. He was still recovering from the emergency heart-bypass surgery that had weakened him considerably. His surgery had been a surprise. He was the kindhearted person in the family who kept everyone coming back. Alexis had noticed how his body had slowed, but was glad to see that his mind was as sharp as ever. The people around him were continuously breaking out into fits of laughter.

Walter was with the group when Alexis walked in and joined her two friends on the floor. After a few minutes, he looked over his shoulder and saw her sitting there. His steps were almost soundless on the wooden floor as he left the room. The women were speechless as he passed them without speaking.

Paris was the first to speak up. "Okay. What is this effect you have on men and can we have some of it? What did you do to him?"

"Nothing." Alexis shook her head. "He wanted to apologize and be friends."

"What's wrong with that?"

"Nothing at all. Except I don't have time for him. I'm done."

Sarah sipped her martini, then stretched to set it back on the small table near them. "I hear you, girl. I love Walter and all, but you have been done a long time ago, if you ask me." It had been obvious to her that Alexis and Walter were just going through the motions, even before they moved in together. "And speaking of being done, what did you decide to do about your boss? Now there went an asshole. I don't think I have ever seen you so shook up."

Alexis opened her mouth to answer but Paris interrupted her.

"What? What did I miss?"

"Nothing. I had a disasterous dinner with my boss. He somehow decided that I was fair game since I was suddenly single. I knew it was coming, but I just didn't know how to handle it. You know that little voice that we all have but we somehow manage not to listen to?"

Paris's mouth dropped open in surprise. "What are you talking about? Isn't he married?"

"Since when has that mattered? I kicked him on his ass,

too." She shifted in her place, crossing her legs to the side. "Fortunately for me, Sarah happened to be in Z Tejas, too, so she rescued me before I fell apart."

"Why didn't you tell me about it? She just told me that you'd had a bad day."

"You were otherwise involved."

"And when you say you kicked him on his ass, you don't mean literally, right? I mean if my employee——"

"No, of course she doesn't mean literally, Paris." Sarah's eyes glowed. "What she meant was she grabbed him by the balls and pulled until he kissed the ground."

Alexis nodded slowly. "And then I quit. I went to the office and cleared out my shit yesterday morning."

A hush fell over the group. Paris looked at her cousin in disbelief. "Oh. My. God. I have two words for you. Anger. Management."

"I'm tired of hearing it." Sarah rolled her eyes at Paris. She was forever the drama queen. "Good for you. So what is your plan?"

"I don't know yet. I thought about it a long time. I filed a sexual harassment claim, but I just know that a bunch of lawyers fighting over sexual harassment could be nasty business. It was time to move on."

"You could have done it more gracefully though. What is my mother going to say?"

"About what?"

They hadn't heard Athena come in, but there she was, larger than life, standing less than two feet away from them. "What am I going to say about what?"

"Well, Aunt Athena." Alexis braced herself for the lecture

she knew was coming. She stood up. Might as well just get it out. "I quit my job."

"Excuse me? So, did you get a new one somewhere? Where are you going to be working?"

"I don't know yet."

The men on the other side of the room stopped talking and turned to listen.

"That was a bit rash. And ridiculous."

"Excuse me? You haven't even heard the rest of the story." Alexis felt like a teenager being scolded for staying out past her curfew.

"Your side? There is only one side, Alexis. This family sacrificed for you and you have thrown away everything you have accomplished in one move. Like you did with Walter."

Alexis was perplexed about the Walter comment but was prepared to let that one slide.

"We worked too hard to put you through that damn fancy law school for you to talk about just quitting your job. It's not as if jobs like yours were a dime a dozen. I'm sure whatever the problem is, you could have worked it out. I know."

"No, you don't know. You obviously don't know anything about me or my needs." Alexis suddenly became aware that all eyes in the room were on them. It wasn't that they wouldn't eventually know all her business and talk about her. This family was like that. But there was no need to give them a show, too. "We can discuss this later."

Athena grabbed her by the arm. "No, we will discuss this now. What are you going to do? We certainly can't support you—"

She yanked her arm away. "I am a grown woman. I can

take care of myself. Why do you have to be so overbearing? I can handle this. You raised me that way."

"Overbearing? How dare you talk to me like that. When I was a child I would have gotten slapped for talking to my elders like that." Athena crossed her arms in front of her. "Well, I obviously failed because I raised you to be ungrateful, too. We rescued you and you would think that you wouldn't disrespect us like this. What are people going to say, Alexis? You have thrown your career away."

Alexis seethed with anger. Rescued her? What kind of nonsense was that? She fought not to get too upset. "If I had known that you brought me here just so you could wear me like a badge the rest of our lives, I wouldn't have come. I was not your project. I'm still not."

"Your mother was my little sister. We did our best."

"Did you? I have spent my whole life not being good enough for you. You made us feel like there was forever a race between me and Paris. I can never be Paris. Life isn't a race."

"How can you say that? We did not."

"Not we. Uncle Brian wasn't the cause. You were."

The room was silent as Athena looked around for help. "Are you going to let her talk to me like that?" she yelled in the direction of the men. They turned away. There was not a soul in the room willing to interfere with this argument. "This is crazy. Alexis, you can get your job back, just tell me what happened. We can work it through."

She shook her head. "None of us are children anymore, Aunt Athena. I think it's time for me to go."

No one said a word as Alexis left, not even Paris, who usually had a retort for everything. Alexis knew she was right.

Taking control of her life after Walter left was only part of her transformation. Athena might think she was crazy, but if she was going to make her own decisions, she had to do it all the way. This time, the only little voice she would be listening to was her own.

self-help 101

The Texas sun was high in the sky and Ayzah still had no idea where Prince was. Ma'dear was right. Everybody had a plan except her. Remedy had obviously moved on with his life. Even Prince had a plan, one that was supposed to have included her, but Ayzah wasn't so sure that it did anymore, or even what that plan really was.

She washed her hands and froze as she watched the water flow down the drain. A metaphor for the way she had pissed her life away. First, she had been too busy running the streets and partying to think past high school, and then she had spent too much time trying to find a man to be with her because of what she could possibly get from him. Now she was spending what precious time she had left sitting around waiting on Prince or someone else to make her happy, tell her how she should live her life. What had that gotten her but frustrated? And she didn't even know where Prince was.

Ayzah turned off the water. Remedy not coming home last night hit her hard. It was one thing for Angel to say he had a date, but it was something else altogether for her to find out it was true. She was sure it wouldn't take Remedy long to figure out who had keyed his car. She cringed as she thought about the sound of metal against metal as her key ran the length of his car. It wasn't smart and it wasn't nice, but she had been so angry. *Stop kidding yourself.* Keying Remedy's car was downright mean even for her. If she had learned nothing about him in the short time they were together it was that Remedy was crazy about his car. It might not have fancy rims or any of that shit that some of the gangster cars had on it, but he owned it, free and clear.

Afterward, Ayzah had been stunned and didn't know what to do. She'd stood there for a minute and tried to catch her breath and get it together. Prince was gone, and then she couldn't find Remedy either. She'd been paralyzed. When she'd finally come back to her senses she'd left fast, then gone to the library. There had to be a book somewhere that would tell her what she needed to know. After relying on other people so long, now she needed to take matters into her own hands.

Ayzah's thoughts were interrupted by the sound of a key turning in the door. She stiffened and felt her anger start coming back. She tried her best to take deep cleansing breaths. More than anything, she wanted to keep a level head this time. She expected Prince to have a story, but she was going to stay strong. She was tired of being pulled back and forth like a yo-yo and was determined not to be charmed, bought, or sexed into submission.

He looked like he was trying to sneak in even though it was broad daylight. Ayzah watched him quietly, her arms folded against her chest and her legs crossed like armor, the way she had so many times. He turned around and gently closed the door, then locked it. He was still wearing the same oversized pants he had left in, but his white T-shirt was no longer white. It was wrinkled and dingy-looking.

Anger blazed from Ayzah's eyes. He jumped when he saw her.

"Why you looking so evil?"

"Am I?" Ayzah choked back her anger and forced her voice to sound calm. "Do I have something to be evil about?"

He looked perplexed. "Don't play games."

"You don't be defensive."

He headed toward the kitchen. His steps were heavy.

Ayzah followed him and leaned in the doorway. "So how was your *business?*"

Prince opened the refrigerator. "What do you mean?" He was so predictable it wasn't funny, Ayzah thought. Every time he came in the house, he did the same thing. Played uncomfortable the same way. It almost felt like he was waiting her out, trying to see what she knew or didn't know, how she might react. The strange thing was she always fell for his trap. Not this time. "Your business, remember, that you had with Deon. The business that took all night and half the day and kept you from calling me or answering your phone."

"Why you trippin', Ayzah? I'm tired. I was up all night——"

"Doing what?"

Prince closed the refrigerator. His eyes widened. "What?"

"You heard me. Doing what? What kind of business keeps you out all night and half the day where you can't call or answer your phone?" Ayzah glared back at him. She'd been intimidated and manipulated for too long. He might hit her, but she was so fed up, that was a chance she was willing to take.

"I can ask you the same thing. Where were *you* last night?"

Ayzah recognized the tactic. Prince couldn't get her into bed so now he was going to try and turn the spotlight on her, making it her fault. "This isn't about me."

He glowered, his fists opening and closing.

Ayzah's stomach jumped. She looked away, refusing to take the bait. She had finally made up her mind about something and was not going to be bullied.

Prince shifted. He turned partially away from Ayzah and ran his hand across his forehead, as if wiping away sweat that wasn't there.

Ayzah inched away, keeping her eyes on his hands. "I was doing my research." She paused. "I have figured out what I need to do to get custody of Jamal." Ayzah crossed her arms in front of her.

"What are you talking about? We already know that. I thought we decided what we were going to do."

"I. Have. Been. Doing. Research. I went to the library. I know I can't afford a lawyer right now, so I went to the library on my own."

"Since when do *you* know how to research anything?"

Ayzah ignored his dig. She didn't want to go off on any tangents. "I know a lot of things you aren't aware I know."

"I see." Prince paused. "What brought this on? You didn't seem to be too into the idea before. You thought he was fine where he was."

"And he is fine. I still believe that Remedy is capable. But I was talking to my mother."

Prince nodded his head. "Your mother. What did she tell you? That you needed to repent and God would make it okay?" He snorted, almost laughing at the suggestion. "Trust me when I tell you that God got bigger problems to worry about than you and your shit. I'm tired, Ayzah. I don't really have time for all this. I need to get some rest."

Her face darkened. He needed rest? She was the one who had stayed up all night waiting for him. "You need to make time. If you want me around."

"What are you saying?"

"I'm saying that most of the fucked-up shit that has happened to me has been because of messing around with you, including not having custody of my son."

Prince raised his hand as if to surrender. "I'm sorry. Go back. Tell me what your mother said. What the library said."

Ayzah turned and took a few steps away, putting some distance between her and Prince. She sighed, then began. "Basically, from what I can tell, I need to have a stable home life. You too, if we are a couple. That means a job, and probably no stripping. A real job."

"You can do that." He grinned. "I know you got skills."

How convenient that he ignored his part. "But the other thing is, Remedy got custody on grounds of abandonment."

"We both know that is bullshit. He wasn't abandoned. He was left with his father."

"That may be, but we were so busy celebrating being together and all, I didn't contact anyone for almost a year." She paused. "In order to get formal custody, I am going to have to tell them that I was basically almost kidnapped, maybe afraid to call or contact them because of what would happen to me."

"I didn't stop you from calling."

"You don't remember telling me to wait?"

"That's not coercion."

"Maybe not in your book, but it felt like it in mine."

Prince looked pensive for a minute, then shrugged. "I don't see a problem with that."

"You don't understand. No judge is going to buy that if I am still living with you. If we are still together." Ayzah cringed automatically, waiting for the explosion she knew was coming.

It dawned on Prince slowly, what Ayzah was saying. "So, we can be apart for a while, just until things start going and the child support starts coming in."

"Don't you think that is a lot of trouble for a little bit of money? Wouldn't it be easier just to do the honorable thing?"

"Honorable? I have never walked away from free money and we are not about to start now. Since when have you had this burning desire to be *honorable?*" Prince leaned against the wall. "You plan on turning into a church lady now, getting a respectable job? Take a good look, Ayzah. What can you do?" A beat. "I was being nice earlier, but really, you got no skills. You probably couldn't even hold down a fast-food gig." Prince ran his hand across his face. "You ain't the only one doing research. Do you know how much child support Remedy would have to pay if you had primary custody? Try twenty percent of what he makes. And we both know that your boy is pulling down bank. Two of those fancy smoking bars and heaven knows what else. He is living large and we live in this dump. Do the math, Ayzah. You can figure it out better than anyone."

Her patience was wearing thin. "You know, Prince, it wouldn't hurt for you to get a job. I don't want to run a scam anymore. I want to get custody of Jamal because I am his mother and I want him to know me in a normal way. If child support comes with it, okay, but I don't want it to be a source of stress between me and Remedy. Besides, if Remedy gets married or something, his family will seem more stable than mine. What kind of a way is that for a child to remember his mother?"

"So, I don't see what the argument is. My plan is fine."

"You don't have a plan. You want me just to steal him away in the night. I don't want to do that." She had known that he would react this way. Prince had never held a job in his life for more than six months. He wasn't about to get one now. Ayzah measured her words, trying to understand why Prince had such control over her. If he had been anyone else, she would have lost her temper already. Normally, she was strong, or at least she thought she was. Ayzah sighed. She just might as well say it because it was obvious that he was not getting what was on her mind.

"Prince. I'm leaving you. You are standing in the way of me and my future."

The rage that was in Prince's eyes hit Ayzah hard. He yelled, "What?"

"I'm leaving. I have to. I can't say that I left with you against my will and still stay with you. It won't work. And I'm not interested in getting back together. I don't want to scam anyone. I can't deal with not knowing where you are or if you even plan to marry me." She tried to sound as firm as possible.

Prince grabbed Ayzah by the arm. His fingers dug into her flesh. She tried to pull away but he jerked her to him. "How can you say that? We are a team."

"You. Are. Hurting. Me."

"You're hurting me. That plan isn't going to work. You are mine, you understand?" His fingers dug into her arm deeper, jerking her back and forth as he yelled.

Ayzah pulled away. Anger kept her from being afraid. "You get your hands off me." She swung at him, and her fist caught Prince in the side of the head.

They both froze. Prince raised his hand and felt his cheek where Ayzah's hand had struck him.

"I'm sorry. . . ." She braced herself, expecting Prince to strike back. He didn't.

"You have lost your mind, obviously." His voice was strangely calm.

Panic began building inside Ayzah's stomach. The look on Prince's face was frightening. She needed to get away from him, not just because of Jamal, but because he was crazy. There was no doubt in her mind that if she stayed with him, he would hurt her, one way or another. "I think I should go to my mother's for a few days." The words tumbled out of her mouth.

He rubbed his cheek. "A few days. But that is all."

She nodded, then went to the bedroom to pack a bag.

Prince followed, but didn't stop her. He watched her in silence, almost as if he were guarding her.

Ayzah purposely only took a few things that she would need to make it through a few days, nothing that would upset Prince any more than she already had. She could come back for the rest later, when he wasn't home.

She threw in a few more things, then zipped the bag.

"I suppose this was your mother's idea? She never liked me anyway. Tell me the truth. Did *Stacia* tell you to leave me?"

Ayzah cringed. She could talk back to her mother and do all sorts of things to her, but Prince had stepped over the line. Calling her mother by her first name was the ultimate sign of disrespect. From the look on his face she could tell that he knew that, too.

"No, she didn't."

He laughed. "No, I guess she probably told you to let her God solve your problem, I bet."

Ayzah waited until she was at the door to answer. "You're right. She has never liked you. Actually, Ma'dear was very helpful."

"That's a switch. Did she offer to pay for your lawyer or something like that?"

She shook her head. Ayzah almost felt sorry for him. Prince was always looking for the easy way out, for someone else to foot the bill or solve his problems. Why hadn't she been able to see this before? "No, she repeated something that she has been saying for years, only for some reason I heard her this time." Ayzah opened the door. "Ma'dear basically reminded me that God helps those who help themselves, and that's what I'm doing."

She didn't wait for him to comment. Ayzah stepped through the door and down the three steps that led away from the porch. She didn't look back until she was in her car with the engine running. Prince was still standing there, looking pitiful when she drove off. He meant it when he said she could leave for a few days, Ayzah knew that. That wouldn't be the end of him, but at least she was away. That was a start.

don't let the high heels fool you

I t had been a long time since Alexis had been able to meet anyone for coffee without stress. She would normally feel as if she were sneaking away, shirking some duty that just had to get done. The new, single Alexis devoted as much time to her job as possible. She'd been leaving very little time for socializing, especially downtown. Watching all the self-employed and unemployed sipping their java felt strange. It was an alien lifestyle, one that Alexis was going to have to get used to. She was one of them now.

She glanced around the coffee shop as she approached the counter. Several people had computers and were taking advantage of the free wireless Internet the café offered. She wished she had brought hers, too. She was going to have to take advantage of free Internet, newspapers, whatever worked to find her next job or come up with some kind of game plan. Her argument with Aunt Athena had been a wake-up call. She was going to have to get started on her own Web searching and job hunting because she was certainly not going to be able to live on her good looks alone. Her bank account was

only going to take her so far. She'd done some figuring last
night and decided that she would be okay for six months tops,
and then she was going to have to sell her blood, her shoes, or
both. It was a major step when she quit her job. The look on
everyone's face had been priceless, and remembering it
brought a smile to her face.

Saturday mornings were light in the office. There had
been only a few other people in, three lawyers and a few
clerks. Alexis hadn't expected Monty to be there, but he was.
He'd surprised her and walked right up to her desk, just as she
had finished putting most of her belongings into a cardboard
box she had brought with her.

"What are you doing?" he'd asked.

Alexis had barely looked up. "I'm putting my things in a
box to make them easy to carry."

"You going somewhere?"

The question had annoyed her immensely and made her
skin crawl. "You know better than to ask me that. I'm quitting. I can't work here."

Alexis felt as if her voice had carried through the entire
office. Everyone there seemed to stop in their tracks and tune
in to what she was saying.

"I think you are overreacting." Monty had stepped around
her desk and put his hand on her arm.

"If you don't want me to call the police right now, you will
remove your hand, and don't you ever touch me again." She'd
paused, and Monty had let his hand drop.

"You need this job."

"You don't know what I need. Just get the hell out of
my way."

He'd run his hand over his face, but he'd moved.

Alexis remembered how angry she'd felt as she had stormed out of the office with her pitiful little box. It had seemed like a good move then, but now, she wished she had a better plan. Although she hated to admit it, her Aunt Athena had been right when she'd said that she must not have thought much beyond quitting. Alexis refused to go back and grovel though. She was just going to find a way to live with her decision, and eventually she would let Aunt Athena know what had happened. That is, if she could get her to stop yelling and passing judgment long enough to get a word in edgewise.

Alexis ordered her coffee and then wandered into the bookstore that was attached to the coffee shop. She was going to meet Sarah and Paris in the back for some big, secret pow-wow. At the comfy chairs was what Sarah had said. Alexis chuckled to herself. She couldn't have made a better choice herself. They most certainly would be talking about uncomfortable things, so they might as well be comfortable while they did it. There was no way the three of them could get together and not continue to talk about her latest drama, but that was okay. Alexis needed to talk to someone. They would talk about that and Sarah's surprise, whatever that was.

Sarah had been so happy when she'd invited them here, but mysterious, so much so that neither Paris nor Alexis had any clue what it could be. And she had stormed away from Aunt Athena's so they'd never gotten a chance to pry whatever it was out of her.

The comfy seats were not as difficult to find as Alexis thought they might be. She turned the last corner in the bookstore and there they were. Four luxurious-looking, tan suede chairs, sitting off by themselves. Unoccupied, too, that was a good thing. Alexis knew she would be the first to arrive—she always was—and was prepared to stand too close to whomever might be sitting there, making mean faces to "persuade them to move."

She slid into the one chair facing the front just as her BlackBerry buzzed. Her face split into a wide grin. Remedy. She could still smell his scent on her.

"Hey. Glad that you got home okay." His voice sounded sensuous and full.

"I did." She didn't think she would hear from him for another day or two. This was a good sign. Barely twenty-four hours had passed.

"Everything okay?"

"Why shouldn't it be?"

"I thought you would have been in the office, that's all."

She laughed. "You worried about me? I'm fine." She'd been having such a good time that she'd forgotten to tell him about her job. "I won't be working there anymore."

"Really? Was that a sudden decision? You didn't mention it on our date."

"You could say that." She paused. "I didn't want to talk about me. I'm not that interesting. I'll tell you about it some other time." There was no need to get into it with him now. He would get all riled up for sure, and she planned to handle her business herself.

"I hope that is a promise, but that's not why I called you. I wanted to say thank you for the wonderful evening we had."

"Really?" Alexis was sure she looked like an idiot. Her face was plastered with a grin she couldn't stop. She looked down and covered her mouth with her free hand.

"Yes. And to tell you to be careful."

"Careful?"

Remedy sighed. "When I got home Sunday, my car had been keyed. I'm pretty sure I know who did it. The car was parked in my locked garage."

"And you think that someone will assault my car, too?"

"Look, we should have talked about this more. I'm reasonably sure that Ayzah keyed my car, although I'm not quite sure why. You remember meeting her, right?"

"Your ex." Alexis remembered their chilly meeting at the hospital. Ayzah wasn't an easy person to forget.

"That's the one."

"Why would she do something like that? That sounds kind of childish." She bit her lip. *Ghetto would be a better word.* "What does that have to do with me?"

"Nothing, probably, but I thought it would be unfair to you if I didn't tell you what kind of person I was dealing with."

Alexis smiled. "I can take care of myself, you know."

Remedy gave a deep, throaty laugh. "Yes, I do know. But still."

Paris cleared her throat and then slid into the chair across from Alexis. She crossed her bare legs at the knee and stared. She wore a white leather skirt and her ankle-wrap, open-toed shoes matched perfectly.

"Hey, I gotta go, my nosy cousin is here. And thank you." Alexis pushed the button on her BlackBerry and closed her phone, just as Sarah joined them.

"My," Paris said, "you look awfully happy for someone who just broke my mother's heart." Her mouth was set into a hard line.

"Hey, Sarah." Alexis turned to Paris. Feelings of guilt over the incident came rushing back. Paris would have to go there first thing. "I am happy. And stop exaggerating. I didn't break her heart. She got what was coming to her, forever meddling in my life and yours, too. I'm a grown-ass long-in-the-tooth woman. I can handle my business. Besides, I am tired of her trying to make me into something I'm not."

"Uh-huh. Mother is meddlesome, but you were more than harsh. She is devastated. She said she was cutting you off."

"Riiight. It will all blow over and we will be one big happy family again." *She hoped.*

"But it wasn't clear to me if you were mad at her for meddling or because she called you out." Paris raised her eyebrows. "You and I both know she was speaking the truth." She paused. "I'm not used to you being so intense and making rash decisions. What happened to Miss Nosy Alexis, my favorite cousin and best friend?"

"She finally got serious about her life. And I don't think I was being rash. I had good reason to quit." Alexis opened her purse and put her BlackBerry inside. She snapped it shut while an uncomfortable silence lingered over them.

Paris took the hint and changed the subject. "So, who was that on the phone? That man you were *nursing* the other night?"

"I knew one of you would have something to say." Alexis put her purse on her lap as if it would protect her from Paris's assault. "Yes, it was. He was calling me to thank me for a wonderful evening."

Paris raised one eyebrow. "Hmm. You musta put a hurting

on him then. Wasn't that yesterday? He didn't even wait the required two days to call you."

Sarah sat back in her chair. "I'll never understand you guys and your rules. Barry and I never followed any rules and we have been married for a long time."

"Exactly. You two have been together so long that the rule book has been rewritten. Several times." Paris flipped her hair over her shoulder and smoothed it down with her hand. The diamond ring on her hand glittered in the store lighting.

"Make jokes. Before long you are going to be an old married woman, too. Speaking of that, is Tyson wearing those dreadlock things in the wedding? How does your aunt feel about that?" Sarah contorted her face as she spoke about Paris's fiancé.

"Yes, he is. I happen to like them. That is the way he was when I met him and we intend to walk down the aisle with him looking *just* like that. I don't give a damn what anyone else thinks. Besides, I think long hair on a man is very sexy." Paris pouted.

Alexis cleared her throat, drawing the attention back to her. "To answer your question, Paris, Remedy called to tell me to be careful. Apparently he had a little problem when he got home last night. I told you I thought his ex was a psychobitch."

"And he felt he had to *warn* you?" Paris's mouth dropped open. "I wouldn't be getting involved with no *Fatal Attraction* kind of stuff like that. Girl, you need to move on before you get in too deep."

Alexis's stomach jumped. She hated to admit it, but it was already too late for that. In one date, she got the feeling that

Remedy Brown had securely ensconced himself in her life. "Things aren't always that simple. And you set a fine example. At least one of us had a bad feeling about that man you were dating, yourself included, and you didn't run until he pissed you off, and not even then." Alexis distinctly remembered warning her cousin that there was something shady about that guy, but no one had believed her until he tried to pull a Kobe Bryant on her. "No crazy exes for you, just criminals and embezzlers and the like, right?"

"You had to go there." Paris crossed then uncrossed her legs. "You're right. I *knew* something was wrong with him in the first place. It was my *mother* that liked him. If I remember correctly, in the beginning, you were pushing me to get with that man, too. All of you were caught up because you thought he had a great job and was pretty, remember? The only sane one was Sarah." She winked at Sarah. "And my baby, Tyson. They were willing to do anything to make sure I was okay. They had some kind of plot going, like *Mission: Impossible* or something—" She was gushing.

Sarah held up her hand. "I wouldn't say all that. I like who I like and I didn't like him. We just checked him out, that's all. His own past caught up to him. That whole fiasco had nothing to do with me." She paused. "Look, before we get carried away with this memory lane thing, I called you both here to share some changes I'm going to be making."

"Not like I had anything better to do. This is convenient for Paris though."

"I didn't pick this location because I was trying to be convenient for anyone but me. I wanted the two of you to be the first to see the location for my new office."

A puzzled look spread across Paris's face. "Obviously my head is so far into this wedding that I am out of the loop. They didn't tell me anything about a new location. I missed something. Why would DBA Ventures need to be downtown? Most of the high-tech companies are up north now. You did mean around here, right?"

Sarah smiled. "This has nothing to do with them. This is space for *my* business. I was serious when I said that I'm leaving them."

Alexis chuckled. "Sweetie, you didn't have to quit your job because I did, although I appreciate your togetherness. But how in the hell do you stop working for a company that your husband is part owner of anyway? Besides, I thought you said you were going to be doing home shows or something, like Avon."

"You two give me no credit whatsoever. Do I look like I might sell Avon? I'm not eighteen." She sighed, shaking her head. "After I did some research, I decided that I wanted to go ahead and open a real business, although I do plan to have a heavy e-commerce aspect to it. I'm opening a specialty boutique."

Alexis and Paris exchanged glances. Neither one of them could believe what they were hearing. Sarah had worked for DBA Ventures before it was even really a company, doing a lot of the legwork for her husband and Walter, before they could afford to quit their jobs. She had even drafted most of the early business plans. It was as much her baby as it was theirs.

Sarah threw her hands up in the air. "I know you don't get it but I needed something of my own. I couldn't take working with my husband anymore." She paused. "I found this great space, and it was really cheap. Guess where it is?" She didn't wait for them to answer. "Right up the street. On Eleventh."

"That's near my office."

Sarah nodded. "It is. And it's part of the redevelopment project—"

"So you get incentives to locate there." Paris finished her sentence for her. She knew all about the redevelopment of the east side. She was always filling her friends in on it. Her firm and its community development efforts were one of the driving forces behind the project.

"I'm happy for you," Alexis said. "But what does your hubby think about all this?"

Sarah shrugged. "You know how men are. He's doubtful. A little mad that I'm leaving. But he will get over it."

"If you say so. You are the one that has to live with him," Paris said. "And just what are you going to sell in this boutique?" She stirred uneasily in her chair. "This area isn't exactly known for its high-priced fare. I mean, there are a couple of restaurants over here that people frequent during the day, but that's about it."

"You know better than anyone that that is why businesses are trying to locate over here. Anyway, I plan on selling mid- to low-priced things, like handbags and accessories. I did my homework. My plans are almost done. I think it will work."

"Don't let Paris get you down," Alexis said. "She's mad because she didn't think of it first. You know we will support you in whatever you do. Just remember that discount we talked about." She winked.

"Are you going to show us the space? I need to know where I am going to be meeting you for those future lunch dates. I have to get back to the office soon anyway." Paris stood up and smoothed her skirt. "I think I have a lunch appointment later, so I have to get some things done before the day gets too old."

Alexis and Sarah stood, too, and Sarah reached into her small handbag. She pulled out two index cards, handing one to each of her friends. "This is the place. Meet me here. I'm going to run to the rest room, but promise me you will just drive by it on the way, okay? I'll meet you over there."

They both took the cards. A mixture of emotions hit Alexis all at once. She was happy for Sarah. It seemed like she had been in her husband's shadow ever since they had gotten married. This would be a good thing for her. Probably for them both. She had often been the one with ideas that made a big difference in the company when it was starting out. But Sarah's news made her feel even more like a nitwit. She had all the fancy education in the world and still had no clue as to what her next step was going to be.

♥ ♥ ♥

The address that Sarah had given them was only a few blocks away. Most of the morning traffic had subsided, so Alexis was there in no time. She turned right into the deserted but clean-looking street, driving under a new wrought-iron arch designed to look old and stately.

She parked and stood in front of the building. It was brick, inlaid in places with limestone, a stark contrast to some of the older, wooden structures typical of the area. She smiled. It was nice-looking, and most of the spots were still vacant. There were still Realtor signs in all but one of the windows.

Across the street, a colorful mural decorated what was to be some kind of plaza, surrounded by a few historic buildings which had recently been renovated. This would be a great location for Sarah's business. But it didn't really matter. Sarah was the type who did well at whatever she tried. A twinge of jealousy hit her. Paris and Sarah really would get to hang out quite a bit. This was within walking distance of the offices of Benton & Associates, the small lobbying and community consulting firm that Paris had taken over after her stepfather's heart surgery a few months before.

Alexis walked to the corner and down the side street to look at the building from all sides. The street was more narrow than the one she had come in on, and although it was paved and a new sidewalk stretched from one end of the block to the other, it was still strewn with small gravel. There was an underground parking garage, still roped off. Away from the main street, it was ultraquiet. A lone cricket chirped. She imagined that would change when the building was fully occupied. No one would be able to hear that poor cricket anymore.

The crunching sound of gravel met her ears as she peered down into the garage. She looked behind her, expecting to see Paris, complaining as she usually did. She hesitated, surprised. Unless Paris had changed quite a bit, this was not her. Alexis was positive that Ayzah Brown was standing less than one hundred feet from her. The clothes were different, but it was her. How could you never see a person then run into them twice in one week? Remedy's caution echoed in her mind. She took a few steps toward the woman and stiffened. Ayzah's face was hard, unflinching.

Alexis nodded. She wasn't afraid, just curious. Surprise bloomed over Ayzah's face as she realized that Alexis was far from intimidated. "Were you with Remedy?"

"What?" Alexis returned her stare. It was now obvious that Ayzah must have been following her, waiting to confront her.

She crossed her arms. "I ain't going nowhere. I just want you to know that."

Voices floated from around the corner. Sarah and Paris followed. They stopped suddenly as they spotted Alexis and Sarah. "Is there a problem?" Paris asked.

Ayzah was startled. She hadn't expected Alexis to be with anyone.

"No, I don't think so," Alexis said. Challenge blazed from her eyes. "You have something you want to say to me?"

"I was saying that I don't want you messing up my family. Remedy's a daddy. He can't be staying out all night and things like that."

Sarah cleared her throat.

"I'm sure Remedy can take care of himself," Alexis replied. The venom in her voice surprised her. She took a step closer. "Were you following me?"

Ayzah didn't answer. "I have to watch out for what's mine."

"What's yours?"

Paris spoke up. "Alexis—"

"I said that I got this." She turned her attention to Ayzah. "Don't let the high heels fool you. I'm not one of your little girlfriends." She paused, studying Ayzah's tired-looking face. "You must think very little of yourself if you feel you have to fight over a man."

"I didn't—"

"No, you came up in my face so you let me finish. I have too much respect for myself to fight over any man. For anything. If he don't want you, move on. There is always another." Alexis took another step toward Ayzah.

She stepped backward in response.

Alexis was angry now. "Now, don't sleep. I will protect myself, and you know I can. Don't think I won't kick off my shoes in a minute and—"

"Alexis!" Paris yelled.

"I just wanted to make sure that Ms. Brown here understood where I was coming from. I'm not one of those soft women that run for cover at the slightest bit of trouble."

Ayzah was visibly upset. This wasn't exactly what she had planned.

"Are you done?" Alexis asked. "We had some business we were going to take care of."

Ayzah nodded.

Alexis walked past her, joining Sarah and Paris, leaving Ayzah alone. They spoke in hushed voices as they walked back around the corner.

"You want to tell me what that was about?" Paris asked.

"She thought I was someone else, obviously. She better ask somebody."

"I can't believe you just said that. Ask somebody? What are you, twelve now?" She paused. "You are really on a roll. First my mother, then her." Paris shook her head.

"Yeah, poor lady. She had no idea." Sarah jingled the keys in her hand.

"Obviously she didn't. I made a vow to myself that I was going to take care of business. I spent so much time counting on Walter and now that is time wasted. I'm not wasting any more time being walked over or kowtowing to anyone else."

"Kowtowing?" Paris snickered. "New words, too. How do you go from ask somebody to kowtowing in the space of two minutes? Seriously, I was afraid you were going to get rough on her. Remedy, your boss, Athena. You have turned into one violent lady lately."

"Not violent. I'm just asserting myself. And all those things together, that has just been a string of weird coincidences."

"If you say so."

They reached the front of the building and Sarah put the key in the front door and turned it. It responded with a loud click and she pulled it open, ushering her friends inside. "This is it." Her brow was furrowed with concern. "You two can joke if you want to, but that could have been bad. Alexis, you make sure you take care of business."

They stepped inside. "You know I will. First thing tomorrow. I may be angry, but I am still me. I'll be at the courthouse first thing. I am going to get an order of protection against that woman."

boo boo the fool

It was time for *Oprah* again. Ayzah threw her comforter over her legs and got comfortable in her chair. She felt warm, cozy, and sad. Most of her day had been spent right where she was, sitting in her mother's favorite chair, watching an endless stream of talk shows. She'd gotten up exactly two times since she'd woken up this morning, and those were only to go to the bathroom. Her cell phone had rung about eight times. She no longer even bothered to look at the screen after the second, and had turned the ringer completely off on the house phone. There was no one she wanted to talk to and she knew without looking that most, if not all, of the calls would be from Prince. She certainly did not want to talk to him.

The sound of a key in the front door caused her to jump. A plain, white clock hung on her mother's wall, right in between the pictures of John F. Kennedy and Martin Luther King Jr. Ayzah managed to glance over at it long enough to figure out that Ma'dear was early today. She hadn't expected her for at least another few hours. The thought of moving crossed her mind and then disappeared. What would be the point? She didn't have the energy to hurry up and do anything, or even to make it look like she had been doing anything but what she had, so she just stayed put.

Ma'dear came into the house, letting a flood of light in with her. She didn't speak to Ayzah. She looked around the room and sighed heavily, then put the bags she was carrying down into a corner. She kicked off her shoes and placed them neatly by the front door, then began to walk around the room, opening the blinds on the windows. "We need some light in here. I don't understand why you are sitting up here in this dark room with all this stale air."

Ayzah covered her eyes to protect them from the light. She blinked and tried to let them adjust.

"And you know what else? Another few hours in those pajamas and we are going to have to air out this house." Ma'dear looked at her daughter in disgust. "What is wrong with you?"

Ayzah didn't answer, but instead picked up the remote. She liked to watch both *Oprah* and *Oprah After the Show* if she could. The women in the audience made her feel better. They seemed to have bigger problems than she did.

Ma'dear came around to Ayzah's front and pressed the button on the television. She stood in front of Ayzah with her hands on her hips. "I said, what is wrong with you, girl? I know you ain't up in my house moping over no man."

"I ain't moping."

Ma'dear cocked her head to the side. "No? What would you call it? You don't wash, you don't look for a job. You do nothing. Don't you have some friends to talk to? You left him, right? Hell. You made the right decision. I would hate to see what you would be like if *he* had left you."

Ayzah let her go on. She didn't have the strength to argue or debate. This wasn't about Prince anymore. Or Remedy either. She had gotten herself into a place that she just didn't have the energy to get out of. There was so much to do that it seemed overwhelming. That Alexis woman had said things that put her over the top, made her realize that she had been putting Prince first for too long. Yes, she had left him, but it was the things that came next that seemed daunting. "Ma'dear, I don't know what to do." Her voice was low, almost like a whisper. Ayzah sounded as defeated as she felt.

"Hmph." Ma'dear glared at her daughter. She was annoyed at her, but she felt sorry for her, too. She'd been her thirty years ago. She'd tried, but couldn't figure out how to pass her life lessons on to her daughter. If she could have somehow saved her the heartache she wouldn't feel like such a failure as a mother, but she couldn't live Ayzah's life for her. "Well, I didn't raise you to mope about things. You been through some tough times, but you are going to have to get yourself together. You can't sit up in my chair the rest of your life."

"Ma'dear, please don't talk to me like I'm a child or something."

"When you start acting like an adult I'll treat you like one. If your problems seem too big, break them down into manageable chunks. The way I see it, there are several parts to this thing. Remedy, Jamal, Prince, and you. Deal with them. Talk them through with someone."

Ayzah balked. Ma'dear had been making sense up until then. There was no way she could share what she was feeling with her mother. "No offense, Mother, but I am not prepared to give you things to line your I-told-you-so's with later."

Ma'dear's face softened. She regretted being so hard on her daughter all the time. She acknowledged that she had been a hard mother sometimes, but she had only been trying to stop Ayzah from going down the same path that she had. It was a hard road, best avoided if possible. Ayzah never could understand that. She sighed. "Well, talk to a friend then." Ma'dear patted her on the shoulder. "Why don't you take a shower and get yourself fixed up. You'll feel better, I promise. And if you want me to, I'll help you with that Ayzah part. I can talk to my manager and maybe get you on at the Wal-Mart. It ain't a fancy job, but it has good benefits." She wrinkled her nose. "And you'll probably smell better, too."

That brought a slight smile to Ayzah's face. Her mother was right. She had done nothing for long enough. The hours certainly had to be better there, and there would be no one pressuring her to get breast implants to keep her job. And since Erica wanted to be friends so badly, she was as good a candidate as any. Not that she could really share anything with her. She wasn't ready for that yet. "I think I'll leave all that touchie feelie stuff to you, Ma'dear. But I do think it's time for me to get up from here. Some girl talk might do me good."

Ma'dear nodded. "Good. I was starting to get worried about you. You think about the job part."

She had been sitting in the same position so long that her body ached. Warm mustiness rose from her as she stood up. Ayzah's head swam, but she made her way to the shower slowly, like someone at least twenty years older. Her mother had good ideas sometimes. It would be good for her to see

Erica. At the very least, she might be able to figure out what was over there that had been keeping Prince so mesmerized.

♥ ♥ ♥

No one answered the door. Ayzah rang the doorbell again, then waited. She had second thoughts about having come over to Erica's house in the first place, but once her mind was made up it was almost as if she was drawn there. Still, just for a minute, she wished she was back in her mother's house, sitting in that easy chair, wrapped in her favorite blanket. If Erica didn't live so far from her mother, she would turn around and head right back to east Austin.

When Erica first moved up to northwest Austin, Ayzah remembered that she had made a big deal about it, acting like she was better than everyone else. She'd tried to show Ayzah and anyone else who would listen their new fancy house and had invited half the neighborhood up to see them. The way she carried on, you would have thought they were the Jeffersons or something, moving on up and leaving everything else, including their friends, behind. She and Deon had made the move some time ago, right after his business started doing well. *Whatever.* A thug was a thug, no matter where he lived, right? Deon was nothing but a small-time numbers runner who had done well at maximizing his connections. So well that he used those same connections to become a mark for the police department. In Ayzah's mind, he was lower than low, a professional snitch who got paid for bringing misery to other people, and if that was the kind of business Prince was going to be in, she wanted no part of it. Everybody knew that folks who let the police use them to set other people up just didn't have a lot of friends around. Sure, Deon had done well, but he and Erica really had to move because everyone knew what he did for a living and he really couldn't even show his face in the 'hood anymore, much less live there. Now he did most of his work in surrounding cities where people didn't know him.

Erica was a ride-or-die kind of woman. Every time she saw Ayzah, she let her know that she had been rewarded for sticking by her man, no matter what. She loved to look down her nose at her girlfriends like they were still little kids, comparing them to herself as if they were schoolgirls. She always wore the best gear, and made sure Ayzah and everyone else knew it, too, reminding her that because of what Deon did, the two of them never had to struggle for anything.

Lights inside the house shone through the thin curtains. There was obviously someone home, but there was no movement at all in response to the bell. There was always a good chance that the doorbell was not working, Ayzah thought. On a whim, she reached up and turned the doorknob. The door swung open. Ayzah could not believe that the door was unlocked. She shook her head. It was bad enough that she could walk right up to the door and look through the curtains into the living room, but they obviously felt so safe over here that they had no problem leaving their door unlocked, too. *Dumbasses.* Not smart for someone in the business Deon was in. He certainly had enemies, people whom he'd pissed off enough that they would want to hurt him and Ayzah, or worse. And everyone knew that the truly criminal-minded would hightail it to the better neighborhoods first to do their deeds.

Ayzah yelled her hellos then listened for a response as she peeked around the doorway. No one answered, but she took a few steps inside the house anyway. She stood in the front room, shifting from foot to foot. The entry was nice. Tiled floors. No grungy eighties carpeting that needed stretching like her mother's house. Lots of light. There were a few pictures on a single console table and a coat rack.

"I'll be there in a minute," Erica finally answered. Her voice came from the back of the house, down a hallway that seemed to stretch straight through what seemed like miles of high ceilings and more tiled floors.

Loud thumping and knocking followed Erica's answer. Ayzah jumped. *What in the world was she doing?* It sounded like something or someone had fallen. "It's me. Ayzah," she announced. Didn't want to disturb them if they were back there getting busy. Give them a little time to get decent before they rushed out into the hallway or something like that.

Things slamming. More banging. "You okay?" she asked.

Ayzah tensed. No answer again, but she could certainly hear voices. There was a bad feeling in her stomach. Her lips had gone dry. She licked them, then took a few more steps toward the back of the house. The voices got clearer. She listened hard. If Ayzah didn't know better, she would swear that one of the voices sounded like Prince. She shook her head. Obviously, she was so bent out of shape about their breakup that she was hearing things. She must be. Why would he be here this time of day, anyway? Her spine tingled.

She knew she shouldn't be, but Ayzah found herself standing outside the door to the room. She listened. Erica's voice sounded happy. She was laughing. It almost sounded like someone was rushing around the room, scurrying or something. Ayzah was about to ask if she should come back later and then the knob turned and the door swung open.

Ayzah and Erica stood face-to-face. The air hung heavy with the smell of sex. They both gasped at the same time. The light cocoa-colored skin of Erica's face flushed. She stared straight ahead at Ayzah's throat.

Unconsciously, Ayzah fingered the diamond that dangled there. She felt hot and her eyes were drawn behind Erica, across the room, to the bed. She expected to see Deon, but instead Prince was lying on the bed, under the covers, propped up by pillows. He smiled as if this were one of the most normal situations that he could possibly encounter. One of his hands was behind his head. The other was on top of the sheet that covered him, over his groin. His eyes met Ayzah's and he grinned.

"Hey, babe," he said. "It's good to see you."

Erica stepped away but looked at the floor.

Ayzah's stomach quivered. She hadn't spoken to him since she'd left the house, although he had called her cell phone and her mother's number several times. It dawned on her that he had most likely been right here all the time. "I suppose you are *working.*" She spat out her words as if she were trying to rid herself of a bad taste in her mouth. Anger blazed in Ayzah's eyes. She felt like she was Boo-Boo the Fool or something, the one who never sees things like this coming. Used. She'd thought she was smarter than this.

The covers moved as Prince crossed, then uncrossed his legs under them. He shrugged. "I guess ain't no use in hiding it now, huh?" He paused.

Ayzah thought she saw a flicker of something that looked like guilt cross his face. Why could she not see before that he was such an arrogant son of a bitch?

"You left me." He stated that as if he were giving her an explanation, a reason for him to be in the position he was in. "Me and your girl Erica been kicking it for a while now. I guess you could say she has been consoling me."

Consoling him? "You don't exactly seem too upset. Where's Deon?" She spoke through clenched teeth.

Erica cleared her throat. "I haven't been with Deon in a while. He was having some problems. He had to go away for a while. I have no idea where he is. Disappeared. Poof." She stared Ayzah in the face, hard, as if daring her to say something about it or to make a move at all.

Then just as suddenly as it had appeared, Ayzah's anger faded away. A strange calmness spread through her, lifting a weight from her shoulders. All of this really didn't matter anymore. Not Prince, not Erica. None of it. The truth was, things had just been made easier for her. She didn't have to feel guilt about leaving Prince or even miss him because he was gone. There was no longer any need to do what he wanted, or to worry about what he was going to do next or where he was. He and Erica had just made that none of her business.

She smiled slowly at first, then bigger. "Well, it is really good to see you, Erica." Ayzah spoke in her most gracious voice. Both Erica and Prince looked confused. Ayzah felt in control for the first time in months.

"Don't do anything crazy, baby." Prince's face was riddled with confusion. He sat up on the bed.

"I'm not. All the craziness is over for me. I have to tell you the truth. I was really struggling over this. But that's over now. I hope the two of you are very happy together." She turned to Erica. "You are going to have to watch out for him. He doesn't like to work too hard."

"I can explain. This didn't mean anything. Erica doesn't. It was just sex. I don't love her."

Erica's head whipped around, her brow furrowed in anger. She opened her mouth to speak and then closed it again, folding her arms.

It all came rushing back to Ayzah. All the fake apologies, the begging and explaining. He had not grown up one bit over the past few years. She shook her head. "No need to explain. I meant it when I said I was done, so you are free to do whatever you want. I came over here looking for some friendship. Someone to talk through my problems with. But it looks like they have worked themselves out."

unpleasant necessities

Sometimes the necessary things were the hardest. Alexis hated to go to the EEOC office and stand in line, but she put it first on her agenda anyway. It was important that she file a sexual harassment claim against her boss. She couldn't sleep calmly if she didn't make sure what happened to her was on record. She knew what to expect; she was a lawyer and well schooled in bureaucracy.

The small downtown office was just as she suspected. White tile floors with a few hard plastic seats lining the walls. Government workers behind glass. It was strange being on this side of the law for a change, sort of eerie. Alexis knew they'd heard it all, so she expected that she would fill out her forms and they would listen to her complaint with blank faces, barely caring. She anticipated that a little old lady with blue hair would ask her all the questions that were sure to be on her questionnaire form, write down her answers, assign her a case number, and then send her on her way.

She was almost right, too, except that her examiner was

the largest man she had ever seen. He called her name, then signaled for her to follow him to his office. He gave her a smile that was warm and genuine-looking, then led her back to a small half cubicle with a door at the back of the room. It was almost unfurnished and so tiny that he was barely able to close the door once they were inside. It reminded Alexis of the study carrels she had used while in law school: basically a desk, a chair, and a door. There were no personal items in sight and Alexis guessed that it was a community interviewing room that he shared with other examiners.

He sat back in the chair looking tired, as if he had heard tons of cases just like hers even though the day had just started. She blushed, suddenly feeling like she was a whiny baby for even coming.

The feeling left as soon as he opened his mouth. His voice was somehow reassuring. He didn't follow a script at all, just asked her to tell her story in her own words. She was so comfortable that before she knew it, her story just poured out. She didn't know him from Adam, but by the time she was done, it felt like things had been made that much easier, as if telling it made it go away. They stood at the same time.

"I know I don't have to tell you how to proceed. You are doing the right thing. You know that though."

Alexis smiled. "I believe I am. I just wanted my complaint to be on record. I haven't decided yet if I am going to take any other kind of legal action. I just want the bastard to take notice."

"This office will send the firm a formal letter and let them know that a complaint has been filed against him and his company." He paused. "I have to tell you though, the story about grabbing the man's nuts is the funniest I have heard in a long time. It was all I could do to keep a straight face."

She chuckled. "I know. It was kind of comical. *After* it was over. I was terrified. That is the only reason why I reacted the way I did."

"Believe me, men notice you when you have a hold of their balls. I would."

Alexis thanked him and left the office, feeling surprisingly upbeat after retelling her story. She'd thought it would be more exhausting than it turned out to be. After checking the city hall directory, she moved on to task number two on her list: a protective order against Ayzah. Alexis knew for certain that she wanted no part of that woman in the future if she could help it. It wasn't that she was afraid of Ayzah; she was afraid of what her own reaction might be.

The new city hall building was surprisingly easy to navigate. Alexis had never had much business past the first floor since it opened a few month before, but she found where she wanted to go with no problem. She filled out the required forms and prepared herself to stand in line yet again. Alexis bit her lip. She knew the drill as much as anyone. She'd had countless clients get protective orders against violent spouses or soon to be ex-spouses. In most cases, they needed evidence, evidence which she really didn't have right now. If she called, she knew that both Sarah and Paris would come be her witnesses. But she would get to that. She had to file the papers before she could even hope for a hearing.

Alexis stood to the side and looked at the line. There were at least thirty people ahead of her trying to do the same thing she was. This was a line of scared and pissed-off folks, so there would be very little small talk. Alexis tried to see how far it went but she couldn't be sure. The only thing she could tell was that it snaked out of the office and down the hall. She rubbed the back of her neck. Doing this had seemed like a good idea before, but from what she could tell, she would most certainly be standing there for a while. Not her idea of fun, but running into Ayzah again wasn't her idea of fun either. She might be paranoid, but there was no doubt in her mind that Ayzah would hurt her if she could, and Alexis wanted that to be on record. There was no telling what people might do when they felt threatened, and from the way Ayzah had tried to approach her, she was most definitely feeling threatened by her and Remedy's relationship. Alexis checked herself. *Friendship. Whatever it was.*

"Alexis?"

She spun around at the sound of her name.

"Aren't you in the wrong line?" Judge Kennedy was dressed in plain clothes.

Alexis was so used to seeing her in the courtroom that she almost couldn't place her at first. "I don't think so."

"You file divorce papers in room 207. This is where they take protective orders."

"That's what I'm here for."

The judge's face softened. "Oh, those clients with violent husbands. That is always tough. You sure give people personal service. I wouldn't expect you to be down here doing it for someone. You short on interns?"

Alexis shook her head. "Oh, it's not for a client. It's for me. Had me a little run-in."

The judge looked surprised. "Really? Client's husband or something like that?"

Embarrassment flooded her face. "Nope. New potential boyfriend has a crazed ex-wife. Standard thriller movie kind of fare." She managed a weak smile. "I'm just taking some precautionary steps."

"I know you know better than to get mixed up in some soap opera–type stuff. There are fish in the sea with a lot less baggage." She smiled. "Isn't that what you told me?" The judge had been one of Alexis's clients herself about two years prior. Alexis remembered that she had enjoyed working with her. She truly was a nice woman who had gotten the short end of the stick. "I'll tell you what. Let me take care of those for you." She took the papers from Alexis's hand.

"But I thought I had to stand here so the examiner could log this in, then wait for a hearing and all that. That is what we tell clients."

"That is how it goes. In the textbooks or if you don't have a friend behind the scenes. You do. And it's the least I can do to save you an hour or two. You saved me a lot."

♡   ♡   ♡

She'd let herself be led for so long, having finally made a decision felt really good. Ayzah felt happier than she had in quite a while. When she'd said she'd be back for her things, she wasn't sure she'd meant it. There was a part of her that thought she might give in if Prince said the right thing. But after seeing Prince and Erica together, she had no other choice. There was no way in hell she had any intention of living in this raggedy house with Prince ever again.

Ayzah flitted around the small house that she'd shared with Prince. He hadn't even worked for this. It had been his father's house. Prince's daddy never gave him a dime, but when he moved out to the country, he let Prince live in his old house rather than sell it. The two of them had lived in it together on and off for a long time. In her head, she counted the number of nights she had spent there without him, busy trying to make their house a home, and wondered how many of those very same nights he had spent with Erica. With another woman, period.

Most of the house had been decorated from money she'd earned. It was hard to distinguish things that truly belonged only to Prince. Ayzah grabbed a few things that she considered to be hers and dropped them into a few small boxes Ma'dear had helped her scrounge up.

Ma'dear was actually her lookout. She was sitting outside Erica's town house, watching Prince's car to make sure it wasn't moving anywhere. If Prince did leave, she was supposed to call Ayzah and give her time to get out of the house. She had no desire to talk to him ever again. That would be all she needed. Prince showing up and acting a fool over her leaving. He'd been blowing up her cell phone since she'd left him at Erica's. A pang of anger and humiliation hit her again, but it lasted only a second. There was no need to waste her energy on looking back or mulling over what Prince had or had not done. His true colors had always been easy to see, just as Ma'dear had warned her. She'd just refused to open her eyes and look. Ayzah sighed.

He and Erica truly deserved each other. He'd probably thought she wasn't serious about leaving, thinking perhaps that he could try and charm his way back into her good graces. Again. Not this time. Ayzah didn't plan to give him that opportunity at all. She was done with him. It wasn't like he

could claim Erica was an accident or even that it only happened one time. She was using him the way he had been using Ayzah, and he probably couldn't even see it. They were
leeches, the both of them, feeding off of other people whenever they could.

Her phone rang again and she didn't answer. Her lips
puckered with annoyance. Once again, she knew that it was
Prince. It was his turn to be calling all over town trying to
find her for a change. *Let him wonder.* The sad thing was that
she knew he was calling from Erica's house. They had both
just used her. He'd probably been taking care of Erica for a
while with money she constantly found a way to come up
with whenever Prince said he needed it. Anger knotted inside
her. She probably would have quit stripping a long time ago
had it not been for Prince convincing her that they needed
the money. Ayzah knew without asking that he had not saved
one thin dime as he'd said he would. It was clear to her now
that he'd never been planning to move with her to L.A. at all.
If she had gotten custody of Jamal, it would have been more
of the same. Prince would probably have taken Jamal's child
support money just like he did her money from her job and
used it for heaven knows what. It was almost like he was her
pimp, only she wasn't really out on the street.

One last trip to the bedroom confirmed that every stitch of
her clothing was gone from the closet over which she and
Prince used to fight. Ayzah even took her hangers, then made
her fourth and final trip to her car without even looking back.
There was only so long that she would be somebody's fool,
and Prince's time was up.

Cure for what ails you

Remedy began kissing Alexis right under her jaw, then made a trail of tiny kisses down to her collarbone.

It felt good to have him so close to her. Alexis hummed, filled with the shiver of awareness. She wanted to pinch herself. Things were moving way faster than she would normally have allowed before. But this felt somehow right. "You know I was going to come over here to tell you that I couldn't see you anymore, right?"

He licked her ear gently. "No, you weren't. You just think you were. If you really didn't want to see me anymore you would have called me on the phone."

Alexis chuckled lightly. He was right. "I'm not the kind of woman who would just kick a man to the curb without giving you a chance to say your piece. Someone did that to me and it didn't feel good."

"Is that right?" Remedy pressed a kiss to her neck again.

Alexis closed her eyes, savoring his kiss, then opened them. "I hope you are going to get a protective order against Ayzah. I did and as a lawyer—"

"You aren't my lawyer," he said. "I can handle Ayzah. But I want to handle you right now."

She wanted him to handle her, but first things first. "I wasn't going to see you anymore because I don't need a whole bunch of mess in my life. I can't deal with that."

Remedy pulled away from Alexis, just far enough back so that they could look each other in the eye. His face was serious. "You shouldn't have to. I can't tell you what to do. Ayzah does have issues, yes. And I can't ask you to put up with her. We aren't married or anything so you shouldn't have to. But I do know that I find you really attractive and plan to keep pursuing you."

"Is that what you are doing? Pursuing me?" *How could she possibly walk away from such honesty?*

Remedy cocked his head to the side. The expression on his face said it all.

"I have a lot to worry about now. Things to get done," Alexis said. "I have to find a new job, and let me tell you, I have no idea where to start. The last thing I need to worry about is some woman trying to cut off my head or something because she thinks I'm messing up her life."

Remedy sat all the way back on the sofa. It was obvious that Alexis was overwhelmed. He just wanted to hold her in his arms and help her in some way, but he didn't want to add to her stress. "I'm sorry about that. I thought she might try to mess with you or something. She has never been the type to give up easily."

"You can't apologize for her. You didn't send her."

"But in a way I did. Ayzah isn't interested in preserving a family like she told you. How can she preserve something we don't have? What she is interested in is money. My money, period. She doesn't want anyone around that she thinks might mess up her chances of getting custody of our son and the child support she thinks might come with it, that's all."

"I guess it boils down to money for a lot of people. My ex was like that. He put money before all else, even me." Alexis looked at the floor, remembering the frustration she'd felt as she had tried in vain to get Walter's attention.

"Yup. And she is putting money before our son." He pulled Alexis to him. "But I prefer not to talk about that right now. I have to enjoy every minute I get with you, considering that you may be leaving me at any minute." He smiled and raised his eyebrows. "Let's talk about you. What is your plan? Find another law firm to work for?"

Alexis shrugged. "Not sure. I haven't exactly been the think-ahead type where my career is concerned. I never thought about working until retirement or anything. The only thing I was working toward was being someone's trophy wife, and I didn't even know it. That is what my family would have liked anyway."

Remedy nodded, but he didn't even crack a smile at Alexis's comment. "Nice job, if you can get it."

"So they say. But in the meantime, the rest of us have to figure out ways to eat." Her answer was thick with her confusion.

"Have you considered that the reason you can't seem to figure out your options is because maybe none of them are what you would do if you could do anything in the world?" He paused. "Maybe you can't consider another law firm because it's just not in your heart."

"Is that how you live? By what's in your heart?"

"I try to."

"What about responsibility and all that?"

"Sometimes you have to be responsible to yourself and the things *you* need, not worry so much about other people."

She marveled at the idea of not worrying about what other people thought or needed. It sounded like quite a luxury to be able to do that, certainly something that she was just beginning to be able to think about. "I just know I feel trapped in my own life sometimes. Its stressful."

Remedy looked at her, and the desire Alexis saw in his eyes startled her. "Let me release some of that stress, then." His mouth covered hers and they kissed, so deeply that Alexis lost her sense of balance. The room swirled. Remedy's hand roamed her body, exploring her breasts, her hips, and her thighs. Alexis shivered as his fingers probed further underneath her skirt. He caressed her thighs with the tips of his fingers and her legs involuntarily parted.

He rose and pulled her to her feet. Remedy opened the zipper to her skirt like an expert. It dropped to the floor and Alexis stepped out of it, kicking it to the side. Her body felt hot all over and she stood before him in her blush lace underwear. Alexis heard him catch his breath as his eyes roamed freely over her near-naked body.

Remedy ran his hand along the outline of her behind, pulling her closer to him, then unhooked her bra and removed it, trailing wet kisses down her breasts. She gasped. He sucked first one nipple then the other. Gently, he lay her back on the couch, continuing to kiss her breasts and her stomach. She arched her back in response. Remedy slipped his arm under the small of her back and lifted her gently toward him. He paused his kissing around her navel, gently swirling his tongue in the small hole.

Alexis moaned again. He moved the small strip of fabric that was her underwear to the side with his tongue. Her vagina spasmed as the warmth hit it. "Remedy. Oh my god." Alexis gasped his name and inhaled sharply. She grasped the back of his head and her hips lifted to meet the caress of his tongue.

A flood of pleasure spread through her. He paused, dropped his pants to the floor and slipped on a condom in what seemed like one motion.

Alexis gasped as he lowered his rock-hard body over hers. She was eager to touch his skin. Her heartbeat pounded in her brain as he entered her. She moaned loudly, surprising herself.

He moved slowly and methodically, savoring every movement as if it were their last. They found their rhythm and Alexis moaned at each thrust. Remedy enjoyed Alexis like this. Totally uncovered and unreserved.

She wrapped her legs around his body and cried out for release. Their eyes locked, and for a minute, it was as if she could see past Remedy's outside layer to the tender person he was underneath. Waves of pleasure, like nothing she had felt before, washed over her.

Remedy tensed, then moaned in concert with Alexis. They came together, then lay still. Their sweat intermingled as they listened to each other's breathing. Their eyes locked in silent embrace.

Their breathing slowly returned to normal. Remedy slid off of Alexis and sat on the floor in front of the couch. She joined him on the floor and they snuggled together. Alexis was shocked by the intensity they had just shared. Aftershocks still pulsed through her body.

He touched her, and she jumped in response. Her skin was at the height of sensitivity. Remedy put his arm on her shoulder, brushing his lips across her head. "If you could find some way to take some of that there and channel it, you'd be able to figure out what your next step is."

"You think?" Alexis leaned into him. She savored the way his warmth surrounded her.

"And you have family and friends that love you. It should be easy."

"It should be." But it wasn't. Nothing would be easy until she at least tried to apologize to her Aunt Athena. Her mind was clearer than it was before.

"You are the one that needs to take some of what you have and find a way to bottle and sell it. I think I am actually less stressed than I was before." Alexis ran her hand down Remedy's arm.

He smiled. "I told you, I can take care of what ails you. All you have to do is let me."

She leaned back into him, enjoying his warmth. Remedy was just what the doctor ordered.

too little, too late

"I don't see why you even have to go back over there," Erica pouted. "She knows about us now, so what would be the point?" She paced slowly back and forth across her bedroom. She nibbled on her acrylic nails.

"Why do you have that look on your face?" Prince finished drying himself with the towel that was wrapped around his waist, then let it drop to the bedroom floor. He wouldn't even try to explain things to her. Erica would never understand his relationship with Ayzah.

"This ain't a look. I'm thinking. I have a lot on my mind." She paused. "You got everything you need right here. You don't need her. She is just a helpless bitch anyway. Can't you see that Ayzah is just bringing you down?"

"Please. Can't we just make this pleasant? I will be back to see you as soon as I make her feel a little better." Prince really didn't want to have this discussion. Erica was good in bed, but after it was over, he always wanted to run screaming from the building. He just didn't particularly like her. She gave him everything he wanted and took care of his needs in bed. Not to mention that she sucked a mean dick. But Ayzah took care of him otherwise.

He didn't know what he was going to do when and if Deon ever showed up again and wanted to get back with her. Erica was the kind of woman you enjoyed when you needed to, but from whom you didn't really expect anything long-term. The way he saw it, they didn't have a "thing," just a series of one-night stands. Booty calls. Since Deon had been gone, she had been clinging to him, wanting to make more of it than it was. But what Erica didn't understand was that Ayzah had always been there for him, no matter what he did. They had history, and he had always known that she would have done anything for him. Erica, on the other hand, was only out for herself. This time, he had the feeling he had gone a little too far.

What had he been thinking? There had been times when Ayzah had suspected that he had other woman, Prince knew that. But this was the first time he had thrown it in her face as he had. His expression was serious and somber as he thought about it. It had been a mean thing to do, even for him. He just had been so angry that she had talked all that crap about leaving him and moving on. And then she wouldn't answer his calls. What was that about? She wasn't going anywhere without him. She loved him and would eventually give in. But he had made it that much harder on himself by being with Erica. It would have been so much easier if it had been someone she didn't know. And now Erica was tripping, trying to make this whole thing into something other than what it was.

Erica stopped pacing and disappeared down the hall into the kitchen. He really didn't have time for her nonsense. Prince pulled on his clothes and then picked up his watch, snapping it onto his wrist. It was getting harder and harder to leave Erica. She had been very accommodating at first, but lately she had become more demanding, clingy almost. He picked up his bag.

She appeared at the doorway, slipping her arms around his waist.

"So, you promise you'll be back?" She hugged him from behind, pressing her body against his.

Prince held onto her wrists and tried to pry her away from him. "Soon as I get things squared away. I'll be back."

"It won't do any good for me to tell you that I just want you to stay, right?"

"I thought we had an understanding, Erica. We weren't going to make too much of this. Keep it in perspective."

She nodded. "We did. But it feels like so much more to me. I thought you felt it, too. When we are together—"

Prince grabbed Erica's arms, pulling them from around his waist.

She stiffened and tossed her head in defiance. His black eyes impaled her and she froze.

"Don't get it twisted. It's still just sex." Prince released her and stepped back. His voice had a ring of finality. "But I'll be back to fuck you if you want."

Erica's eyes smoldered with anger. She crossed her arms in front and nodded slowly. He was more to her than a good fuck. She would make him see that. Soon.

♡   ♡   ♡

Things were not right. The moment he walked through his door, Prince knew she was gone. His throat tightened. No matter what else happened, Ayzah had always been there, even for the hot minute that she had been married to Remedy. If he needed her, she would come. If he said he was sorry, she would forgive him. But something was different now. It almost felt like she didn't need him anymore. He walked through the house and surveyed what had changed.

In the front room, there were just a few things out of place that he could see. He narrowed his eyes and gazed around the room. There was a picture missing. One of those silly cat statues that Ayzah liked so much was gone. He walked from room to room, trying to confirm what he already knew.

It was obvious that she was pissed off. Prince's mind raced. He must have tried to call Ayzah twenty times, and not once had she answered any phone. Not that he really expected her to miraculously answer it after about the tenth call. By then, any hope that he had of wearing her down had passed.

It wouldn't be hard to find her. Ayzah was fairly predictable and he knew where to look. He knew Ayzah better than she knew herself. She would be in one of a few places. The club where she danced. Her mother's house, or with Remedy. And her mother's house was at the top of the list.

see through sins

She had to work tonight. Ayzah pulled on her jeans and prepared to lie to her mother. Ma'dear let her move in but was under the assumption that she had stopped dancing at The Yellow Rose. Ayzah sighed, then reached for her makeup bag. She hadn't exactly told her that, but when Ma'dear had mentioned it, she hadn't told her otherwise.

Work in Wal-Mart. *Ugh.* The thought disgusted her. She couldn't imagine herself wearing one of those damn vests, slaving for barely more than minimum wage. She'd tried that normal job shit before, after Jamal was born. Besides, she'd been too fat then to dance anyway. No one would have wanted a lap dance from a fat girl. She'd worked in retail, in the mall. But she'd barely been able to make ends meet. As soon as she'd gotten her body back in shape, she was right back up in the club again. The money was good, and it was one of the few things in her life that made her feel in control. Ayzah smiled. She started moving, and the men did almost anything she asked.

Ma'dear knocked on her door and then poked her head into Ayzah's room. She smiled. It felt good to have her daughter here, like old times. It almost felt as if she had her baby back again, the way she used to be when she was a child, before she got mixed up with Prince.

Ma'dear's eyes narrowed. "I'm back from bible study." She paused. "I thought you'd be getting ready for bed or something. You look like you are getting ready to go out."

Ayzah tried to remain steady. She didn't want to give herself away. She looked down at her jeans and T-shirt. "You think so? No big deal. I sort of have a date."

Ma'dear gave Ayzah an appraising look. "A date? Really? I hope you aren't going out with Prince again." She'd seen her daughter go running back to that fool more times than she could count. She could do so much better.

She shook her head. "No, I'm not. I'm going to the bookstore and then I'm going to meet up with some friends." Ayzah licked her lips nervously. Hopefully Ma'dear wouldn't ask too many more questions.

"The bookstore?"

Ayzah nodded.

Ma'dear sighed. "Will you be back late?"

She nodded. "Probably. You told me to get my mind off of things, right?" She zipped up the small tote bag she had packed.

"That's an awfully big bag. You gonna get that carpal tunnel thing from carrying that." Ma'dear's eyes seemed to bore through the bag. Ayzah swung it around behind her as if she was trying to hide it. The small smile on her face vanished for a moment.

"I know. It *is* heavy. But I promised Erica I would return some of her things. Tonight. She's meeting me at the bookstore."

Ma'dear looked away. She wasn't born yesterday. "Okay then. I won't wait up. You have fun with your friends." She watched Ayzah as she headed toward the front door. There was so much she wanted to say to her daughter, but she held her tongue instead. There were some things that she was going to have to learn on her own.

face-to-face

I
t didn't take as long as she'd imagined it would. Monty had obviously gotten the notification that she had filed a complaint. He'd left her several messages and had sent her a few e-mails, all of them marked as urgent. She read the first one and deleted it from her BlackBerry just as soon as she was done, and didn't bother to open any of the others. Alexis felt no obligation to him whatsoever and she refused to be harassed. Let him explain to his partners why she had filed a complaint against him.

Alexis walked down her short driveway to her mailbox. It was barely midday and the hot sun was already beating down. She picked up her newspaper on the way and daydreamed, not really paying attention to her surroundings.

"Alexis." There was a sense of urgency in the voice she heard.

She stiffened and looked up, just as Monty stepped out of the shrubs outside her front door. *When had he gotten between her and the house?* Alexis didn't recall passing him on the way to the mailbox or anything.

Monty wore clothes similar to those Alexis remembered seeing him in every day in the office, except his pants were wrinkled and dirty and his white shirt had a brown spot in the front, as if he had spilled part of his lunch on it or something. His hair, usually gelled perfectly into place, looked tousled all over his head.

"What are you doing at my house?" Alexis looked around for an alternate way into her house. This was not the way she wanted to meet with Monty.

"Why are you doing this? Why did you file that complaint? Were you trying to ruin my career or something? Ruin my marriage?"

"I could ask you the same thing. What in the hell were you thinking? You should have been worrying about your marriage before."

Monty's eyes looked desperate, almost crazed. "I didn't do anything you didn't want. You think I don't notice the way you look at me?"

Alexis couldn't believe what she was hearing. Monty was obviously overcome by stress or something. "You are not making sense."

"I need you to withdraw that complaint," he said. "I hope you aren't thinking about suing or anything. I have no money and the firm won't pay. You'll just eat up your savings paying a lawyer."

"Leave. Now." Alexis gripped her mail tightly.

"And you have no proof. None at all."

A sinister-sounding laugh escaped from Monty's throat. Alexis didn't answer. It wasn't about proof and they both knew it. If she didn't withdraw the complaint, it would always be there, on the record. "You should have been worried about spots on your otherwise sterling career when you were *harassing me.*"

Monty took a step forward and then stopped.

"Think of the damage a protective order on top of that complaint would do." Alexis held her ground. They shared an icy look, but she didn't want him to think she was afraid. "You should leave," she said again.

Monty seemed to contemplate what to do next. He took a step forward, then stepped back again.

Alexis clutched her mail even tighter and stood as still as possible. She hoped that he would make the right choice. She had done it before, and had no doubt in her mind that she would defend herself against him again. And this time, she might not be so polite. She cleared her throat, waiting for him to make a decision. Where in the hell were her neighbors? Why did no one see her distress?

"Withdraw the complaint." Monty stepped out of her path. "This isn't the last time you'll see me." He walked a wide path around her as he headed down her driveway to the curb.

Alexis exhaled loudly. Her heart was beating so hard that she could feel the pulsing in her fingertips. She opened her door and stepped inside, then closed and locked it behind her. She leaned against the door for a minute. When she'd decided to file the EEOC complaint, she had just thought she was doing the right thing. She'd also thought that she was getting even for what Monty had done. She remembered thinking that her boss was an idiot if he thought that she would do nothing about what had happened. She had thought he would be angry, but they would all learn from their mistakes and move on. But Monty was obviously more than dumb and arrogant. He was crazy. She had not counted on that.

$\vee \quad \vee \quad \vee$

When they were done for the evening, a bouncer always walked the girls to the car. That was a rule, and Ayzah always obeyed it. You never knew when a semi-intoxicated patron was waiting around in the parking lot, counting on getting more than a lap dance. Sure, there were some girls who did that kind of thing, slept with the guys who came into the club for money, but Ayzah was not one of them. Her employment at The Yellow Rose was strictly about dancing.

She waited impatiently for OJ to get back. She shifted her weight from foot to foot. It had been a long night and she wanted to get home before Ma'dear woke up and started asking questions. He was probably out in the parking lot, talking trash with some girl or something. She decided she could get to her car alone this one time. She was parked right in front anyway and the place was on Lamar. It wasn't like Lamar Boulevard was deserted at any time of day.

Ayzah threw her bag on her shoulder and pushed open the heavy door. The neon and fluorescent Yellow Rose sign still glowed, humming in the night. Ayzah walked through the parking lot quickly. Her high-heeled flip-flops made a thwacking sound against the bottom of her feet that seemed to echo, blending in with the humming sound that came from the sign. Ayzah looked around. OJ was nowhere in sight. She twisted her mouth in annoyance. Where in the hell was he?

They shouldn't have to wait until he was ready to walk them out to go do whatever it was they did next, she thought. There would be no Yellow Rose without them.

There was a shadow by her car. Ayzah froze just as a figure stepped into the light cast by the one streetlight illuminating the nearly empty lot. Ayzah gasped.

"You shouldn't be walking out here alone," he said. "I've been worried about you. You ready to go home?"

Ayzah's heartbeat slowed down as she recognized Prince. For a moment, she thought she had made a mistake by coming out by herself. She thought she was about to become the next club urban legend, the girl who disappeared in the night, never to be seen again. "Why are you here, Prince? You trying to give me a heart attack or something?" She placed her hand over her heart.

"I came to take you home."

Ayzah had known he would be back, she just hadn't expected to see him tonight. She'd been sure he would keep calling or show up at her mother's. "I think I can get there by myself."

Prince smiled, a look of relief on his face. "I knew you would come around eventually. We need to go talk about getting custody of Jamal some more."

"You can drop that. I'm not that dumb. You are not interested in me or Jamal at all. It's only about the money for you, and I know it." Ayzah opened her car door. "You know, I should have come around a long time ago. I have no idea why I kept falling for your shit. Just leave me alone, Prince. I meant it when I said I was done."

It dawned on Prince then that he hadn't won anything.

She wasn't coming home with him after all. Ayzah had meant that she was going home to her mother's.

She didn't give him time to answer or go crazy or anything. Before Prince could think of what his next move was, Ayzah had jumped into her small car and started the engine. He saw her put the car in gear and by the look in her eyes, there was no doubt in his mind that the best thing to do would be for him to get the hell out of her way. Period.

run to the future

The parking lot near the Fiesta Beach entrance to the Town Lake running trail was almost completely empty. Mesquite trees cast shadows on a lone car parked a few feet from the water's edge. It was quiet here. Few walkers and runners and the occasional biker. Alexis pulled in and looked for Paris's car. She swore at no one in particular. Since taking up tae kwon do, she had not been running as much as she used to, and when she did run, this side of the Town Lake Hike and Bike Trail was her least favorite. She had no idea why she'd let Paris talk her into meeting there in the first place, other than that a long run might do her good. She had a lot of energy that she needed to burn.

She picked up her BlackBerry to call Paris and cuss her out for being late yet again. Since Monty's impromptu visit the day before, she was wary of being in deserted places like this. She obviously had to keep her wits about her and wasn't as able to spot someone following her as she would have thought she might be. Alexis didn't want to be stuck in the middle of nowhere alone. This end of the trail was in the shadows of one of the city's power plants and it might be a prime location for a murder mystery. She certainly had no desire to be a player in that.

There was a call she had missed, from a number she didn't recognize. From what she could tell, the caller had not left a message. Again. This was about the fourth call like that this morning. Alexis had no doubt now that these were from Monty. His behavior surprised her. He knew the law and he was still harassing her. She was probably going to have to get a lawyer after all.

Paris knocked on her window sharply. Alexis jumped, her heart racing. She pushed the button and opened her window, scowling at her cousin. "You could have announced yourself," she snapped. She stashed her handbag and phone behind her seat.

"Stop being so melodramatic." Paris was not concerned with Alexis's reaction. "You should have had some coffee before you came. Took care of that attitude you have." She tugged at her hot-pink shorts, trying to bring them further down.

"That little bit of fabric is only going to go so far over that piece of flesh, so you can just stop pulling." Alexis raised her eyebrows. They were there to run and, as usual, Paris had come dressed for a fashion show. "Your ass is going to be hanging out as soon as we move."

Paris rolled her eyes. "Whatever. Don't hate. Let's go. You are starting to sound like my mother."

Alexis was silent at the mention of her aunt. She got out of her car and locked it. The two women headed for the gravel trail, walking gingerly to avoid slipping. Alexis was used to running on the other part of the trail, the part that ran through the more populated areas of downtown. She was wary as she glanced around. There was a reason this end was less popular, she thought. This was obviously not the best-maintained portion of the trail. There were other spots where the gravel had been packed down and was firm. Here, there were fewer people than on the other side because the trail was more uneven. There was almost no one on the trail at all that Alexis could see.

"Have you talked to her?"

They started to run, a slow jog. "No, you know she won't even take my calls." Alexis had tried to call her Aunt Athena a few times at first. When she wouldn't answer, she'd stopped calling. "She is taking this being done with me thing very seriously."

"You know how intense she can be. You brought it on yourself. She probably won't talk to you until she knows you have a new job. *As a lawyer.*" Paris cleared her throat.

"What else would I be?" A light sweat had found its way onto Alexis's forehead. "Look, what I did made sense. The man harassed me in a big way."

"You need to tell her that. She might understand more. But that doesn't excuse you blowing up at her." Paris shrugged. "Everybody seems to be changing careers, maybe you might be, too. That would kill Athena if you came home and said you were not going to practice law anymore. I hope you aren't thinking about doing something like becoming the bra woman in Nordstrom or something."

"You are bizarre." She snorted. "You come up with the

most obscure stuff." She smiled. She'd missed that. "I *have* been exploring my options."

"You'd better be interviewing. This is the state capital. There are literally hundreds of law firms here. There has to be a job for you."

"It's only been a few days. Besides, I have been thinking about doing something different."

"That is exactly what I am talking about." Paris stopped in her tracks. "Here we go." She threw her hands in the air and tilted her face toward the sky. "Not you, too. Lord, have mercy."

Alexis began to laugh at her antics. "Stop. Who's sounding like your mother now? It's not like I just said I'm going to become a fishmonger or anything. I have been thinking about going into practice for myself."

"This is the first time I've heard that. You do know that if you do that, that is your own business. You have to actually work."

"Stop it. I actually work anyway. I got the idea from Rem."

"He's Rem now?"

"Remedy. He didn't actually say that I should go into practice for myself. He just made me realize that I need to be doing what I love. So I'm thinking about it."

Paris nodded but didn't speak. They ran over the top of the Longhorn Dam in silence, staring down at the murky water below. Alexis's stomach trembled. She wasn't sure if it was because she hated being so far up in the air, making this her least favorite part of the trip, or because she had finally given voice to the thoughts she had been having since her conversation with Remedy. "So, what do you think?"

Paris pursed her lips and took a deep breath as if she were measuring her words. "Well," she said, "if you think it will make you happy, I think it's a great idea. Just how much thought have you given this? Have you started a business plan yet?"

"To tell the truth, I haven't gotten that far. I can't get past the fact that it would take a whole lot of time and money to do it. And since I now have no job, that presents a problem."

"You see how I work. How much time I spend. Running a business is no walk in the park. You are a lawyer, but you would have to run your business, too, do all of that stuff that I have to do that you consider tedious and boring. And more, really, because my parents were the ones that laid the ground-work for me, and I stepped in after all the hard work was done. You won't have that luxury. It's not like we have a law firm in the family that you could just step into as a partner."

"I know all that."

"You asked my opinion and I'm giving it." She paused. "You should get on that business plan. And if you are worried about how family—"

"Athena."

"Athena is going to take it—"

"I'm not worried. It just would be so much easier if I had her support. And everyone else's, too."

Paris slowed her run down to a fast walk. "You should have thought of that before." Beat. "Tell her your story. With-out yelling. That is all you can do. But if you are going to worry about what everyone else thinks you won't get past square one. Forget about them. All the other stuff will fall in line."

Alexis was pensive for a minute. She knew that Paris would have her back. Sarah would, too. Maybe Paris was right.

"I can help you with that business plan, if you want me to. You know that is a service we offer at Benton & Associates now."

"What don't you do? You seem to do everything."

"It's all about fulfilling a need. The business plan is actually one of the easier parts of what needs to be done. You need clients. Back office people, but there are services that can do that, too. And office space. That could be the most expensive piece."

"I think I already know where I want to be located. I want to be right there in the redevelopment project if I can."

"Well, good for you. You let me know what you need then."

Alexis didn't answer. She kept her eyes on the trail flowing underneath her. They reached their turnaround point and began to run back in the direction they had come from. She knew she should feel good. Talking about her decision was half of the battle. "Could you talk to Athena for me?"

"Anything but that. I can give you my support, but you know her almost as well as I do. You are going to have to win her yourself. I can tell you right now that she isn't going to be crazy about the idea. She likes a sure thing. That bird-in-the-hand thing is one of her favorite sayings."

Alexis looked worried. Paris was not saying anything she didn't already know.

"Don't stress. It's *your* life. All you can do is apologize to her and hope she accepts. And the truth is, you really do have to live your life for yourself. If I were you, I would do my thing, hang my shingle, and not worry about anyone else."

"We'll see."

"I guess we will. You all have to be civil for my rehearsal and rehearsal dinner. You'll either work it out or you won't."

done in the dark

Ma'dear was up waiting. Ayzah tried to be as quiet as possible as she entered the house. She closed the door softly behind her, then took off her shoes at the front door. She placed them gently by the door, then tiptoed toward her room. She was halfway across the living room when Ma'dear cleared her throat.

Ayzah fell back against the wall. "Why didn't you say something?" she shrieked. "This is just too much for me. Two times in two nights." She had not fully recovered from Prince's surprise visit at the Yellow Rose yesterday.

"You are the one sneaking up in my house for the second night in a row."

Ayzah sighed heavily. She'd had a bad night, again. Prince harassed her yesterday, now OJ had been on her about her breasts again. "Do we have to do this tonight? I'm really tired."

"Really? What were you doing to get that way?"

"I'm grown, Ma'dear." She stood with her back to her

mother, talking over her shoulder. Ayzah didn't want to turn around and look her in the face.

"Yes, you are. But you are living in my house." She paused. "I'm tired of this, Ayzah. You need to have some respect if you are going to stay here."

"What are you talking about?"

Ma'dear lowered her voice. "I'm talking about you. You stay out all hours and you have no visible means of improvement, at least not any that you want to talk about during the light of day anyway. That Prince keeps calling here all hours, too. He damn near called me out by name, too."

Ayzah spun around. "What?"

"He called here demanding to know where you were. Said I was hiding you when I told him that you weren't here." She stood up and came over to her daughter. They stood face-to-face and Ayzah could see the anger on her face. "He is stalking you. You'd better deal with it."

Silence. She bit her lip.

"Let's talk about all this and the karma you are throwing out into the world, Ayzah. I talked to Remedy. He told me about his car and how you have been treating him. You'd better get that together. What is this I hear about you accosting his girlfriend?"

"Ma'dear, I haven't done anything to that woman. I just—"

The tension in her jaw conveyed Ma'dear's frustrations. "Ayzah, this is not high school. You can go to jail for shit like that."

Ayzah's mouth dropped open in surprise. When was the last time she had heard her mother swear?

"You can't live under my roof acting like you are fifteen years old." She paused. "Fix it, Ayzah. You better at least give Remedy some peace and do the right thing. You can't control what Prince does, but you can control your own actions. You need to stand up and do the right thing for once in your life. If not for you, then for Jamal."

She opened her mouth to speak but couldn't think of any smart retort. Their eyes locked, and Ayzah could suddenly see the truth in her mother's eyes. She could see her tiredness and her deep frustration. Ayzah closed her mouth and looked away, ashamed. Ma'dear went to her room, leaving Ayzah to stand in the hallway alone.

♡ ♡ ♡

The location wasn't a bad one, Remedy thought. It just presented some challenges. With a little work, this would be the perfect spot for his new club. He donned a hard hat and walked inside the gutted building. Some of the floors were okay, he noted, but parts of the second-floor loft would have to be redone completely. He walked around the perimeter of the first floor, making notes about what he wanted changed. In this area, he wanted most of the seats to be low to the ground, just like the place in Dallas, so the floor would have to be fixed. He could see where the construction crew had already started on demolition. They had moved some of the debris away and sanded in spots, but there was still a lot of work to be done.

A narrow stairway led to the second-floor loft. Remedy was cautious as he climbed up them. The building inspector said it was all good, but he couldn't tell what was sturdy and what wasn't. He didn't want to end up with anything else broken.

There were a few closed-off rooms on the second floor. These looked as promising as they did when he first saw the property. Perfect for private rooms. He envisioned private parties, even things like bridal showers up here. The room on the end was almost totally open to the floor below, a true loft. Remedy stood in the center of the room. This was perfect, a spot for his VIPs. It was still rough, but he planned to test it out on his first dignitary. Alexis.

thicker than water

Paris crossed over Interstate 35, heading toward her office. A nervous look played about her face. Low music hummed in her car while her mother chattered on endlessly.

"I don't see why I needed to go with you to the office today. I haven't been there in ages, certainly not since your father's surgery. You don't need me."

This whole thing was proving to be more trouble than it was worth, Paris thought. "You do need to go. I am going to need you to pop in every now and then while Tyson and I are on our honeymoon. If you don't then nothing will get done. Besides, I've made some changes I want you to be familiar with."

"You could have just taken your father and explained all that to him. He'll be in the office anyway."

They turned onto Eleventh Street, moving through the arches and slowly down the newly paved and refurbished streets. The stone buildings stood proudly, guarding the entrance to the east side. Paris stopped short of her office, turning left onto the side street near the location for Sarah's soon-to-open business.

"Where are we going?" Athena asked. "I really don't have a lot of time. I have a luncheon later today."

"You will have plenty of time for your luncheon. I wanted to stop in and see how Sarah's place was coming along. She has begun receiving her inventory and you know that if something is there for me, I have to see it first. Besides, I'm getting my bridesmaids' gifts from her. To give her some business."

Athena's lips were curled in contempt. She was fond of Sarah, but certainly not of the east side. "You know how I feel. I believe in progress. We should all be moving forward and leaving these neighborhoods to themselves."

Paris pulled into the garage and opened her window to take a ticket from the machine. "Mother, you say that like you weren't from here at one point. I'm surprised at you."

"I don't see why. You have known me all your life. Can I stay in the car?"

Paris wasn't really surprised. She knew her mother better than she knew herself. Athena could be so predictable. *That is why I had to resort to subterfuge to get you down here.*

"No, you cannot," she said. "It's too hot. I'm not having the authorities lock me up for elder abuse." Paris smiled. She knew her mother hated being referred to as an elder. But the dig was too delicious to refuse. "C'mon."

She led her mother to Sarah's store. The door was locked, but Sarah was inside, surrounded by tons of boxes. She held a clipboard in her hand and looked up as soon as Paris and Athena made it to the front door. She smiled broadly, then unlocked the door to let them in. "Well, hello. Nice to see you, Mrs. Montague." She stepped away to let them in.

Sarah and Paris spoke while Athena looked around. Her

mouth was drawn into a semiscowl as she looked around the room critically. Both women were silently amused as they watched her. Sarah was used to Paris's mother. Her bark was far worse than her bite. She knew that, and was prepared for any comment she might come up with.

"What do you think?" Sarah followed her around the shop, letting her look as carefully as she knew she would.

Athena cleared her throat. "I think you ought to make sure you have good security."

"Mother." Paris shook her head. She would never change.

"I don't think it is going to be a problem."

"This *is* out of the way. Do you think people will come here to buy these types of things?"

"Mrs. Montague, I want Necessary Things to be a destination. It will be fine. We have lots of boutiques in Austin that people drive all over town to visit. But I'm sure you are aware of that since you are a boutique shopper yourself."

"What does your husband think about this? I find it hard to believe that he is letting you—"

Paris gasped.

"What?" Athena looked wide-eyed and innocent.

Sarah ground her teeth together, then took a deep breath. "I assure you that we have a relationship built on trust and mutual respect. I am an adult and he doesn't have to *let* me do anything, the same way I'm sure your husband treats you. He's become very supportive."

"That is enough, Mother. I just wanted you to see it, that's all." Paris's face flushed. Her mother could be so exasperating sometimes.

"Did you see I have a new neighbor? There is a new business opening next door, too." Sarah crossed her arms in front and raised her eyebrows. She looked at Paris knowingly.

"People are really jumping at the chance to gentrify the old neighborhood, huh?"

Paris and Sarah didn't comment. Their gazes locked. "Maybe we will take a peek over there on our way out. Do you know what it is?" Paris asked.

Athena was already on her way to the door. "You have a nice place. Nice things." She picked up a handbag that was sitting on the counter on her way out, then put it down again. Sarah and Paris looked at each other again, surprised. They both knew how hard it was for Athena to give a compliment of any type, no matter how small.

♡   ♡   ♡

Alexis gasped when she looked up. She had been surveying the office she had just rented. It was small, but only one door away from Sarah's boutique. Other than a small desk and a phone, the room was filled with several vases of flowers for which she'd just finished finding a place. Paris and her Aunt Athena were outside her door, getting ready to knock. She cursed under her breath, wishing she had put that brown paper in the windows as she had originally planned. The place was barely furnished and Paris was playing games. She knew it was her doing without asking; there was no way her Aunt would come there of her own volition. It would have taken a team of horses to drag her down there to see this place. Besides, she hadn't even told her yet.

The surprise on Athena's face as she gazed into the space was obvious. She had no clue that she would be seeing Alexis today. Paris looked at her through the door, too, only she looked more smug. Alexis made a mental note. She would pay for this one. Her plan had been to talk to her aunt on her own time, when she was ready.

Reluctantly, she opened the door and stepped aside to let them in. Athena would certainly know what her plans were eventually. "What a surprise." Her face was flat and she glared at Paris.

"We were just in the neighborhood—"

"Right, Paris." She paused. "Hello, Aunt Athena. What do you think of the place?" *Might as well dive right in.*

"So, this is your place. Obviously your cousin thinks of this as some kind of joke or something. Why didn't you tell me what you were up to?"

How could I when you won't take my calls? "I wanted to wait until it was perfect. Until I could explain to you what happened with me and my boss."

Athena waved away Alexis's comment. "I know all about that. It's not like your cousin can keep a secret. You should have screamed and pressed assault charges, too."

Alexis should have known that Paris would have repeated just about every word she'd said to her mother. She followed Athena as she walked around the small space. "As you can see, the office is barely furnished and—"

Athena cut her chattering short. "So, just what do you plan to do here? There isn't even a sign up on the door."

"I'm going into practice for myself." She folded her arms.

They all paused. It was so silent that Alexis could hear everyone in the room breathing.

"Here?"

"You know of a better place?" Alexis tried to smile.

"I could think of several. You don't want to be associated with any of those storefront ambulance-chaser–type lawyers, do you?"

She counted to ten. "Well, this is as good a place as any. I'm close to downtown and easy to get to, and the rent is in the right range to keep my overhead down."

Athena nodded slowly, but didn't speak.

Paris cleared her throat and jumped into their conversation. "I think this is a wonderful idea, Mother. Don't you?"

"It doesn't matter what I think, now, does it? Miss Alexis already let me know her opinion. You really think there is a need for a divorce lawyer here? How will people find you?"

"I'm expanding just a bit, to family law. And yes, I think there is a very big need. Here as well as anywhere else."

Athena didn't comment further as her conversation was interrupted by a persistent knocking at the door. Alexis peered past her aunt and Paris to see who it was. They all turned in the direction of her gaze.

Alexis recognized Monty at once. He looked as disheveled as he had a few days before in her yard. Her eyes narrowed.

"I thought you said you weren't open for business yet," Paris said.

"I'm not." Alexis's eyes were riveted to the door. She wasn't sure if she should open it or if she should call the police. She couldn't think of one reason why he would be outside her door, or how he had even figured out that she had a door at all.

Athena made the decision for her. "For goodness sake. Aren't you going to let the man in?" Before Alexis could protest, her aunt had turned the key in the lock and held the door open for Monty to enter.

He barely looked at Athena or Paris, and only took a few steps inside the doorway. He stared directly at Alexis. "Have you given any thought to what I said?" His voice was courteous, but held a strong suggestion of a threat.

"What are you doing here?" Alexis didn't take her eyes off of him. She had one hand on the phone.

"You didn't think I was making idle threats, did you?"

Paris looked from the man in front of them to Alexis. "Alexis, aren't you going to introduce us?"

"This is my ex-boss." Beat. "The one I told you about." She was suddenly glad they were there. She felt safer. "Meet my Aunt Athena and my cousin, Paris. They were just checking out my new offices."

"If that's what you want to call them." He paused, his eyes darting around at the other two women. "We can make sure that you are scraping by on very few clients, you know. You need to retract your complaint. You have no proof. No one to back up your story."

Alexis felt a surge of anger. "You know what, I have news for you. There is at least one other person that is willing to come forward and tell what kind of boss you really are, so don't threaten me. Matter of fact, I think it is time for you to go. Again."

Athena and Paris watched with open mouths. Alexis stepped forward.

"Do we need to call the authorities?" Athena asked.

Monty held up his hands. It seemed as if Athena's mention of calling someone made him come back to reality a bit. "I'm going. There won't be any need for that." His eyes were dark and angry. "I was just trying to talk some sense into Alexis, that's all." He backed toward the door.

"I think she has quite good sense." Athena had moved closer to Monty, too, in between him and Alexis.

No one moved. The few seconds that Monty paused in the open door felt like an eternity. Alexis, Paris, and Athena all stared at him, daring him to take even one step forward. He glared at Alexis one last time, then left through the open door.

Alexis came around from behind the desk and locked the door behind him. Collectively, they all exhaled.

"I thought I was going to hit that man upside his head with my purse. He would have been in a world of hurt then, let me tell you. There is no telling what is in here."

Paris and Alexis laughed together.

"I wasn't trying to be funny," Athena said.

"But you are, Mother. I don't ever remember you talking like that. You sounded tough."

"Don't let the fine clothes fool you. I can get down with the best."

"Get down?" Alexis said. "That doesn't even sound right coming from your lips."

The two women looked at each other and held their gaze. Athena's standing up for her was as if a truce had been called.

Athena spoke in a more hushed tone. "You'd be surprised what comes out of your mouth when someone threatens one of your babies."

One of your babies. That was music to Alexis's ears. She smiled, then hugged her aunt. That was as close to an apology or a blessing as she was going to get.

dead elephants at dinner

The traffic on Cameron Road was light. The rush hour was over and a few neighborhood people appeared now and then. Alexis knew the address well. She was to meet Remedy for a celebration dinner, he'd told her. The only problem was that Alexis thought that the building that had been at the address he had given her had been destroyed by fire several months ago.

The small strip mall was in various states of repair. The fire had been all over the news and this was the first time that Alexis was seeing it in person since then. Recovery was slow. Being small, the strip mall had only held a few businesses before: a hair salon, an insurance office, and the night club. All were gone now. There was only one other car in what was left of the parking lot; the rest was covered with construction debris.

It wasn't quite dark as Alexis pulled into a space right next to the car she recognized as Remedy's. He was nowhere in sight. She turned off her car, debating whether or not she should even get out of the car. Most of the day, she'd been spooked and could not help looking over her shoulder, half expecting a crazed Monty to leap out of the shadows. She'd gotten several empty messages from a number she thought might be his today. Alexis was considering another protective order, this time against her boss. In deserted places like this, you could never be too careful.

Alexis grabbed her BlackBerry to call Remedy just as he stepped into view. She threw the phone into her bag and placed it on her arm as she got out of her car. He waved, then smiled an irresistibly devastating grin. Alexis walked toward him, returning his smile. His cast was gone.

They hugged and she felt a warm glow flow through her.

"Wow. Two arms." She put her face in his neck and inhaled.

"Amazing, isn't it. It came off today. Turns out it was only a fracture." Remedy placed his hand on the small of her back and tried to guide her into the building he'd come out of, but Alexis hesitated.

"It'll be okay," he said.

Alexis looked doubtful. "I thought we were meeting for dinner."

"We are. I have it in here."

"An abandoned building? This used to be Midtown Live."

Remedy chuckled. "I am well aware of what it used to be." He paused. "You have to get used to expecting the unexpected from me. I will explain everything. Promise."

Reluctantly, Alexis followed him inside the building. She was cautious, but she was also overwhelmed by curiosity. The news had made a big deal of showing the padlocked building, and Alexis noticed that the padlock had been replaced with a real estate–type lockbox. Inside, she expected the smell of charred wood, but instead the thick aroma of fresh paint hit her nose.

It was dimly lit inside, and there were signs of construction everywhere. A new wooden floor was being laid and there were piles of wood flooring in several spots. Construction tools and boxes were sitting around the room and rebar poked through the floor on one side.

"So, what do you think?" Remedy studied Alexis's reaction.

"I think I am in a construction zone. I'm waiting for you to tell me why I'm here."

"Well, we are going to have dinner, like I said." Beat. "Up there." He pointed up to the loft above their heads, then reached behind him to an alcove in the wall and grabbed two hard hats. "You have to wear this." He put one on his head and handed the other to Alexis.

Doubt filled her, but she put the hat on anyway.

"I wanted you to be the first to see it." A mischievous look came into his eyes.

"I could have waited a few more weeks. Like until after the floor was in."

"If you haven't already figured this out, welcome to the new Midtown Hookah." Remedy smiled from ear to ear.

"You bought this place?"

"Not exactly. The old owners needed money to restart, more than they could get, so my partners and I became investors and in exchange, the concept is tweaked a few nights a week. Hookah."

"Remedy." Alexis was breathless. "I'm so happy for you. And for the place. This is a great idea."

"I went online and read all about the debate in the community. This was the opportunity we were looking for."

"Are we really going to eat up there though? It doesn't look like the railing is completely finished."

He glanced in the direction of the loft. "Yes, we are. It's safe. Really. And we are going to be far back from the ledge. There is an alcove up there you can't see. It's going to be our new and improved VIP area."

"I'm—"

"If you are not comfortable, then we can go elsewhere."

Alexis was uncomfortable, but didn't want to spoil their evening. Remedy had obviously gone to a lot of trouble to get her here and to get food inside, too. There were no kitchen facilities that she could see anywhere. There was a small light glowing from the balcony, and from the way it was flickering, she guessed that he had set up quite a spread, complete with candlelight and everything. Going up to see it, even if it was just for a minute, was the least she could do.

She was more comfortable when they actually got there. Remedy had made the balcony so inviting, it felt warm, cozy and secluded, although it was in a half-built building. The eeriness that seemed to permeate the rest of the place did not exist here. As she looked around and admired what he had done, the tension melted from her back and shoulders.

Remedy led her to a small table in the corner, similar to the one they'd sat at in Dallas, at The Velvet Hookah. It was also low to the ground, but Alexis could tell that this one was much newer. It had one large pillow off to the side of it. He sat down, then extended his hand back up to her, helping her down beside him.

There were two candles in the center of the table, giving off the candlelight that Alexis had seen from below. An old-fashioned, *Wizard of Oz*–type picnic basket was off to the side. Remedy opened it and pulled out a bottle of wine, fol-lowed by two glasses.

Alexis leaned back on the pillow, watching him. She was surprised again at his spontaneity, marveling at how he had been able to create yet another perfect evening. This was their third date and he was three for three.

"Did you straighten everything out with your aunt?" he asked.

"I wouldn't say that. It's going to take more than a day to straighten all that out."

"A dead elephant between you, huh?"

"More like a whole damned menagerie." They fell into a fit of laughter.

"I've never heard it put quite like that." He finished filling her glass and he handed it to her.

"Our relationship is not like anyone else's, that's for sure. This mother-daughter thing is very complex. My aunt is the closest relationship I have to one of those. It is what it is, I guess."

"I'm glad you were able to reach some kind of equilibrium then." He had his share of family issues and knew exactly what she was talking about. He sipped his wine, then reached over to open the picnic basket again. The sound of something metal clanging caught his attention. He sat up straight, listening.

Every pore in Alexis's body was suddenly at attention. "What was that?" she asked.

Remedy shrugged. He listened hard, but the only sound he heard was the two of them breathing. "Probably some-thing that the workmen left falling or something. We are the only ones here, so there is nothing to worry about."

Alexis bit her lip. She hoped so. In the past few weeks,

she'd had more people yelling at her than she cared to talk about, and now she found herself constantly looking over her shoulder.

Remedy reached into the basket again, pulling out boxes of Chinese food this time.

Alexis laughed nervously. "Where did you find a place in town that still has those old-fashioned white boxes? I'd thought most places had given those up a long time ago."

"I told you I had skills."

She reached over to help him, separating the paper plates that he pulled from the basket next.

"Remedy." Ayzah's voice intruded on their private moment. They both turned toward her voice. Light streamed around her body from the stairway beyond her, framing her in the doorway.

They scrambled to their feet. "What are you doing here?" Remedy gave her a black, layered look.

Alexis backed up. "Weren't you served, Ayzah? You do know what that means."

"Yes, I do." She stepped forward. "But you won't have to worry about having me arrested. I came here because I have some things to say to Remedy and he won't return any of my calls."

"I have nothing to say to you. We can talk through our lawyers."

"I came to apologize. For the way I have been acting." Ayzah came toward them, onto the balcony.

Alexis glanced over her shoulder, immediately more uncomfortable with the situation. There were too many people in the small half room for her taste. "Look. I'm going to go. You two can talk, do whatever you need to." She grabbed her bag.

Ayzah stepped to the door to let her pass.

Alexis could hear them begin to argue before she was even through the door fully. Remedy's exasperated voice followed her as she clunked down the winding stairwell. She chastised herself for getting involved with him so fast. He obviously had more baggage then she realized. Remedy was smooth, and the sex was damn sure good, but his main problem was that his ex hadn't made up her mind to really be an ex yet.

She reached the bottom of the steps when she came face-to-face with another woman she didn't recognize. Alexis nodded tensely and forced a smile as the woman pushed past her.

She didn't return the gesture, instead moving back up the steps to where Alexis had left Remedy and Ayzah.

Alexis paused. If she'd had a bad feeling when Ayzah had shown up, she had a terrible one now. That woman had the angriest scowl on her face, and she didn't seem too steady on her feet. For a second, she thought of going back up to the balcony, but quickly pushed that thought to the back of her mind. Whatever else Remedy was involved in, she didn't want to know. Knowing would make it that much harder to get her butt out of there.

Her steps echoed as she crossed the floor to the door. Just as she reached it, she looked up to where Remedy and the other two women were arguing on the balcony. Their voices echoed throughout the building, and it looked like Ayzah and the other woman might come to blows. The new woman had somehow gotten past Ayzah and Remedy, and had her back to the ledge, and she and Ayzah were yelling, talking right in each other's face. Ayzah was back to being the woman she'd met that day in the hospital, cursing and gesturing in the air wildly. Alexis searched the balcony for Remedy, but was unable to see him.

Ayzah took a step forward, yelling something that Alexis couldn't understand. Every part of her body screamed that she should hop in her car and go without looking back, but she was riveted to the spot. Her evening had started so wonderfully and had disintegrated into something on par with a bad daytime talk show. Just as Alexis willed herself to turn away and leave, things began to move in slow motion.

Alexis could clearly see the other woman's slender hand reach toward Ayzah's neck, grab something, and yank it away. Ayzah drew back her hand and slapped the other woman. It sounded as if a whip had cracked.

Alexis gasped and her mouth dropped open in surprise.

Ayzah lurched forward, trying to retrieve what the other woman held in her hand. The woman stumbled, then struggled to regain her balance. Her arms flailed in the air, flapping as if she were a bird trying to make its first flight. She fell backward off the balcony and landed on the first floor with a thud.

Remedy had followed Alexis and now stood beside her. They stood frozen and silent as the noise of the woman's fall and the shock of the two pieces of rebar protruding from her chest hit them.

Alexis blinked, then looked up into the balcony.

Ayzah stood near the edge, peering down over the precipice at the gaping rictus of her friend's mouth, frozen in a silent scream of surprise. Her hand was tightly closed around the diamond necklace she had ripped from Ayzah's neck. The building was entirely quiet, except for the echo of slowly dripping water. Ayzah began to whimper, then let out a long, slow whine.

"Erica."

what goes up

It took a minute for it to hit her that Erica was dead. When the paramedics came, they'd pronounced her dead at the scene. Ayzah's first thought when she realized that Erica had fallen was that she was going to jail.

How had things gone from bad to worse? It was suddenly clear, the realization that there were some things she had to do for herself, without Prince, and it was all a mess. Her hands trembled. If that wasn't a sign from God, Ayzah didn't know what was. It was time for her to get her shit together. Her heart pounded in her ears so loudly she could barely hear anyone talk. The cops took her statement and then told her she could go. She was stunned. They weren't arresting her. Yet.

She was in the middle of a crime drama, down to the last statement from the policeman. "Don't leave town," he'd said. *Shiiit.* She had nothing to run from. She hadn't done a thing.

She'd tracked Remedy down with good intentions. She had no idea that things would end up the way they did.

Ma'dear was right. You reap what you sow, and Erica had sown her last evil seed.

Her rickety car seemed to drive slower than usual as she left, headed for work. It was a wonder that they weren't carting her off to jail. It was also a wonder that Remedy and his girlfriend had told the truth. They could have told the cops that she had pushed Erica just to get rid of her, but they didn't. Yes, she'd slapped her, but Erica had fallen on her own. Ayzah was astonished. It would have been too easy for them, not that Remedy hadn't wanted to have her arrested. The misery and hatred that she saw in his eyes had chilled her to the bone. Ayzah sighed. It was like she didn't deserve it. Because of her, his date was ruined and his club . . . who knew when that would open now.

She was an hour late for work. OJ would have her head, but she had to go. She could pick up a few hundred dollars tonight and then quit. It was for the best anyway. Her so-called thinking time was over and there was no way she was going under the knife to please him. How many years of this could she possibly have left?

It occurred to her that she had not heard from Prince in a couple of hours. He'd been calling her repeatedly, and then suddenly his calls had stopped earlier today. Ayzah couldn't help herself. She had to call him. How could she pass up being the one to tell him that his little sex buddy was dead?

♥   ♥   ♥

The parking lot was filled with light. Floodlights brought in by the cops mixed with the blaze of headlights from several police cars that had responded to the call. Alexis leaned on her car, watching in disbelief as they swarmed over the site like ants. She'd given her statement at least four times already and there was no doubt in her mind that she would be doing it again.

They had taped off the building with that awful yellow tape. Erica's body had already been moved, and Alexis didn't doubt that if she went inside, there would be a chalk outline on the floor. She shuddered at the thought. Remedy came over to where she was standing and put his arm around her shoulders. Alexis didn't want to be hugged, she just wanted to go home. Alone. Immediately after that girl's body hit the ground, she realized that she and Remedy had reached a point where they were going to have to take a step back and take a long, hard look at their relationship. Sure, he was attractive to her, but she was going to have to take some time and examine her own motivations.

"Let me take you home."

Her head swirled with doubts. "You know what? You are going to be here awhile, and I need to get home. I'm going to go as soon as they say I can."

"But you are trembling. It won't take long."

"Rem. I think that is a normal reaction." She paused. "I'm going to be okay. Besides, I have a long day tomorrow. My office is officially open now and the rehearsal dinner is tomorrow night. I'm going to look like shit."

There was a silence between them then as Remedy took in the full and hidden meaning behind Alexis's words. "When can we see each other again?"

Alexis fought hard to keep the tears that had welled up in her throat from falling. She shook her head. "I don't know, Rem. Let's sleep on that, okay? I think you have some business you need to handle first."

endings and new beginnings

Her eyes were puffy and tired-looking. Alexis took the stack of mail she'd picked up on the way in and dropped it on her desk. The newspaper headline on top screamed out the news of Luther Vandross's death. Alexis felt a double loss. Luther's death added to the sadness she was feeling because of what had happened with Remedy. She sat down, then ran her hands across her face, resting her head in them. Her lack of sleep was taking its toll. She still couldn't believe what she had witnessed last night. Remedy had called her first thing this morning, but she didn't have the energy to talk to him. There was just too much to do. She pushed the mail around. Most of it was junk mail.

A billboard had been erected announcing her new practice just off Interstate 35, a few blocks from the office. It should have made her happy when she drove past it this morning on the way in, but all it did was make her more tired. And it was only going to get worse. Although she had only planned to come in for a few hours, then leave and run errands, Alexis knew that what she really needed was a nap. After all was said and done, she still had to get to the rehearsal dinner tonight and then the wedding tomorrow. There was just no time for sleep.

Alexis called her service and started to write down all her messages. She had quite a few. There was no way she could afford not to return calls; she needed the business. A shadow caught her eye just as she reached for the phone and she jumped. Sarah came through the door, smiling from ear to ear.

"So, you want to tell me the photographer you used for that billboard ad? I must say you are looking fabulous on it." She handed one of the cups of coffee in her hand to Alexis.

She took it gratefully. "I don't have the energy to joke. Let's just hope it works."

"It will. It's wonderful. Lots of people need family lawyers. Just think of all the women who need to track down child support or something like that."

Alexis groaned.

Sarah's eyebrows shot up. "Was that upsetting?" A beat. "I'm sorry. That reminds you of last night, right? Bet you are glad that is over."

Alexis slurped her drink loudly.

"So, what are you going to do?"

"Do? What's to do? I have already made up my mind. Me and Rem are going to cool it. We have to."

"I think that's wise."

"He was like a Band-Aid, something to ease the pain with. Like tae kwon do and the new hair."

"But you seemed so happy for a minute—"

Alexis nodded.

She hadn't seemed happy; she'd been happy. She shrugged. "Contrary to popular belief, there is no knight in shining armor."

The door jangled again and they looked up as a woman walked in. Alexis recognized her immediately. She was too surprised to do more than nod at Shana, Monty's assistant.

Sarah stepped back. "I'm going to go."

Alexis held up her hand to stop her. "Shana," she said. "This is a surprise."

"I'm sure it is." She paused, looking around nervously. "I have been trying to call you for a while."

"You didn't leave any messages."

A beat. "Have you opened your mail yet?" She nodded in the direction of the stack of mail that was still on Alexis's desk. There was a pensive shimmer in the corner of her eye.

"I have just glanced at it. Why?"

"They want to offer you your job back if you withdraw your complaint. They think you might sue." A beat. "I mailed the paperwork for Monty so I know."

"Okay, so—"

"So, I want to come forward." The normal bubbliness that was in Shana's voice was gone, replaced by a matter-of-fact tone that Alexis was not used to from her. "I couldn't afford to be the only one sticking my neck out, but if I know you are there with me—"

Alexis stared, surprised. "To tell the truth, I hadn't really given too much thought to pursuing anything beyond the complaint. I just wanted to move on."

"But you said you had other people." Sarah was confused.

"Couldn't he tell I was just bluffing to get rid of him? He was looking all crazy."

"Well, I'll come forward. I'm willing."

It took a minute for Alexis to regain her composure. Maybe this wasn't going to be such a bad day after all. She grabbed a pen and a pad and motioned toward a seat near her desk. "Can I get you some coffee or something?" She nodded at Sarah, who made a dash for the door.

Shana took the seat she was offering. "We have some work to do."

♥ ♥ ♥

Insistent pounding awakened Ayzah from a deep sleep. She put her head under a pillow. Ma'dear would be getting that any minute, she thought. The pounding continued, and she took a peek out at the clock. It took a moment for her eyes to focus. It was almost ten in the morning. Ma'dear would be long gone by now.

Ayzah had half a mind not to answer the door at all, hoping that whoever it was would go away. After she'd been late to work, OJ had worked her extra hard, then laughed when she'd tried to quit. His gravelly voice had mocked her. "You ain't giving this up," he'd said. *That's what he thought.* It was time to move on.

She pulled a terry cloth robe around her and shuffled to the door, pausing before she opened it to peep through the small window in the center. She didn't want that fool Prince to be showing up at her door. He'd probably heard about Erica by now and wanted someone to lick his wounds. She'd be damned if that person would be her. That asshole had given her jewelry that belonged to Erica. Ayzah rubbed her neck. It was still sore from where Erica had ripped the necklace from her neck before she'd fallen from that ledge.

It wasn't Prince, but two police officers. Ayzah shuddered. They must have decided to arrest her after all. She sighed, then reluctantly opened the door.

"Ayzah Brown?"

She nodded.

"We need to ask you a few questions. Can we come in?"

She stepped aside to let them enter. "I already told them everything last night."

The two men looked at each other, then back at Ayzah. One of them held up a picture of Prince.

Ayzah's face clouded with uneasiness.

"Do you know this man?"

"Yes. I do. I . . . we used to be involved."

"Used to?"

"I broke up with him a few days ago, and he kept calling me for a couple of days." She paused. "I found him with another woman, the one that died last night, actually. He kept calling me and then the calls stopped a few nights ago. I haven't heard from him since. Is he in trouble?"

"Parole violation. He didn't show up to his appointment."

She hesitated. "I didn't even know he was on parole. I tried to call him but he didn't answer his phone."

"We tried that, too. And his car is missing."

"There is no telling where he is. He had recently started working with someone, Deon—"

"Deon Whitfield?" One of the officers scribbled on his pad.

"That's him. And he was staying out all night. That's how I found out he was seeing Erica."

"Do you know what Deon Whitfield did for a living?"

Ayzah nodded. "Everyone around here does. He is a snitch. A mark. He helps cops catch people or something like that." The two officers were silent as Ayzah looked from one to the other. "I haven't seem him in awhile."

"You wouldn't have. Deon Whitfield was relocated months ago. For his protection." A beat. "And then he was killed three weeks ago in a construction accident."

It took a moment for their words to sink in. Prince had lied. Again. He couldn't have been working with Deon. He was probably just sleeping with Erica the whole time. "I don't know where he is. That is what I was told."

They studied her face for a minute, then one of them took out his card and handed it to her. "Call us if you hear from him."

Ayzah took it. She nodded, but she doubted she would ever hear from him again.

scout's honor and white horses

The letter was drawn up and hand delivered by noon to Alexis's former offices by courier. The plan had been simple. In order to get what she wanted, the firm was going to have to pay up and give good references for both Alexis and Shana. Thoughts of Monty and Shana had almost eclipsed last night's fiasco of a date. If Alexis hadn't been so dog tired, the day would have been a great one.

She pulled her car into the parking lot below Mt. Bonnell. It looked like most of the others were already here. It was seven p.m. and still above ninety degrees, so the steps leading up to the summit looked quite formidable. She swore. She understood the significance of getting married on the highest point in the city, but didn't Paris realize that her guests were going to be hot and sweaty before the ball even got rolling? It was going to be one funky reception, that was for sure, and not because the music was good either.

The summit of Mt. Bonnell was perched high over Lake Austin. A stone gazebo stood in the center of the small park.

She was hot from the climb, but Alexis couldn't help but catch her breath as she got a glimpse of the sun shining on the nearly still water. Athena greeted her at the top of the steps. She looked as frazzled as expected for someone whose daughter was getting married the next day.

"Good. You're here. I know you had a rough night, but I'm glad you could make it. We are almost ready to start the rehearsal." She turned to leave. "Would you please talk to Paris and convince her that she really does need a stand-in for this? It's bad luck to actually rehearse at your own rehearsal."

Alexis searched in her purse for a tissue to wipe her brow. Good thing she was into the minimalist look these days, otherwise her face would melt.

"Heard about your new boyfriend and his drama last night," Walter said behind her.

Alexis turned so she could see him. Her mental preparation for seeing Walter again had worked well. His presence didn't even upset her. "It was on the news."

"Too bad. Having Midtown back would have been great. But you know what they say, you can't go back, right?"

"I wouldn't count Remedy out yet. He's not the quitting type."

"We'll see. He's not even from here. I don't understand how he could even get sentimental about a place like that."

Alexis frowned. *A place like what?* When had Walter become so negative? Maybe she had just been unable to see it before. Obviously, she hadn't realized just how selfish he was. "Remedy has a good heart."

Walter chuckled. He looked around nervously. "That may be, but I bet it's over for you two now. I know how you don't like drama. I wouldn't think you'd want to be associated with all that." A beat. "So, if you don't have a date for the wedding now, I'd still be willing. It would be good since I am your escort in the wedding party."

The last thing Alexis wanted to do was fight with anyone right then. It would make it more stressful for Paris, and Alexis was sure she didn't need any of that. She fought to restrain herself and wondered how she could have possibly rallied so hard to be Walter's wife at one point. They hadn't been talking ten minutes and he was already disgusting her. "You're kidding, right?" She smiled. "Like I said, I wouldn't count Remedy out yet." Her BlackBerry rang, saving her. "You know what? I need to take this." She pressed the track wheel to connect the call. "I think I'll pass. You said it right when you said you couldn't go back." She put the phone to her ear and walked toward the rest of the wedding party gathering under the stone gazebo.

It was Shana. Alexis listened intently. She was talking so excitedly that Alexis could barely catch everything she was saying.

"They are offering a settlement. Cash." Shana sounded as if she were going to hyperventilate at any moment. "They don't want to be embarrassed by a public lawsuit. I don't know what you put in that letter, but it worked."

"Okay. You are going to have to calm down."

Shana chattered on, relaying what had transpired when the package was delivered.

"We are going to have to go slow. I suggested that we try to mediate." The firm was offering more money than Shana made in three years, and much the same for Alexis. She grinned from ear to ear. If it panned out, that money would really help her get her new practice off the ground. And provided that the rehearsal went well, the day was going to end on a higher note than she expected. She could barely contain her own excitement.

Sarah and Paris both stared at her with questioning looks on their faces. Alexis smiled, then motioned to them that she would fill them in later.

Athena was at her wits' end as she gave a slew of instructions. No one was listening. Both Paris and Sarah were staring now, and she frowned at them, pointing at Athena. If they didn't do what she wanted soon, she might have a heart attack.

She finished on the phone and disconnected her call, still smiling. Sarah raised her eyebrows, but didn't speak. Alexis looked at the puzzled expressions on her friends' faces and realized that they were not looking at her, but behind her. She took a tentative glance over her shoulder, then turned around completely. She came face-to-face with Remedy Brown.

Mixed feelings surged through her as their eyes met. "What are—"

"I thought I was your date." He paused. "I know what you said, but I figured you still needed a date, right? I don't know one person who wants to go to a wedding alone."

Alexis thought about it. She didn't want to go to the wedding alone, but that didn't mean she wanted to date Remedy. At least not right then. "I'm not sure."

Everyone was quiet, watching.

"I'm not asking you to marry me. I know what happened would be a lot for anyone. But you have to admit that it wasn't my fault, not directly." He licked his lips.

It really wasn't his fault. She could see Walter out of the corner of her eye. He was looking over at her and Remedy, an angry scowl on his face.

Something clicked in her mind. Although Walter and Remedy were very different, they had served similar purposes in her life. She had tried to use each of them to fill a hole, something no other person could do for her. Before she could be in a relationship again, she was going to have to get comfortable with herself and fix up her own wounds. Sarah was right. There was no knight in shining armor. She was going to have to ride that white horse herself, but that did not mean she had to go solo to her favorite cousin's wedding.

"This doesn't mean that we are going to be dating or anything, you do understand that?"

There was the hint of a smile in his gravelly voice as he spoke. "It can be what you want. Scout's honor."

Alexis met his smile and the hand he offered. Remedy Brown *did* have a good heart. "Is that a fact?"

He nodded.

And that was good enough for her.

Want More?

Turn the page to enter
Avon's Little Black Book—

the dish, the scoop and the
cherry on top from
NINA FOXX

Acknowledgments and Notes

It has been over 100 degrees in Central Texas for what seems like an eternity, making it almost impossible to do anything outside. This is a good thing; I needed more incentive to sit down and churn this one out. After *Marrying Up,* the minor characters in the book still intrigued me. Usually I can wrap them up and write them away, so to speak, but not this time. Alexis was still there when everyone else was gone, screaming at me to give her adventure.

At the same time, I wanted to write a character who was more gritty than the others, someone not from the same place, from a different type of upbringing. Not better, not worse, just different. I wanted her to be more urban, but not cartoonish. That was Ayzah. And then I put them together and the fun began.

This was the first time I outlined a book from beginning to end, and I have to say I didn't like it. I usually use about one line a chapter, describing what the action in the chapter is to guide me forward. I tried to use a more detailed step-by-step guide this time and it just didn't work. Ayzah and Alexis screamed at me that they just didn't want to do that. If you play The Sims, you know what I mean. I kept trying to write them into action, like I was controlling them with my PlayStation joystick, and they fell down on the floor and cried, doing whatever the hell they wanted.

Again I tell you that this is fiction. It's all made up, even if I did use real settings. A word about places. Midtown Live: real place. Nokonah (Remedy's Austin residence): real place. The

Velvet Hookah: real place. I am no country bumpkin (or so I like to think) and I went there and had no idea what a hookah was. Thank you to my new friend Jami Ervin for introducing me to it. Her brother Jei is one of the proprietors and he set up the hookah for us and even showed us how to do it. He then held his laughter while we perpetrated. It's all good.

Jei is something else. He oozed sexiness like Remedy did in the book (girl, don't front, you know what I mean), the kind of man you just can't take your eyes off. He wore spurs like it was nobody's business. And I still am not sure if he would be able to fly anywhere with them, and I don't care.

A lot of people will ask me why I made one friend not black. Honey, it's simple: Life isn't always black and white. Sometimes it's gray, and that is okay.

Denise Davis gave me an antique apron that makes me look like June Cleaver. I love it. I don't necessarily wear that to cook. TMI, right? Okay, there were a lot of people who said things that helped me figure out where the story was going next and they just didn't know it. Jami, you are a character, all by yourself, you church lady. It makes me happy that we can be friends and be so different. Kevin and Judith Enders. (She didn't smoke the hookah, Kev, it's all good.) Peter Arnel, anchor-reporter at CBS Radio Network in Dallas, and my girl Jill Hubley (welcome to Texas).

Then there are those whom I just asked point-blank, "What the hell? I don't know what should come next," and they were patient with me through my anxiety, like Lori Bryant Woolridge and Eric Jerome Dickey. Thanks y'all for answering my questions. The multitude of others, including the Femme Fantastik (catch us while you can): Lori, Carmen Green, Marissa Monteilh, Jacquelin Thomas, and Victoria Christopher Murray. Your support and friendship is like a light on the darkest days. Pam Walker Williams (What? You can't drink before noon? Well, then let's move the clock), Peggy Hicks and the TriComm crew, Carrie Feron and Selina McClemore, Tessa Woodward, Gena Pearson (over in the UK), and the Elaine Koster Literary Agency: thanks to you all.

The myriad of readers and book clubs, independent bookstores like Black Images Book Bazaar in Dallas—without you it just couldn't be done. The Austin chapter of Jack & Jill of America and Alpha Kappa Alpha Sorority . . . 'Nuff said. Thank God and the Ancestors for your never-ending guidance. And last but not least, my family. Lynda, Dina, Stephanie, Jo Anne, Brian, Roger and Butchie, Robert, Brandie, Sydney, Kai and Maria, and most of all, my husband, Major. Thanks. I'm going to find me a new pair of shoes and do the happy dance now. Much love.

July 7, 2005, 11:36 P.M.

After I was done writing *Just Short of Crazy,* I got to thinking. Where in the world would my characters be a few years from now? The following is an interview with Ayzah after Remedy becomes famous, say five or ten years down the line. The reporter is trying to get information from those who knew him way back when. And, well, Ayzah is still quite the character.

An Interview with Ayzah Brown

"So, I should just talk?" She tapped the microphone. "Is it on?"

"Yes, it is. We want to get everything. This is going to be a big story. Talk about you and Remedy and your life after you two split up."

"It's true, I was married to Remedy before he got really rich. I mean, he was well enough off when I met him, but I hadn't franchised his hookah idea or anything. Who would have thought that such a thing would be so popular, but I guess they said that about Hooters, too, and look at it now. They even got a Hooters airline flying all over the place."

"Continue, please. Are you still a stripper?"

A peal of laughter. "For goodness sake, no. I would be one old stripper, you know what I mean? This ain't New Orleans or anything. I took a trip there once and saw a lady so old I swear her G-string was made from Depends and she had no teeth in her mouth at all. Her breasts had sagged to nothing and it just wasn't pretty, you know what I'm saying? She swung around the pole and looked like a toothpick riding a swizzle stick or something. Ugly. I moved on from that a while ago."

"How old are you?"

"You should never ask a lady that. But you know what, I'ma tell you. I ain't ashamed of my age. I think I look damn good. I'm forty. Okay, forty-one. But I am still fine."

"Yes, you are. If I didn't know the history I would have put you at much younger than that. Your, ah, your . . . they don't look flat at all."

She cupped her breasts. "These? That's 'cause I took old OJ's money and bought me some that were guaranteed for ten to fifteen years. I figured if it's good enough for society ladies, it's good enough for a simple girl like me."

"They look good."

"Anyway, me and OJ got married. I never knew he had a thing for me, but he did. He ain't that great-looking, but ain't no joking about his stroking, if you know what I mean."

"Did you work at Wal-Mart?"

"Hell, no. No offense to those that do. My mama worked there a long time and the benefits are good and she is very happy. When she retires she will get a pension bigger than some of her friends that have worked for NASA down in Houston for over twenty years. And they got all sorts of education and shit like that that she don't. No, my OJ set me up real good."

"Set you up?"

She nods. "Hell, yeah. I started my own business. Striptease Aerobics. We are in the process of franchising now and last year we released our first video."

"Really?"

"Yes. It's for women only. So it can be in a nonthreatening environment, sort of like Curves or one of them other kinds of women-only gyms. But the idea is that you get in shape while exercising your feminine wiles, too."

"I see. And has it been successful?"

"You ain't got no idea how many women need to be taught how to shake their asses. You would be surprised at the number of suburban housewives that have got a freak in 'em, down deep. I teach them to bring that out." She laughs. "I'm like a therapist."

"I'll bet you are. How about Jamal?"

"People don't always agree with me on that. I got myself together, but I realized that Remedy really had made a good home for him. We share custody now, but he lives primarily over at Remedy's. He's a good man and he knows how to raise a boy."

"A lot of people think that a child belongs with his mother."

"A lot of the time that is true. But you have to think of the child's needs first."

"Seems like you did quite well for yourself without Remedy, then?"

"Most definitely. What I needed was inside me all along."

"You want to add anything else?"

"Could you put the address of my aerobic gym in the article, too? It's on Lamar. We'll give you some free passes for the lady in your life."

"Of course."

From the Journal of Nina Foxx

Monday, May 23, 2005
Peace Pipe

The highlight of my Oprah weekend was not what you would expect. First, Dallas was in for record heat. If you know Dallas, you know then that it was hot as hell. We thought we might walk the block and a half from our hotel to the convention center, but after we took three steps outside we quickly changed our minds and hopped in a cab. Staying dry an extra minute was well worth the two-buck ride. We spotted lots of folks we knew while we waited in the throng outside. At two minutes past ten, they began to let us into a big expo-like setting. There was a warning on our tickets that said no one would be admitted after 11:30 even though Oprah wasn't set to speak until one. Perhaps this was to make sure you went through every Walt Disney World–length line to get coupons or small gifts from the sponsors. Most of them were cute things, things I might use. Diet Rite gave us samples and coupons. Maybelline was doing makeovers (I passed on that one. C'mon, was I really gonna let them take off my MAC and Laura Mercier to put on Maybelline? I think not). Toyota gave away a car (or so they say, I didn't stay to find out.) I didn't win.

And then came Oprah. She spoke for well over three hours and kept everyone's attention, too. She was quite poised in her Manolos and didn't sit down until she got to the question-and-answer period. Then, she looked like she was trying to get them off her feet but thought better of it. There was maybe one meaningful question. Most of it boiled down to the fact that people were in awe of her and starstruck and just wanted things from her. After she was done, they tried to herd us back into the expo area, but we opted instead to grab our goodies and go. A martini in our hotel seemed like a much better offer.

The best part of the weekend came much later. My traveling buddy took me to an establishment owned by her brother. The

Velvet Hookah in Deep Ellum offered an interesting aside from the regular club scene. The enclosed patio gave the illusion that there was no front door and the walls were covered in red velvet. We sat on the floor on pillows in the front patio porch area and smoked a *hookah*. Dallas being a nonsmoking city, this was the only place where smoking was allowed. Our host welcomed us by sending over an impressive-looking hookah filled with a blend called "foreplay." He thought we might like it, although I kept wondering, foreplay for what? We were a group of four very straight women on a girls' weekend getaway sans husbands or boyfriends. Now, I have never smoked anything in my life and have to admit that I didn't inhale, but it was a cool experience. It turned out to be the best part of the trip: just four women hanging out, watching the sights and laughing at the passersby gawking at us.

NINA FOXX

Lynda Scott

Previously an industrial psychologist, **NINA FOXX** authored several patents before writing her first self-published novel, which sold more than 13,000 copies. She is the author of the novels *Going Buck Wild, Marrying Up,* and *Just Short of Crazy.* Her work is also featured in *Wanderlust: Erotic Travel Tales,* and she had contributed reviews to *Black Issues Book Review.* Nina is a founding member of the Femme Fantastik Authors on Tour. Originally from Jamaica, New York, she lives in Austin, Texas, with her family.